ABOUT THE AUTHOR

Sarah Mayberry lives by the beach in Melbourne, Australia, with her partner (now husband!) of nearly twenty years. As well as writing romance novels, she writes scripts for TV, loves cooking and reading and shopping, and is learning how to be a good fur parent to her brand-new black Cavoodle, Max.

Books by Sarah Mayberry

HARLEQUIN SUPERROMANCE

1551—A NATURAL FATHER
1599—HOME FOR THE HOLIDAYS
1626—HER BEST FRIEND
1669—THE BEST LAID PLANS
1686—THE LAST GOODBYE
1724—ONE GOOD REASON
1742—ALL THEY NEED
1765—MORE THAN ONE NIGHT

HARLEQUIN BLAZE

380—BURNING UP
404—BELOW THE BELT
425—AMOROUS LIAISONS
464—SHE'S GOT IT BAD
517—HER SECRET FLING
566—HOT ISLAND NIGHTS

Other titles by this author available in ebook format.

Every book is hard. No matter how much I plan in advance, I always make missteps and reach a point where I feel as though my head is going to explode. The people who stop that from happening are Chris, my real life hero, and Wanda, the best editor a writer could have. Thank you both for always having my back.

Also a big thanks to Shane Saw for my beautiful new website, Lisa for awesome Community Kitchen, and Joan for listening to me ramble and moan.

And tummy scratches for Max, for being the cutest fur ball under the sun.

PROLOGUE

ANGELA BARTLETT STRODE up the path toward her best friend's house, very aware she was running late. It was a warm October day and only the screen door barred her way when she arrived on the front porch.

She rang the doorbell, then leaned close to the screen. "It's me. Sorry I'm so late," she called into the house.

"So you should be." The voice echoed up the hallway, followed by the sound of footsteps.

A petite, pretty woman with pixie-cut blond hair appeared, a baby balanced on one hip. She was dressed in hot-pink capri pants, an aqua T-shirt and bright yellow sneakers with hot-pink laces.

She sounded grumpy, but her brown eyes were smiling and Angie knew she wasn't really in trouble. They'd been friends long enough that Billie could easily forgive a few minutes' tardiness.

"Happy birthday, sweetie," Angie said, dropping a kiss onto her friend's cheek as she opened the door. The baby stared at her with big, liquid eyes and she dropped a kiss onto his forehead, too. "Hello, Charlie-boy."

"Shh. We're pretending it's any old party so one of us doesn't get all maudlin about getting old," Billie said.

"Thirty-two is not old," Angie said, as they walked into the spacious country-style kitchen.

Sunlight streamed through floor-to-ceiling windows

that opened onto a deck. The adjacent open-plan living room was also flooded with light, the brightness accentuating the brilliant jewel tones of the furnishings. Like Billie herself, this was a house full of color and life and vibrancy.

"Where's Michael?" Angie asked when there was no sign of Billie's husband.

"Where do you think?"

Which Angie guessed meant he was in his study. An architect, Michael often brought work home with him, something Angie knew Billie sometimes resented.

"Auntie Angie." A small body launched itself at Angie and Billie's five-year-old daughter wrapped her skinny arms around Angie's hips.

"Hi, Eva."

Eva looked up at her, adoringly. "I thought you were never going to come."

Angie sank onto a crouch. "I was late. Sorry about that." She hugged her goddaughter close, breathing in the smell of berry shampoo and Barbie perfume.

"Don't let it happen again," Eva said mock-sternly. She was a cheeky little thing, funny and smart as a whip.

"I will make a concerted effort, I promise," Angie said solemnly.

"Okay, time to get this party started," Billie said, crossing to the sound system and hitting a button. James Brown's "Get On Up" blasted through the house. Billie started dancing, holding Charlie out from her body and shaking her backside as only she could.

Angie smiled at her friend's antics. "Here's an idea— you could just ask Michael to come out of the study like a normal person," she yelled over the music.

Billie simply grinned and kept dancing.

Eva giggled, thrilled to be part of the conspiracy to flush out her hardworking father. Angie grabbed her hands and they joined Billie, doing their best to match Billie's moves.

A minute later, a tall, broad-shouldered figure appeared in the doorway. Michael Robinson's dark, curly hair was ruffled. His feet were bare, his jeans old and faded, his white T-shirt well washed. He crossed his arms over his chest, the expression in his gray-green eyes equal parts amused and frustrated.

Billie sidled up to her husband and passed him their son before starting to dance in earnest, her small body moving smoothly to the beat. She shook her booty, jiggled her small breasts and wiggled her hips until Michael lost the battle and his mouth curved into an all-out grin.

"Okay, message received. No more work. What needs doing before everyone arrives?"

A flurry of activity ensued. Billie took Angie on a whirlwind tour of her birthday present from Michael, the small wooden studio in the backyard designed to give Billie the space to pursue her current passion for all things ceramic. They had barely returned to the house when a couple of neighbors arrived, along with a few other friends. Michael entertained them on the deck while Angie helped Billie put the finishing touches on the food in the kitchen.

"So… How are things with the hot Greek guy?" Billie asked as she mixed oil and vinegar for the salad dressing.

"Nonexistent," Angie said.

"Don't tell me it's over already?"

"It's over."

"Angie, I swear. What are we going to do with you?"

Angie frowned, irritated by the despairing note in

her friend's voice. "Being single is not a disease. I love my life."

"I want you to be happy."

"I *am* happy. A man does not happiness make. Sometimes, in fact, he makes unhappiness."

Billie opened her mouth to say something, then obviously thought better of it. Angie was glad, since she suspected her friend had been about to say something about Finn, and that would have really pissed her off. They had talked Finn to death years ago. There was nothing new to be said, no new conclusions to come to. He was firmly in the past.

Where he belonged.

"I'm not giving up on you," Billie said after a short silence. "There's a new guy at Michael's office. I haven't convinced Michael to find out if he's single or not yet, but if he is, I want you to meet him."

Common sense told Angie to let the comment slide— Billie was like a runaway freight train when she got an idea in her head—but her own stubbornness demanded a response.

"Let me get this straight. You don't know this man at all, haven't even set eyes on him, I'm betting. Yet you want me to go out with him?"

"I'm only thinking of you."

"I'm curious. What, exactly, is his qualification for being a good prospect for poor old Angie? Having a pulse? Walking upright?" She put down the knife she'd been using to focus all her attention on her misguided friend.

In the loaded silence after her speech Billie slid the knife out of Angie's reach. "Just in case," she said, poker-faced.

Angie laughed. Billie was too damn irreverent and likable and her heart was so obviously in the right place. "You are hopeless."

"So are you."

They took the salads outside and the next few hours drifted by in a haze of sunshine and white wine and laughter. Angie kicked off her shoes and sat back and listened to the others talk around her, occasionally pitching in a comment of her own, but mostly happy to watch Billie do what she did best—shine and sparkle and glow.

When it came time for dessert, Michael produced a white box sporting the logo of Billie's favorite bakery and they all oohed and ahhed over the giant chocolate-and-coffee mousse cake inside.

Angie fished a small box from her handbag and handed it to her friend with a smile. "Something for your collection."

"You spoil me, but I'm not going to say no," Billie said.

Angie watched as Billie lifted the lid to reveal a delicate black-pearl necklace, the pearls suspended on hand-beaten gold wire that had been curved into delicate, impossible spirals. As always when she first revealed a new piece, there was a little stab of nervousness in the pit of her stomach. After nearly ten years of being a professional jewelry designer, she'd resigned herself to the fact that that small moment of self-doubt would probably never go away.

Perhaps, in some way, it was essential to her craft.

"Oh, Angie." Billie pressed a hand to her chest, her gaze glued to the necklace. "It's so beautiful… I don't have the words. You've outdone yourself. My God."

Angie smiled, pleased, and accepted her friend's hug

when Billie shot to her feet and rounded the table to embrace her.

"I love you, sweetie. Happy birthday," Angie said, speaking quietly so only her friend could hear.

"I love you, too, String Bean. You talented hussy. I will treasure it always, I swear."

Angie could see all the memories they shared reflected in Billie's eyes as her friend drew back from their hug—the years at boarding school, the mistakes they had made, the highs, the lows. Unexpected sentimental tears burned at the back of her eyes and she blinked rapidly.

Billie sniffed, too.

"Do I need to go get the tissues?" Michael asked drily.

"We're having an intense moment of womance here, do you mind?" Billie said.

Everyone laughed and the moment was gone. Angie helped clear the table while Billie played a game of tag with the children, running around the backyard until they were all breathless. Angie loaded the dishwasher and smiled to herself as she listened to Billie complaining about how she would have to retire from playing tag now that she was an old lady of thirty-two. Angie was rinsing out a salad bowl when Billie entered the house, red-faced, hands on her hips as she labored to catch her breath.

"Wow, you really are winded, you tragic fossil," Angie said as her friend walked to the cupboard and reached for a glass.

"Don't laugh. Your birthday is coming up soon," Billie said.

She was genuinely out of breath and the smile faded from Angie's lips. "You okay?"

"I'm fine. Just need some water." But Billie's hand trembled as she held her glass under the water.

"Maybe you should sit down."

She waved an impatient hand, already walking away with her drink. "I'm fine."

Angie shrugged and resumed rinsing the salad bowl. The sound of glass shattering had her spinning around. She was in time to see Billie press her hands to her chest before collapsing to her knees, the sound of bone hitting wood a loud, resonant thunk.

"It hurts," Billie gasped, fingers pressing into her chest.

Then she hit the floor, unconscious, her body loose and lifeless.

Angie let the salad bowl crash into the sink.

"Michael!" she screamed. She rounded the counter, her bare feet slipping on the floor. She fell to her knees beside Billie's pale, still body as Michael appeared in the doorway.

"What happened?" he asked, his face a stark, terrified white as he took in his wife's body on the floor.

"I don't know. I don't know. *Call an ambulance.*"

CHAPTER ONE

Ten months later

THE FAMILIAR HEAVINESS settled over Angie as she parked in front of Billie's house. Every time she came here, she saw the same image in her mind's eye: the flashing blue and red ambulance lights reflecting off the white stucco facade, the shocked neighbors gathered on the sidewalk, Billie's too-still body being rushed to the ambulance, an EMT working frantically to keep her alive.

Angie reached for her purse and the bag containing the gifts she'd bought in New York and made her way up the drive, noting the mail crowding the letterbox. The lawn needed mowing, too.

A pile of shoes lay abandoned on the porch—two pairs of child-size rubber boots and a pair of adult sneakers. She hit the doorbell, checking her watch.

After what felt like a long time, she heard footsteps on the other side of the door. It swung open and Michael appeared, his features obscured by the screen.

"Angie." He sounded surprised, but she'd emailed him three days ago to tell him she'd be coming by to see him and the kids once she arrived home.

"Hey. Long time no see," she said easily.

He rubbed his face. "Sorry. I forgot you said you

were coming over." He pushed the screen door open. "Come in."

His hair was longer than when she'd flown out six weeks ago, his jaw dark with stubble. He was wearing a pair of jeans and a sweatshirt, both hanging on his frame.

"How are you?" she asked as she kissed his cheek.

"We're getting by." His gaze slid away from hers and he took a step backward, one hand gesturing for her to precede him up the hallway to the kitchen. "How was New York?"

"Good. Busy. Hot and hectic." She'd gone to train with an American jewelry designer and show her work at an arty little gallery in Greenwich Village. She'd also gone to get away, because she'd needed to do something to shock herself out of her grief.

She blinked as she entered the dim kitchen and living space. The blinds had been drawn on all the windows, the only light coming from the television and around the edges of the blinds.

It took her eyes a few seconds to adjust enough to see that Charlie was ensconced on the couch, his gaze fixed on the flickering TV screen as Kung Fu Panda took out the bad guys.

"Hey, little man," she said, crossing to his side and leaning down to drop a kiss onto his smooth, chubby cheek.

He glanced at her and smiled vaguely before returning his attention to the movie. She took in the stacks of books on the floor, the dirty plates on the coffee table, the clothes strewn over the couch.

"Eva should be home soon. She went to a friend's place after school," Michael said. "You want a coffee?"

She returned to the kitchen, her gaze sliding over

the dishes piled in the sink and the boxes of cereal and other foodstuffs lined up on the island counter. Paperwork sat in a cluttered pile, and an overloaded laundry basket perched on one of the stools, leaning dangerously to one side. Everything looked dusty and ever-so-slightly grubby.

"Coffee would be good, thanks," she said slowly.

The house had been like this when she'd visited before she'd flown to New York, but for some reason it hadn't made the same impression as it did today. Then, she'd talked with Michael amidst all the dishes and laundry and not registered the darkness and the mess and his gauntness. It had all seemed normal, because in the months since Billie's death it had become the norm as she did her best to help Michael any way she could.

Today, she saw it all—the disorder, the dullness in Michael's eyes, the air of neglect and hopelessness—and she understood with a sudden, sharp clarity that this wasn't simply a household in mourning, this was a household veering toward crisis.

Her chest ached as she watched Michael go through the motions of making coffee. For as long as she lived, she would never forget the look in his eyes when she arrived at the hospital hard on the heels of the ambulance that horrible day. He'd been sitting in a small side room, elbows propped on his knees, head in his hands. She'd stopped in the doorway saying his name. When he'd looked up the emptiness and grief in his eyes had told her everything she needed to know. The memory of that moment of realization—the death of her last hope, that somehow they had managed to save Billie from what had clearly been a catastrophic major event—was still sharp and bitter and hard, but she knew that her loss was nothing compared to Michael's.

He'd loved Billie so much. She'd been the center of his world and she'd died far, far too young. Was it any wonder that he was finding it so hard to pull himself together and move on?

She swallowed a lump of emotion and lifted the basket off the stool so she could sit.

"How did your show go?" Michael asked as he slid a brimming coffee mug toward her.

"Well, I think. But it's so competitive over there, I'm not holding my breath."

"Your stuff is great. You don't need to hold your breath."

She didn't doubt the sincerity behind Michael's words, but the lack of emotion in his voice was yet another marker of how flat he was. He'd taken a year off work after Billie's death to provide some stability and continuity for the children. As equal partner in an architecture firm with two other architects, he'd been fortunate that he'd been in a position to do so. At the time Angie had applauded the decision but now, with the benefit of the new perspective provided by her six-week absence, she wasn't so sure.

"Did I miss anything while I was away?"

Michael shrugged. "Like what?"

"Eva was talking about starting ballet again. How did that go?"

"She changed her mind."

"But she was so keen."

He shrugged again. "You know how kids are."

The doorbell echoed through the house before she could ask any more questions.

"That'll be her now."

He left to answer the door. Unable to stop herself, she slid off the stool and crossed to the stack of dirty dishes. The dishwasher was full of clean dishes, and she started stacking them in the cupboards. She was as familiar with Billie's kitchen as she was her own and she'd emptied the top rack by the time Michael returned, Eva trailing in his wake.

"Hey, sweetheart," Angie said, scooping Eva into her arms. "I missed you so much."

Eva's arms tightened around her with surprising strength, her head burrowing into her chest.

"I missed you, too, Auntie Angie."

Angie smoothed a hand over her hair and squeezed her as tightly. She met Michael's gaze over his daughter's head and offered him a faint, sympathetic smile. He didn't respond, simply dropped Eva's school bag on top of the rubble on the table and went to the fridge.

"How was school?" Angie asked, tucking a strand of hair behind Eva's ear.

"It was okay. Dad, I got invited to Imogen's birthday today. It's going to be a fairy party. I can go, can't I?"

"When is it?" Michael piled ingredients on the counter—carrots, zucchini, onions.

"Not this Saturday but the one after that, I think." Eva pulled a crumpled invitation from her uniform pocket and handed it over.

He glanced at it briefly. "Okay. Remind me to take you shopping for a present beforehand."

"Okay. I will. And I'll stick the invitation here, too." She gave her father a significant look before using a magnet to fix the paper to the fridge door. "See? It's right here."

"Yeah, I got that, Eva." There was a note of impatience in his voice, but even that was subdued. Angie watched him, worried.

Michael started grating a carrot. He glanced up, almost as though he sensed her regard. "You staying for dinner?"

"Sure. Thanks. Can I help with anything?"

"Nope. It's just spaghetti, nothing fancy."

Eva groaned. "Not spaghetti *again.*"

Michael ignored his daughter's complaint, grabbing a saucepan and filling it with water. Angie felt a tug on the knee of her jeans and looked down to find Charlie peering at her.

"Up, up!" he said, arms held high.

Clearly, Kung Fu Panda's attractions had waned.

She ducked to lift him, receiving a whiff of ripe diaper as she settled him into her arms. "Wow. Someone's been busy." She lifted his T-shirt and pulled his diaper away from his back to do a visual check. What she saw was not pretty.

Michael raised his eyebrows. "Does he need changing?"

"Oh, yeah."

"Right." He started drying his hands.

"I can take care of it," Angie offered quickly.

"You're sure?"

"Of course. We'll be back in five, won't we, Mr. Stinky Bum?" She jiggled Charlie on her hip as she made her way toward his nursery. The blind was drawn in here, too, giving the room an oppressive, claustrophobic feeling. She flicked on the light, then lifted the blind as high as it would go. Sunshine streamed into the room and some of the tightness left her chest.

Poor Michael. And poor Eva and Charlie.

"What you doin', Angie?" he asked in his bright baby voice, eyes wide and inquisitive.

"Letting some sunshine in, little monkey."

She lay Charlie on his change table and tugged off his jeans. She pulled off the soiled diaper and dropped it in the bin.

"Here." Eva passed a fresh diaper to her, along with the box of baby wipes for the mop-up operation. Angie hadn't realized she'd followed her.

"Hey, thanks." Angie gave the little girl a grateful smile.

"It smells." Eva waved a hand in front of her face.

"Yes, indeed, it does. Your little brother has a gift."

She cleaned him up while Charlie stared at her with a beatific smile and Eva hovered behind her.

"Can I ask a favor, Auntie Angie?" Eva asked after a few seconds.

"Of course you can. You can ask me anything."

"Will you remind Daddy about the party?"

Angie dusted powder over Charlie's nether regions, glancing at Eva. "Sure. But I'm pretty sure your dad will remember all on his own."

"No, he won't. He said he'd take me to see the new Miley Cyrus movie and he didn't. And he promised he'd take me roller skating and we didn't do that, either."

Michael had always been a great father. Attentive, playful, protective. He was indulgent when he needed to be, firm when it counted—and he always did whatever was necessary to make his children feel happy and safe. Hearing that he'd let Eva down on more than one occasion recently brought the tight feeling back to Angie's chest.

"I'll make a note in my phone and I'll call him before the party, okay?"

"Thank you, Auntie Angie." Eva hugged her again. "I'm so glad you're back."

They returned to the kitchen with Charlie walking between them. Michael was scraping vegetables into a saucepan before adding a store-bought jar of pasta sauce.

"Can I play with the iPad, Dad?" Eva asked, already sidling toward the couch.

"Half an hour, max."

"Okay," Eva said, rolling over the back of the couch and down to the seat.

It was such a classic Billie move that for a moment Angie was stunned. Grief stung the back of her eyes, and for long seconds she could do nothing but stare at the floor. When she dared glance at Michael, his face was utterly expressionless, but somehow she knew that he had been equally affected by the small moment. Suddenly he looked much older than his thirty-five years— old and weary and defeated.

The impulse to go to him and simply wrap her arms around him was overwhelming, but they had never had that kind of friendship. They were comfortable and familiar with one another, yes, but they both sat toward the shy end of the personality spectrum, especially where physical stuff was concerned. Billie had been the hugger, and she'd trained Angie to first accept and then reciprocate her ready affection, but it was not a skill that had transferred easily to the other relationships in Angie's life.

She started setting the table and after a few minutes Michael spoke up.

"Dinner's about ten minutes away. Would you mind watching the kids for five while I grab a quick shower?"

"Of course not. Go for it." She shooed him away.

He gave her a half smile as he left. She finished setting the table, then started on the kitchen. By the time Michael returned wearing a fresh pair of jeans and a clean T-shirt, she'd stowed the various foodstuffs in the pantry, emptied the dishwasher and whittled the debris covering the counters down to a stack of paperwork.

Michael's gaze flicked around the room before finding her. She tensed, worried she'd overstepped, but he simply gave her a small acknowledging nod.

"Thanks, Angie."

Between the two of them they wrangled Charlie into his high chair. Michael cut his pasta into small pieces and let it cool before offering the bowl to his son. Charlie stabbed at the plate with his Winnie-the-Pooh cutlery, sending food flying. Michael asked Eva about her day at school and her afternoon at her friend's, saying all the right things in response to her questions, keeping up a semblance of normality.

It was all so subdued and colorless and joyless Angie wanted to weep.

Afterward, she gave Eva the I Love NY T-shirt and lip gloss she'd picked up for her, as well as a funky pair of high-top sneakers.

"Fresh off the streets. No one else will have these for months," she assured Eva.

"They're so sparkly." Eva twisted the shoes so their sequined details reflected the light.

Angie handed a plush toy hot dog to Charlie, along with a miniature version of Eva's T-shirt. Lastly, she slid a T-shirt Michael's way. He raised an eyebrow, obviously surprised he'd been included on the gift list.

"I saw this and thought of you," she said by way of explanation.

He unfolded the T-shirt and read the inscription: Trust Me, I'm an Architect. He smiled his first genuine smile of the day. "Very cool."

By eight o'clock the kids were down for the night, despite much pleading on Eva's behalf to "stay up late because Auntie Angie is home." A stern look and a few words in her father's deepest tones sent Eva scurrying off to bed, leaving Angie alone with Michael.

"Sorry, my hosting skills are a little rusty. I forgot to offer you wine with dinner. There's a bottle in the pantry if you want a glass…?" Michael asked.

"I'm good, thanks. I'm kind of detoxing after New York."

"Lots of partying, huh?"

Again, he was saying the right things, but he wasn't truly engaged. Rather than answer, she studied him for a long beat before starting the conversation that she owed it to Billie—and Michael and Eva and Charlie—to have. Even if it made her uncomfortable to force her way into sensitive territory.

"How are you, Michael? I mean, how are you *really*?"

"I'm fine. We're all good." He said it so automatically she knew she was getting his canned response to well-wishers and relatives.

"You don't look good to me. You've lost weight, you're living in this house like it's a cave, you're shuffling around like a zombie."

His chin jerked as though she'd hit him and it took him a long time to respond. "We're fine."

She glanced at her hands, wondering how hard and how far to push him.

"Have you thought about going back to work early? I know you took twelve months off, but they would take you if you wanted to return early, wouldn't they?"

The thought had occurred to her as she'd watched him prepare dinner. Most men preferred to be doing something rather than sitting around contemplating their navels.

Michael's already stony expression became even more remote. "I took the time off for the kids. They need me to be around."

"They need you to be a fully functioning human being first and foremost, Michael. Did it ever cross your mind that having all this time to think isn't good for you? God knows, it would drive me crazy. If you went to work, you'd get some of your life back. Some of who you are."

"I appreciate the sentiment, Angie, but we're all doing fine." He stood, clearly wanting to end the discussion.

Angie hated confrontation—usually went to great lengths to avoid it—but she hated what she saw happening to Michael even more.

"You think this half life is doing any of you any good? When was the last time you left the house to do anything other than drop Eva at school or go to the supermarket? When was the last time you did something because you wanted to rather than because you had to?"

For a moment there was so much blazing anger in his eyes that she almost shrank into her seat. She understood his anger—his wife of six years had died suddenly and brutally from an undiagnosed congenital heart defect, leaving him to raise their two children alone. He'd lost his dreams, his future, the shape of his world in the space of half an hour.

But the fact remained that life went on. Michael was alive, and Billie was dead, and there was nothing anyone could do about it. Certainly living in some sort of shadow world wasn't going to fix things or make them better.

So she stood her ground and eyed him steadily. "I know it's hard. I think about her every day. I miss her like crazy. But you stopping living isn't going to bring her back."

Michael swallowed, the sound loud in the quiet space. He stared at the floor and closed his eyes, one hand lifting to pinch the bridge of his nose. She didn't know him well enough to understand his signals—she'd only known him when he was happy, not when he was deeply grieving, and she had no map to help her navigate this difficult territory.

"If you want to talk, if you want to rage, if you need help around the house, if you want to burn it all to the ground and start again… Tell me," Angie said. "Tell me what you need, Michael, and I will do whatever I can to make it happen."

She held her breath, hoping she'd gotten through to him. After a moment he lifted his head.

"I need my wife back."

He turned on his heel and walked out of the room. Angie's knees were shaking. She couldn't even remember standing, but she must have in those last few, fraught minutes.

Moving slowly, she gathered her purse and let herself out of the house. Her sandals slapped hollowly on the driveway as she walked to her car. She threw her bag onto the backseat but didn't immediately drive away. Instead, she crossed her arms over the steering wheel and rested her forehead against them. The sadness and emptiness that never really left her welled up and her shoulders started to shake.

I miss you so much, Billie. In so many ways. I'm sorry I couldn't help him. I'll keep trying, but I'm not like you. I don't have your touch with people. But I'll keep trying, I promise.

Angie breathed in through her nose and out through her mouth, fighting for control. She'd had these moments off and on for the past ten months; she knew how to weather them. After a few minutes the shaky, lost feeling subsided, she straightened and wiped the tears from her cheeks. A few minutes after that, she started her car and drove home.

MICHAEL STOOD ON THE DECK, breathing in the cool night air. Trying to calm himself.

Angie was so far out of line it wasn't funny. While she'd been off drinking mojitos or cosmos or whatever the cool drink was these days in New York, he'd been staring his new reality in the face. She had no idea how he felt, no clue what he went through every frickin' day.

The moment the thought crossed his mind his innate sense of fairness kicked in. She may have been in New York for six weeks, but before that Angie had been a rock, standing by his side and doing anything and everything she could to make things bearable after Billie's death. More important, Angie understood more than anyone what losing Billie had meant to him, to his life. She and Billie had been more like sisters than friends. They had finished each other's sentences, said the honest thing when it needed to be said and been each other's best cheerleaders. Angie was trying to piece her life together, too. Trying to work out how to live in a post-Billie world.

That still didn't give her the right to critique his life. It definitely didn't give her the right to tell him he was a zombie or that he was living a half life or to tell him what his kids needed.

When was the last time you did something because you wanted to rather than because you had to?

He ground his teeth together, wishing he could expunge her words from his mind. He didn't want to think. He didn't want to lift his head and look around and see that life was going on around him. He wanted...

He wanted the impossible. Billie, with her huge smile and her even huger heart. He wanted her laughter echoing in the house again. He wanted to wake up in the morning and turn his head and find her lying next to him instead of an empty pillow. He wanted to kiss her lips and smell her perfume. He wanted to lie in bed and have her press her cold feet against his calves to warm them.

He wanted. And his want was never going to be satisfied because his wife's aorta had dissected as a result of high blood pressure, a catastrophic cardiac incident that had meant she was dead before they reached the hospital. Billie was dead and gone, turned to dust. All he had left were the children they had made together and his memories and the house she'd turned into a home for them all.

Not nearly enough.

He sank to the deck, pulling his knees loosely toward his chest. It was cold, but he wasn't ready to go in yet. Angie had stirred him up too much.

He stared into the darkness, aware, as always, of the

silence within the walls behind him. Billie had been the noisiest person he knew. She'd hummed when she washed the dishes, sung in the shower, galloped around the house. Getting used to the new quiet had been but one of many small, painful adjustments he'd had to make over the past ten months.

He exhaled, watching his breath turn to mist in the air.

"Daddy?"

He glanced over his shoulder. Eva stood in the sliding doorway to his bedroom wearing nothing but her nightie, her arms wrapped around her body.

"You shouldn't be out here. It's too cold." He pushed himself to his feet.

"What are you doing?"

"I could ask you the same question. You've got school tomorrow." He laid a hand on her shoulder, turning her around and guiding her to her bedroom.

"I couldn't sleep."

They entered her bedroom and she walked dutifully to her bed and slipped beneath the duvet. "Can you tell me a story?"

"You need to sleep, Eva."

His daughter was a night owl and a master of distraction and procrastination. If he let her, she'd be up half the night, demanding stories and anything else to delay putting her head on her pillow.

"Oh, all right." Her tone was hard done by and world-weary and he couldn't help but smile.

He kissed her forehead. "Sleep tight, don't let the bed bugs bite."

He pulled the quilt up so that it covered her shoulders. He started to straighten, but Eva's hand shot out and caught a hold of his sweatshirt.

"You won't forget about Imogen's party, will you, like you forgot about the movies and roller skating?" she asked, her eyes fixed on his face.

He frowned. "What movie?"

"You said you'd take me to see Miley Cyrus's new movie. Just like you said you'd take me skating with my class."

It was on the tip of his tongue to tell her he didn't know what she was talking about—then suddenly the memory was there, clear as day. Eva, cajoling and pleading, her hands pressed together as though in prayer, promising to do all her chores on time without him having to ask if he would please, please, please take her to the movies. He'd said yes, unable to deny her anything that might give her pleasure.

Then he'd forgotten to follow through on his commitment.

They need you to be a fully functioning human being first and foremost, Michael.

Guilty heat rose up his neck and into his face as Angie's words echoed in his mind. He'd been too busy being defensive and pissy to actually listen to what she'd said, but it was impossible to ignore the anxiety in his daughter's big brown eyes now.

"I'm sorry I forgot, sweetheart. I've had a lot on my mind lately."

"I know, Daddy. You miss Mummy, don't you?"

"I do. But that doesn't mean it's okay to let you down. I promise I won't forget Imogen's party, all right? We'll put it on the calendar."

"I asked Auntie Angie to remind you, too."

Michael winced inwardly. No wonder Angie had felt compelled to say something.

"Good idea. And maybe we could catch that movie this weekend."

"It's not on anymore."

"Then we'll watch it when it comes out on DVD. Make a night of it with popcorn and everything. Okay?"

"Okay. Thanks, Dad."

He kissed her forehead again and waited till she'd snuggled beneath the quilt before leaving the room.

He made his way to his bedroom and sat on the end of his bed. He scrubbed his face with his hands, exhausted. A perpetual state since Billie's death. He thought about what Angie had said and Eva's anxiety.

He needed to get his shit together.

It had been ten months since Billie had died and he needed to stop simply surviving and start living again—if not for his own sake, then for the kids. Because forgetting the Miley Cyrus movie hadn't been his first screwup.

Only last week, he'd woken up, pulled on a pair of jeans and a sweatshirt, then made Eva's lunch and set her backpack by the front door, ready for the school run. He'd gotten her out of bed and into her uniform, strapped Charlie into the car. All part of their morning routine, a routine he did without thinking about it, day in, day out. It was only when he'd been backing out of the drive and the news had come on the radio that he'd realized it was a Saturday.

No doubt if he cared to sift through the past few months, he'd be able to find dozens of similar examples. What had Angie called it? A half life.

Highly appropriate, since he felt like half a person.

As though he'd lost some essential part of himself when he'd lost Billie. He'd always been too quiet, too introverted, too inclined to get lost in his own head and his work, but Billie had dragged him into the world and made him engage and taught him to live as though he meant it. As though every moment counted.

But Billie was gone. And he was not, and the kids were not.

Life went on.

He pushed himself off the bed and went into the bathroom to brush his teeth.

He needed to make some changes, to do something to shift things. He thought about Angie's suggestion—that he go back to work early—and forced himself to really consider it as an option, even though his first response had been to reject it, as he'd rejected everything else she'd said.

He'd taken the year off because he'd wanted the kids to have some kind of continuity of care after Billie's death. She'd been a full-time mom and therefore their primary caregiver, and neither she nor Michael had family who'd been able to step in and help thanks to the tyranny of distance—Billie's family were all in England, his own in Perth, a thousand miles and a time zone away. At the time, twelve months had felt woefully inadequate to patch over the gaping hole left by Billie's absence, but the truth was that the kids had been far more resilient than he'd ever imagined.

Not that they weren't affected by their mother's loss—they were, in hundreds of small ways, all the time—but they were far better at living in the now than he was.

He'd needed the time-out more than they had. He'd been

so shattered in those early days, like a shell-shocked soldier, and there had been something undeniably comforting and numbing about the routine of their very limited domestic life—it had become its own form of suspended animation, a holding pattern that they had existed in to get by.

But getting by wasn't enough, not when he was letting his kids down. They deserved better from him. He needed to move beyond merely surviving.

As impossible as that seemed from where he sat right now.

He looked himself in the eye in the mirror, taking in his shaggy hair and gaunt features and bristly cheeks.

Time did not stand still, and neither could he. Tomorrow, he'd call his partners in the firm and talk to them about returning early. Then he'd start setting his house to rights, both figuratively and literally.

The thought alone was enough to make him feel heavy and overwhelmed.

Damn you, Angie. Why couldn't you have left me alone?

He already knew the answer—because she was a friend, and because she cared enough to make the tough call, even when she knew her point of view probably wouldn't be appreciated.

He needed to add apologizing to her to his list of things to do tomorrow.

He finished up then shed his clothes and climbed into bed. Turning onto his side, he closed his eyes. As always as he drifted toward sleep, there was a small, forgetful moment where he slid his hand over to touch

Billie's back, instinctively seeking reassurance as he hovered on the brink.

As always, he found nothing but cold sheets.

A few minutes after that, he fell asleep.

CHAPTER TWO

THE NEXT MORNING FOUND Angie wrestling with the ancient lock on the door to her studio. She pulled the key out, then slid it back in and jiggled it around. After a few tense seconds she felt the latch give and rolled her eyes.

Typical. Like everything else in the Stradbroke building, the mechanism worked just enough to make it difficult to make a case to the landlord to replace it. She locked the door behind her and dropped her bag on the small table and chairs she kept for client meetings, then crossed to the window to let in some fresh air. Next, she pulled on the well-worn leather apron she wore to protect her clothes and hunkered down in front of her safe to open it. Inside were the flat strips of gold, silver and other metals that she used to create the alloys for her pieces, as well as a box containing dozens of small boxes, each of which boasted a selection of diamonds and other gems. She preferred to work with white, champagne and pink diamonds, but she had a small collection of rubies and emeralds and sapphires, as well. This morning she ignored the stones and pulled the gold and silver from the safe. Both the rings for the Merton commission—her first priority this week—were to be made from 18-karat white gold. She checked the design brief she'd created in consultation with Judy and John and did some math to calculate how much she'd need of both

palladium and gold to accommodate their ring sizes—
an L and S respectively—then turned toward the scales
to measure.

Perhaps inevitably, her thoughts turned to Michael
and the kids as she worked.

She'd really pissed him off last night with her unso-
licited advice.

It was so hard to know what to do. Michael may have
been married to Billie for six years, and Angie may have
seen him once a week on average during that time, but
their friendship had always been grounded in their mutual connection with Billie. Not that Angie didn't like
him in his own right—she did, a lot—but in her mind
he was Billie's husband first and foremost, and then Michael. Just as she suspected she was Billie's friend first
to him, and then herself.

Although maybe that assessment wasn't strictly true
anymore. It had been an intense ten months, after all.

The phone rang, cutting through her thoughts. She
leaned to grab the handset.

"Angela speaking."

"Angie, it's Michael."

"Oh. Hi."

"Don't worry, I'm not going to bite your head off
again. I rang to apologize for last night."

"You don't need to apologize."

"Yeah, I do. I was an ass, and I'm sorry."

One of the things she'd always liked about Michael
was that he didn't beat around the bush. He was a man
of few words, but those he did speak were always worth
hearing.

"Apology accepted. Even if it is unnecessary."

"I thought about what you said, and I spoke to my

partners today. They're keen for me to come back whenever I'm ready."

"Hey, that's great. Are you going to take them up on it?"

"I don't know. I need to sort out child care. But you were right. Sitting around here on my own all day isn't helping anything."

She pictured the darkened kitchen and living room and his shaggy hair and too-thin frame.

"It's hard to get into things again. But life goes on whether we want it to or not. Wrong as it seems." She hated how trite she sounded.

"Yeah, I know."

"Have you thought about going back part-time to start with? Maybe three days a week, or something like that? That way both you and the kids would have a chance to get used to you not being around as much."

"Part-time. I hadn't thought of that. But there's no reason why I couldn't do it, even if it meant I worked from home on the other days."

"Let's face it, you're probably going to do that anyway," she said drily.

"True. And that would mean I'd only have to find day care for Charlie three days. And work out something for Eva after school."

She moved to the window, stepping into a shaft of sunlight and letting it warm her skin.

"What about a nanny? I have no idea how much they are, but my friend Gail uses one. She says it's a godsend."

"Yeah? I guess it would be worth investigating. I keep hearing that the day-care places around here have waiting lists as long as my arm."

"I'll ask where she got hers and text you."

"Thanks, Angie. I appreciate it."

There was a humble sincerity to his tone that made her throat tight.

"How would you feel about me coming over on Sunday and taking Eva shopping for her friend's present?"

It felt like a pitifully small gesture, all things considered, but at least it was practical.

"I would feel eternally grateful. I have no idea what to buy a six-year-old."

"Neither do I, to be honest, but we can wing it. What say I swing by to pick her up at two on Sunday?"

"She'll be ready. Thanks, Angie."

"It helps me, too, you know," she said quietly. "Being with the kids. Helping you out."

He was silent for a moment. "Okay." There was a wealth of understanding in the single word.

"I'll see you Sunday."

"You will."

She ended the call and stepped out of the sunshine.

Michael was going back to the firm. A good decision, she was sure of it. Her work had saved her during the early, hard months. She was sure it would help him find himself again now.

At least, she hoped so.

THE REMAINDER OF THE WEEK sped by in a blur. Angie worked late every night, keen to make inroads on the commissions that had been waiting while she was in New York. She allowed herself the small luxury of sleeping in on Sunday before catching up with a friend for lunch. It was just after two when she stopped in front of Billie's house.

She rang the doorbell, then had a horrible moment where she was suddenly convinced that she'd left her phone behind in the café. She fumbled in her handbag. Her fingers closed around her phone's smooth contours as the front door opened.

"Hey. Right on time," Michael said.

She glanced up, a lighthearted retort on her lips. The first thing she registered was his new, crisp haircut and the fact that he was clean-shaven. Then her gaze took in his broad chest in a sweat-dampened tank top and the skin-tight black running leggings moulded to his muscular legs. The words died on her lips and she blinked, momentarily stunned by the change in him.

"You've cut your hair," she said stupidly.

"Yeah. Decided it was time to stop doing my Robinson Crusoe impersonation."

He gestured for her to enter and she brushed past him. He smelled of fresh air and spicy masculine deodorant. He preceded her up the hall and her gaze traveled across his shoulders before dropping to his muscular backside. Billie had often waxed poetic about Michael's body, but Angie had always made a point of not noticing—she didn't want to know that kind of stuff. Now, as he stopped at the kitchen counter, she was forcibly reminded of the fact that he was a very attractive man.

For a moment she didn't quite know where to look.

"Is, um, Eva ready to go? I thought I'd take her to Chadstone," she said, naming Melbourne's biggest shopping center. Her gaze skittered uneasily around the room. It was only then that she noticed the other changes—the kitchen was clean, not a single dirty bowl or plate in sight, and the dining table had been polished to a shine. True, a small stack of neatly folded washing sat at one end, but it looked like a temporary measure this time rather than a permanent fixture. The living room had been cleared of stray books and magazines and abandoned clothes, the cushions on the couch plumped.

Most important, the blinds had been raised, inviting the weak winter sunshine into the house.

She forgot all about her uncomfortable awareness as her gaze met Michael's.

"Look at you go," she said quietly.

He shrugged, but she could tell he was pleased she'd noticed the difference. "Getting there."

It wasn't only his hair that was different, she realized. His eyes were different, too. Brighter, clearer, more focused. As though he'd ceased looking inward and was ready to engage with the world again.

"Okay. I'm ready. Let's get this show on the road," Eva announced as she marched into the room.

She was dressed in a pair of yellow cowboy boots, a bright blue skirt and a poppy-red sweater. Her blond hair had been pulled into two lopsided pigtails and fastened with yellow-and-white polka dot ribbons, and a grass-green handbag hung from her shoulder.

Her mother's daughter, from top to toe.

"You look like a summer's day," Angie said, opening her arms for a hug.

Eva walked into her embrace, resting her head beneath Angie's breasts.

"I feel like a summer's day. We're going *shopping*."

Michael smiled ruefully. "Words to make any man quake in his shoes." He picked up his wallet. "How much money do you need?"

"I have my own money, thank you very much." Eva

pulled an elephant-shaped wallet from her handbag and displayed the two five-dollar bills resting within.

"Not bad, money bags. How about I give Auntie Angie a little extra in case you ladies find something nice that catches your eye?"

Angie shook her head as he offered her two crisp fifties. "I've got it covered."

"You're doing enough already."

Before she could protest again, he closed the distance between them and tucked the bills into her coat pocket. She caught another whiff of his deodorant and a faint hint of clean, male sweat.

She cleared her throat. "Well. We should probably get going, little lady. Don't want to miss out on all the bargains."

Eva kissed her father goodbye and Angie told him they would be back by five and hustled out the door. She didn't feel one hundred percent comfortable until she was sliding into the driver's seat.

Which was dumb. Michael was still Michael, even if he did have an attractive body and a handsome face. Just because she'd suddenly tuned into that fact for a few seconds didn't change anything.

"Weirdo," she muttered under her breath.

"Sorry?" Eva said, her face puzzled.

"Nothing, sweetheart."

And it *was* nothing. A stupid, odd little moment of awareness that meant nothing to anybody. Shaking it off, she started the car and pulled away from the curb.

MICHAEL SHOWERED AFTER Angie and Eva had left, taking advantage of the fact that Charlie was enjoying a rare afternoon nap. His legs ached from the run he'd taken after lunch while his neighbor, Mrs. Linton, watched the kids, but for the first time in a long time his body felt loose and easy.

He soaped himself down and allowed himself to enjoy the simple pleasure of warm water and well-used muscles. His thoughts drifted to the afternoon. The odds were good that Charlie would be awake any second now. Maybe they could go to the park. Charlie could run around to his heart's content and afterward Michael might take a look at the plans Dane had sent over last night.

Michael was still feeling his way toward the whole going-back-to-work thing. He'd spoken to a nanny agency and they were lining up interviews for him for next week and Mrs. Linton had offered to help in the interim, but a part of him was holding back for some reason, not quite ready to commit to the complete resumption of his life. It was one thing to get a haircut and clean the house. It was another thing entirely to draw a line under the past few months and let the world in again.

Dane had clearly taken his imminent return as a given, however—Michael had checked his email last night and found a sizable file waiting for him, complete with brief and draft plans for a luxury beach house the firm had been commissioned to design. One of many projects, apparently, that his fellow partners were happy to hand over the moment Michael returned.

After dressing in jeans and a T-shirt and hooded sweatshirt, he took Charlie to the local park where they swung and climbed and played peekaboo endlessly. There were a couple of other parents hanging around with their kids, one of whom he recognized as a member of Billie's mothers' group. He chatted to her politely for a few minutes before Charlie once again demanded his attention. He walked away feeling woefully rusty at the whole small-talk thing.

Later, he was folding the last of the washing when he heard the door open and the sound of Eva's footsteps pounding along the hall.

"We got the bestest present *ever*," she announced as she burst into the kitchen. She held what looked like a set of butterfly wings.

"Wow. They look pretty cool," he said as Angie followed Eva.

"We had trouble deciding between fairy and butterfly wings. So we got both." Angie brandished her own shopping bag. "Eva's going to decide which ones she thinks Imogen would prefer." Angie's deep blue eyes were shining with laughter. They both knew that Eva's choice would be more about which pair of wings she didn't want.

"Sounds like your mission was achieved."

"We had a great time. Auntie Angie took me to get my nails done, and we had coffee and *bisgotty*."

"Biscotti," Angie said easily. "Which is a fancy-pants way of saying *biscuit* in Italian."

"Biscotti. Bis-cotti," Eva repeated to herself.

Michael didn't even try to hide his smile this time, and neither did Angie. He met her gaze again.

"Stay for dinner?"

"Sure. If you've got enough to go around."

"It's nothing fancy, just pasta. And there's always enough pasta."

"No," Eva groaned. "We always have spaghetti."

"I think you might be exaggerating a little there, sweetheart."

"We had it last night, and Wednesday night, and Monday night."

Michael frowned, ready to correct her. Then he realized she was right. "Those were all different pastas." He sounded lame, even to himself. The truth was, he was a competent cook, but not a very imaginative one.

"Have you made anything yet?" Angie asked.

"No. I was about to start on the sauce. Which will be different from the other sauces we had during the week," he said for Eva's benefit.

She gave him a skeptical look, as well she might. There was only so much a man could do with tomatoes, onion and ground meat.

"If you want to take a break from the kitchen for the night, I could make us Mexican. I picked up a few groceries while we were out so I've got a taco kit and the makings for a salad in the car," Angie said.

"Yes!" Eva jumped up and down on the spot, hands in the air.

"Mexican it is, then," Angie said.

The dinner prep passed quickly, punctuated with lots of laughter. The Mexican feast elicited loud approving noises from his children—a hint, in case he'd missed the earlier message, that he needed to add a little more variety to their weekly menu.

Charlie was rubbing his eyes by the time they had finished eating and Michael took a chance and settled him in his bed. Miraculously, Charlie's eyes shut after only ten minutes of story.

When Michael returned to the kitchen, Angie was seated at the counter, her chin propped on her left hand as she sketched rapidly in a notebook.

"Guess who's already asleep?"

She glanced up, her blue eyes unfocused for a few seconds as she dragged herself back from whatever creative space she'd been in.

"Really? He's down already?"

"The magic of the park."

"Wow. They should put that in a can. It would sell like hotcakes."

"You want a coffee?"

"Sure."

He glanced to the living area and saw that Eva had crashed out on the couch, too. Unusual for her, but maybe the shopping had worn her out. He pulled mugs from the cupboard and grabbed the French press. He turned to check if Angie wanted some chocolates with their coffee and saw that she was once again absorbed in her notebook, this time writing small, neat notes to herself in the margin.

She was so self-contained, one of the calmest people he knew. In fact, he could count on the fingers of one hand the number of times he'd seen her really agitated or distressed. She approached everything with an interested, open-minded curiosity and an unfailing, quiet sense of humor. She was good company, good to spend time with.

All of which made her apparently perpetual single status baffling to him. It wasn't as though she was hard on the eyes. She might not be conventionally beautiful, but her long, oval face and deep blue eyes were very appealing. She had a sleek, subtly curved body that was more athletic than va-voom, but there was no denying that she was an attractive woman. Very attractive.

He knew through Billie that Angie's love life was hardly a barren desert—there were men, not too many, but enough—yet none of them seemed to stick. He also knew via his indiscreet wife that there had been one man years ago who Angie had been crazy about. Was she still holding a candle for him? Or was it simply a matter of her not being interested?

Behind him, the kettle clicked to announce it had boiled. He started to make the coffees as the doorbell rang through the house.

He frowned. It was nearly eight-thirty, and the days of people dropping in unannounced had gone with Billie.

"I'll finish this. You get the door," Angie said.

"Thanks."

He made his way up the hall and opened the door to find the woman he'd run into in the park earlier on his doorstep, a piece of paper in hand.

"Michael. Hi. Remember me? Gerry." She gave a self-conscious laugh.

"Of course," he said, even though he'd forgotten her name the moment she'd reintroduced herself this afternoon. He simply didn't have room for that sort of thing in his head right now.

"Sorry to show up on your doorstep like this, but I was thinking about Charlie this afternoon and I realized that you've probably been out of the loop a bit since we all used to contact Billie for things… Anyway, I thought you might be interested in this."

Gerry thrust the piece of paper at him and he saw that it was a flyer advertising a sing-and-dance event at the local indoor play center.

"A bunch of us are going to make a day of it, take a picnic, that sort of thing." Gerry smoothed a hand over her deep red hair.

"Thanks. I'll see if we can make it. Charlie thinks he's a rock star, so it's all about singing and dancing for him."

She laughed a little too loudly. "Oh, he's adorable. And so is Eva. Such lovely kids."

There wasn't much he could say to that and not sound like a monstrous egotist, so he simply smiled politely. Gerry started talking about the next mothers' group get-together and insisted on passing over another list with everyone's phone numbers, indicating her own.

"Anything you need, babysitting, whatever, you call me," she said. "I'd be happy to help out any way I can. I know how tough it is doing it all alone."

They had been talking on the doorstep so long he suspected he probably should have invited her inside, but just when he was prodding himself to do so she palmed her car keys and took a step away.

"I'll see you around, Michael."

"Sure. And thanks for this, Gerry. I appreciate it."

She waved a hand to indicate it wasn't a big deal and then took off up the driveway, her high heels loud against the concrete. He shut the door and returned to the kitchen. Two mugs sat steaming on the counter. Angie had a small, wry smile on her face.

"One of Billie's mothers' group friends with a play-date thingy," he explained, brandishing the flyer before using a magnet to fix it to the fridge. "I ran into her in the park today."

"Was that what that was about?" Angie asked, eyebrows arched knowingly.

He stared at her blankly. "What else would it be?"

She gave a small laugh. "Michael, she was hitting on you."

"No, she wasn't."

"Um, yeah, she was. Totally hitting on you. Who drops by with a playdate reminder at eight-thirty on a Sunday night?"

He shook his head. "You're wrong."

She didn't say anything, but her expression did.

"She's married, Angie. She has kids."

"She has kids, yes, but not all the women in that group were married, you know. Ever heard of single parent-hood and divorce?"

He shrugged, sick of the subject. "Fine. Maybe she was hitting on me. If you say so."

He grabbed his mug and took a mouthful of strong, hot coffee. Angie had made it exactly the way he liked it.

"She won't be the last, you know."

"I don't care."

She eyed him sympathetically, hands wrapped around her mug, elbows propped on the counter.

"You might eventually."

He set his cup down so firmly it made a loud crack against the marble surface. "No, I won't."

Why was Angie pushing this? She, of all people, should understand that Billie couldn't be replaced.

Afraid he'd say something he'd regret, he went to put his daughter to bed.

CHAPTER THREE

ANGIE WATCHED MICHAEL'S retreat, wishing back her impulsive words.

He'd been genuinely surprised and not a little uncomfortable when she'd pointed out that the woman had been flirting with him. She should have bitten her tongue then, when it was clear that the subject of him being a hot commodity in the singles market wasn't something he was ready to consider.

Her gaze fell on the milk, abandoned on the counter. Grabbing it, she slid off her stool and returned it to the fridge. Michael had looked so grim when she'd hinted that other women might be interested in him. So sad and serious.

He'd loved Billie so deeply, so devotedly. Angie was an idiot for even raising the subject of him moving on.

She turned to find Michael standing barely a foot behind her.

"Sorry," he said simply and sincerely. "I overreacted."

"I'm the one who's sorry. I shouldn't have said anything." She fought the urge to take a step away. She didn't want Michael to think he made her uncomfortable—he didn't—but she was very aware of how close they were standing.

He smiled faintly. "Good old Angie, always letting

me off the hook. Have I told you lately that you've been fantastic?"

"Um…no?" This close, she could see tiny flecks of amber in the depths of his gray-green eyes. She stared, fascinated.

"Thank you, Angie." He reached out and rested his hand on her shoulder. His thumb grazed the sensitive skin of her collarbone as he gave her a quick, light squeeze before moving away. "You want to watch a movie?"

She frowned, unsettled by the small contact and the fact that she could still feel the heat of his hand.

This was Michael, after all.

He glanced over his shoulder, waiting for her answer. The ring of a cell phone cut through the room.

"That's mine," Angie said, crossing to where she'd dumped her handbag at the far end of the dining table. She checked the caller ID but didn't recognize the number. "Angela Bartlett speaking."

"Angie, it's Tess."

"Oh. Hey." Angie frowned. Tess was a fellow tenant in the Stradbroke building, and while they were friends, it was unusual for her to call like this. "How are things?"

"I've got some bad news. There's been a break-in at the Stradbroke. A whole bunch of studios have been trashed."

"What?" Cold shock washed through her. "How bad is it?"

"I have no idea how bad yours is, but mine's a wreck. They stole my computer, my iPod, even my freakin' kettle, can you believe that? And they trashed all of my latest canvases."

Angie could hear the quiver in Tess's voice. She was

a tough nut. If she was teary, things must be pretty bad. Angie closed her eyes. If they had somehow managed to get into her safe, she was completely screwed. She had two sets of rings in there waiting for delivery, and she'd recently received a shipment of gold. Not to mention the thousands and thousands of dollars' worth of gems.

"I'll be there as soon as I can," she said.

"I'll be here. Surrounded by all this crap."

Angie ended the call and scooped up her bag.

"What's wrong?" Michael took a step toward her.

"There's been a break-in at the studio. Mine and a bunch of others have been trashed." She fumbled in her handbag for her keys. Her hands were shaking so much it took a couple of attempts to get a grip on them.

This could be the end of her business.

"Has someone called the police? How bad is it?"

"I don't know. I need to go...." She started to leave, her thoughts racing ahead of her.

"Angie."

Michael's hand caught her arm as she was opening the front door. "Drive carefully, okay? Any damage has already been done, so you speeding there isn't going to change anything." His voice was calm and steady. Grounding.

She took a deep breath and nodded. "You're right."

"Keep us in the loop, okay?"

"I will." She gave him a small, grateful smile before exiting the house.

The moment she was in the car all her worries rose to the surface again but she resisted the impulse to floor it, Michael's words still echoing in her mind. There was no point adding a speeding fine—or worse—to tonight's woes. Whatever they might be.

She found a parking spot around the corner from the building and ran the half block to the entrance. Her footsteps sounded loud in the stairwell as she climbed to the fifth floor. She could see evidence of the break-in as she climbed—graffiti and broken glass—and there was more when she arrived on her floor. Glass glinted on the tiles in the corridor, and every door along this side hung open drunkenly, regardless of the security measures the individual tenants had in place. A couple of police officers stood at the far end of the corridor, talking. One of them started walking toward her the moment they saw her.

"I'm afraid I'm going to have to ask you to leave, miss. This is a crime scene."

"I'm a tenant—studio twenty-three. My neighbor told me my space has been broken into."

The policeman consulted his notebook. "Number twenty-three. That makes you Angela Bartlett."

"That's right."

"You can go in to assess the damage and tell us what's missing, but I need you to not touch anything until our crime-scene people have finished collecting evidence."

"Okay. Sure. Whatever you want, I just need to see my studio."

She was aware of the anxious pounding of her heart as she followed him around the corner. She could see her door hanging open.

"They hit every studio?" she asked, her gaze darting left and right as she inspected the damage to her neighbors' spaces as they passed. What she saw only increased the anxiety tightening her chest—smashed furniture, toppled bookcases.

"On this level, yeah. Downstairs they were a bit more

discriminating." The cop halted. "Okay, here we are. Remember, no touching anything until the team's been through."

She nodded, her gaze fixed on the doorway. She sent up a prayer to the universe.

Please let them have not broken into the safe.

She stepped over the threshold.

The first thing she registered was the black paint sprayed across the wall, a huge, furious four-letter word six feet high. Paint had dribbled down to the floor, which was covered with broken glass from the framed artwork they had torn off the walls. The mid-century sideboard that had housed her books and keepsakes had been tipped over, spilling its contents, and her table and chairs had been smashed.

Her gaze zeroed in on the safe. Relief pounded through her as she saw that while the dull gray metal was scarred and pitted around the locking mechanism and it had been dragged a few feet from its position in the corner, the door remained closed.

"Oh, thank God," she said, closing her eyes for a brief second.

That was one disaster averted, at least. She turned to inspect the rest of her space and sucked in a dismayed breath when she saw her workbench. The intruders had sprayed black paint over all her tools—the leather hammer she'd used for more than ten years, her vernier caliper, her flexi-drive drill, all the drill bits and mops and burrs… Again, she reached out but caught herself in time.

Angry tears burned at the back of her eyes. She didn't understand why anyone would be so destructive. She was a stranger to the intruders, yet they had made a concerted effort to maliciously destroy her creative space.

Her phone rang. She pulled it from her bag. Michael's number showed on the screen.

"Everything okay?" he asked the moment she took the call.

"Yes and no. They didn't get into my safe, which would have pretty much been the end of my business. But they've absolutely trashed everything else they could get their hands on. Including my tools."

"Shit. I'm really sorry, Angie."

"Yeah. Me, too. Stupid assholes."

"I take it you're insured?"

"Yeah, but I think it's mostly going to be cleaning up, not replacing stuff. Apart from what's in the safe, most of the things I had here have value only for me, you know. They're hardly worth claiming on insurance."

"Anything I can do?"

Despite the situation, his offer warmed her. Suddenly she didn't feel quite so alone or overwhelmed.

"Thanks, but there's nothing anyone can do at this stage. The police won't let me touch anything until their fingerprint people have—" Her roaming gaze fell on a spray of dirt on the floor near the window.

The burn of tears intensified as she saw that her Japanese maple bonsai tree had been thrown to the floor and stomped on. The pottery base was shattered, and half the tree's roots were exposed and broken.

"Angie? Are you okay?"

She sank to her knees and reached for the fragile tangle of leaves and tiny branches.

"They smashed my bonsai."

There was a small silence. She knew Michael understood the significance of the loss. Billie had given her the tiny tree as a gift to brighten her workspace, even though Angie had what could only be described as a black thumb. At the time, Angie had given Billie her word that she'd keep it alive, and so far the bonsai had survived almost three years of benign neglect.

She lifted the tree gently. It was crushed, the main trunk almost completely severed. Utterly beyond saving.

"If you want, I can be there in half an hour. I'm sure Mrs. Linton could look after the kids for a few hours."

She sniffed back her tears. "I'm okay. Just angry. It's so destructive. And completely pointless."

"You sure you don't want some company?"

"I'll be all right. But thanks for the offer."

It wasn't until they ended the call that it struck her that ten months ago, Billie would have been the one on the phone, insisting on helping. It was hard facing a crisis without her best support and cheerleader, but it was also nice to know that Michael cared enough to have made the call.

Of course he cares. He's your friend. Just as you're his friend.

She heard footsteps in the corridor and the policeman stopped in the doorway.

"I'm sorry, ma'am, but our team is here now. You're going to have to leave."

"Okay."

She took one last look around her devastated studio. As she'd said to Michael, there was nothing she could do here till tomorrow.

Shoulders straight, she headed for home.

Michael worried about Angie all night until he went to bed and then started again first thing when he woke the next morning. She'd done so much for him and the kids and he hated the thought of her having to deal with the invasion of her creative space all on her own.

After he'd dropped Eva at school, he drove into the city. Charlie was asleep in his car seat by the time Michael found a parking spot. He unstrapped him and carried him the block to Angie's building. Charlie began to wriggle in his arms as he approached the entrance and he set his son on his feet and took his hand.

"You happy now?"

Charlie nodded.

"Shall we go visit Angie, then?"

"Angie?" Charlie's face was a study in delight.

The directory in the foyer told him A. Bartlett was in studio twenty-three on the fifth floor. He eyed the ancient cage elevator suspiciously before deciding to take the stairs. After the first flight, Charlie allowed himself to be carried again, a capitulation which shortened their upward trek by several minutes.

Glass crunched underfoot, and when they arrived at the fifth floor more piles of broken glass were stationed periodically along the corridor, clearly waiting to be collected and disposed of. Michael winced when he saw the damage to some of the studios he passed.

"Down. Down!" Charlie commanded as they neared Angie's.

Michael set him on his feet but kept a tight grip on his son's hand as he searched for number twenty-three. Belatedly it occurred to him that he probably should have called first—for all he knew, Angie might be out arranging repairs or talking to clients. Then he saw that the door to what he assumed was her studio was open and lifted a hand to knock on the doorframe to announce himself. His hand froze inches from the wood as he registered that Angie was inside and that she wasn't alone.

Not by a long shot.

Instead, she was in what looked like a fervent embrace with a tall, muscular man with long dark hair. The other man's hands were splayed possessively over the small of her back, his face nuzzled into the curve of her neck and shoulder. Her arms banded around him, the muscles in her arms flexing as she held him close. Michael couldn't see her face, but it was blindingly obvious that he was about to step into what was clearly a very private moment.

He would come back later. Maybe take Charlie for a walk around the block, then pop in again. Give Angie time to do…whatever with her friend. Or whoever the guy was.

He took a step backward, already pivoting on his heel.

Charlie resisted, straining against his grip. "Angie." He pointed at the object of his affection.

Angie's head came up, eyes wide.

"Charlie." She stepped out of the other man's arms as her gaze shifted to Michael. "Michael. What are you guys doing here?"

She looked and sounded so surprised he suddenly felt a little self-conscious. "We, um, wanted to make sure you're okay. But we can come back later." He tugged on Charlie's arm again. "Come on, matey. You want to go get some chocolate?"

"Don't be silly. You weren't interrupting anything," Angie said.

Long-haired guy frowned, not liking the sound of that.

"I can't believe you came all the way into the city

just to see me. How lucky am I?" Angie bent to scoop Charlie into her arms.

His son happily sat on her hip, despite the fact that he'd squirmed his way out of Michael's arms barely minutes before.

"Angie," Charlie said, reaching out to touch the sparkling earring dangling from her lobe.

"I thought we could help you clean up, sort things out," Michael said.

Angie's expression was soft with gratitude. "Thank you. That's really sweet of you."

Long-haired guy shifted his weight ostentatiously, drawing attention to himself.

Angie looked a little sheepish. "Sorry, I'm being rude. Carlos, this is Michael and Charlie. Carlos has a studio on the fourth floor."

"Good to meet you. I hope things didn't go too badly for you last night." Michael offered his hand.

"I was lucky for once, since they skipped me. But poor Angie was not so lucky."

"No," Michael said, very aware of the other man sizing him up.

Carlos stepped closer to Angie and laid a hand on her shoulder. "I need to get back to my work, but we're still on for lunch, yes?"

There was a faint lilt to his voice, indicating that English was not his first language.

"Can I call you? I really want to get as much of this sorted today as I can. I can't afford to lose more time." Her forehead was puckered with worry.

"You have to eat, beautiful," Carlos said. Then he leaned forward and pressed a kiss to her lips, maintaining the contact longer than was strictly necessary. Almost as though he was trying to make a point—although to whom, Michael had no idea. "Call me, okay?"

Carlos gave Michael a reserved nod before leaving. Angie jiggled Charlie on her hip, making him giggle.

"This is a nice surprise, isn't it? A lovely surprise," she said. Her cheeks were a little flushed, as though she was embarrassed about something.

Michael surveyed the room, taking in the graffiti and the pile of glass and other debris that had been swept into the corner. Pieces of a broken table and chairs lay beside it, and twin piles of books were stacked near the door. A mid-century sideboard in teak veneer lay facedown on the ground.

"They did a real number on the place, huh?"

"Pretty much. If it moved, they smashed it, and if it didn't, they painted it." Angie shook her head with disgust.

Michael crossed to the sideboard and crouched, getting a good grip on it before easing into an upright position. Once it was righted he saw it was still half-filled with books, which explained both why it was so heavy and why Angie hadn't tackled it on her own. There was more broken glass underneath, as well as the smashed remains of what looked like a porcelain menagerie—a lion, a tiger, an elephant and a monkey.

"More casualties." Angie's face was taut with unhappiness.

"No be sad," Charlie said, reaching up to stroke her cheek. "You no be sad."

She immediately smiled, rubbing her nose against his. "It's okay, Charlie-boy. I'm okay."

Michael pushed the sideboard against the wall and crouched to tidy the books on the shelves.

"Don't worry about those. I can do that later," she said.

"We came to help." He was aware of feeling off balance as he tidied the books. It took him a moment to understand that he was thrown by the discovery that Angie had a boyfriend.

She hadn't mentioned anyone to him, not even in passing. The omission left him feeling oddly unsettled. As though something small but significant in his understanding of the world had shifted.

In the months since Billie had died Angie had laughed with him, cried with him, cooked for him, changed his son's diapers and read bedtime stories to his daughter. Yet she hadn't even so much as hinted that she was seeing someone.

Newsflash, buddy—you don't own her. She doesn't owe you anything.

He knew the voice in his head was right. He had no right to feel…*possessive* was the wrong word, but it was close…of Angie. She didn't belong to him and the kids. She was her own person, with her own life and her own dreams and wants and desires. All of which she was entitled to keep to herself if she so chose.

"What does Carlos do?" So much for minding his own business.

"He's a musician, plus he does a bit of sound-engineering work on the side."

"Right."

Shut up. Not another word.

"So how long have you two been…?" He kept his gaze on his task, very carefully not looking at her. He had no idea why he was asking, why he felt the burning need to know what was going on in her life.

Angie laughed, the sound reassuringly startled. "Me and Carlos? I don't think so."

He allowed himself to look at her. "Yeah? The way he was marking his territory just now, I figured you guys must have something going on."

"I have no idea what that was about. We've had drinks after work a few times. But he's not my type. Too brooding and artistic. I like a little less drama in my life."

She might not have any idea what the other man's ostentatious display had been about, but Michael did. For some reason, he'd seen Michael as a rival for Angie's affections. Which went to show how good the other man's instincts were.

Angie took up the broom and resumed sweeping the floor, Charlie clinging to her leg. It occurred to him that bringing a two-year-old to the site of a break-in hadn't been his smartest move. But he hadn't exactly been thinking rationally when he'd turned the car toward the city. He'd only wanted to make sure Angie was okay.

"Here, I'll do that," he said, holding a hand out for the broom.

"I'm almost done," Angie said, smiling at Charlie, who was looking at her with bright eyes.

"Is there a bin where we can dump all this stuff?"

"I hadn't even thought that far ahead." She tucked a strand of long dark hair behind her ear. "There's supposed to be a wheelie bin on each level, but half the time it disappears."

"I'll go see if I can find something." He started for the door.

"Michael?"

He glanced over his shoulder.

"I meant what I said before. I really appreciate you coming in like this."

"Not a big deal."

"It is to me." Her smile was a little wobbly.

He could suddenly see all her hurt and anger and frustration, all the emotions she'd stuffed deep inside in order to do what needed to be done to get her studio back in order.

"We'll fix it, don't worry."

"Okay." Her eyes were shiny with unshed tears.

Before he could stop himself, he closed the distance between them and wrapped his arms around her. She tensed for a second and he thought she would push him away. Then her arms circled his waist and her body softened and she rested her forehead on his shoulder. For a long moment they were silent. He was aware of her knees touching his and the warmth of her body and the faint fruity scent of her shampoo. He rested his cheek against her hair, wishing there was some way he could make things right for her.

After a minute she lifted her head and he let her go.

"Thanks," she said with a small, self-conscious smile as she stepped backward.

"I want cuddle, too," Charlie demanded, both arms raised.

Angie laughed. "Of course you do."

She stooped to pick him up and Charlie wrapped his arms around her neck and pressed a big, wet kiss to her cheek.

Michael smiled. "I'll go find that bin."

It wasn't until he was turning the corner in the corridor that it occurred to him that hug had been his first adult human contact in months.

CHAPTER FOUR

"HEY, CHARLIE, COME away from there. You don't want to touch all that nasty stuff," Angie said, herding him away from the pile of debris in the corner.

Charlie complied readily, trotting off to inspect the safe instead. Angie watched him distractedly. She was still getting over the surprise of Michael's spontaneous embrace.

They had hugged before, but not often, and usually only briefly, in greeting or thanks. And, of course, after Billie's death there had been condolence and sympathy hugs.

Today's hug had felt different, and she couldn't understand why.

Charlie spun the dial, fascinated. Angie thought about the moment when Michael's arms had come around her and she'd found herself pressed against the firm, warm wall of his chest. She'd been surprised at first. But then something inside her had relaxed as she'd understood that she was in a safe place and she'd allowed herself to take comfort from him.

Then he'd shifted slightly or she had and their knees had bumped and she'd become very aware of how well-matched their bodies were—knee to knee, hip to hip, breast to chest.

The realization had been enough to make her step

away then, and it made her feel uneasy now, even though he'd been gone for more than ten minutes.

Because that moment had been about sexual awareness. The woman in her noticing the man in him.

But Michael wasn't a man. At least, he wasn't an ordinary man. He was Billie's husband. He might as well be Angie's brother.

And yet there'd been that funny little moment when he'd opened the door wearing his running gear yesterday and she'd seen him with fresh eyes and registered that he was a very attractive man....

There was a loud rumbling in the corridor and Michael appeared in the doorway, a large wheelie bin in tow. She forced herself to meet his eyes, almost as though she was testing herself, and was relieved to feel nothing. He was simply Michael.

Exactly, drama queen.

"Looks like you hit pay dirt," she said.

"Yeah." There was a flatness to the single word.

"What's wrong?"

"I went to the bathroom."

She grimaced. "Yeah. I should have warned you about that. The plumbing's not great. Might want to wash your shoes when you get home if there was any 'water' on the floor."

"I checked out the ladies', too."

He was so stern, so disapproving, that Angie had to suppress a smile.

"Not up to the Michael Robinson standard?" It was a rhetorical question, because she knew they weren't. Many was the time she'd simply crossed her legs and waited until she went out for lunch to avoid having to set foot in the space.

"This building is a complete shit hole, Angie." He glanced at Charlie to see if he'd registered the four-letter word, but his son was inspecting the wheels on the bin. "Half the lights are out, the roof leaks and I bet most of the windows are rusted shut. The bathrooms are possibly the worst I've ever seen. I'm including the developing world in that assessment, too, by the way."

"It's true, the old girl ain't what she used to be, but that's why the rent's so reasonable. Beggars, by which I mean artists, can't afford to be choosers." She shrugged philosophically.

"Even if that means being exposed to deteriorating asbestos, lead paint and electrical wiring that can't possibly be up to code?"

"Asbestos? What asbestos?" she asked, alarmed.

Michael pointed at the ceiling. "What do you think that is?"

She tilted her head to look at the textured stucco ceiling. "Plaster?"

He shook his head slowly. Grimly.

"I don't like the idea of you working in this building, Angie."

She sighed heavily. "Well, that makes two of us, but I'm afraid there aren't a lot of options in the city. I looked around a couple of years ago, but it was a dead loss."

"Then move farther out."

"Right, and make my clients travel to find me."

"They'll make the trip. You're worth it."

She shook her head. "I need to be central. All my suppliers are in here—my valuer, my metallurgist, my gemsetter, the jewelers' toolmakers…"

Michael's frown deepened. She didn't know whether to be amused or touched by his obvious concern.

"I'll be fine. I've survived eight years in this place."

He glanced pointedly at the debris in the corner and the four-letter word sprayed on her wall. "Just."

She knew what he was saying made sense, but she had formed an attachment to the Stradbroke over the years, decrepit bathrooms and all.

"If it makes you happy, I'll take a look around, see what's out there."

"Good."

Charlie punctuated Michael's words with a thump on the side of the bin.

"I think he's seconding the motion," Angie said.

"Good." Michael moved to her workbench to inspect her tools. "I've never seen where you work before."

"Really?" Billie had been a constant visitor, but there had never been a reason for Michael to come here. "No, I guess you haven't."

He walked over to where her crucibles and welding gear were located. "Is this where you make your alloys?"

"Yep."

He turned and laid a hand on the scarred wood of her stump, a four-foot-high section of tree trunk that had served her well over the years. "And this is where you shape your rings?"

"Sometimes. But I've got a couple of different types of ring benders, too. It depends on what I'm working on." She moved closer, picking up one of the many hammers that sat in the leather loops circling the stump.

"No wonder you have Obama arms," he said.

"Don't forget the calluses."

He raised his eyebrows, clearly surprised. She displayed her work-toughened palms to him.

"I've never noticed," he said.

"I should hope not. A lady likes to have a few secrets."

He smiled, glanced at his watch, then at Charlie. She checked her own watch and saw it was past twelve.

"Someone's going to want lunch soon," she said.

"Tell me about it. Probably needs his diaper changed, too, and I didn't bring any with me." He crossed the room and hoisted Charlie into his arms. "Time for us to go, Charlie-boy."

Charlie immediately began fussing. Michael gave her an exasperated look over his son's head.

"Sorry."

"Hey, I'd cry, too, if I had to leave this palace."

She walked them down the stairs and out the side entrance, kissing Charlie goodbye in the cobblestone laneway.

"Thanks for all your help, little man."

He stared at her, bottom lip trembling, eyes awash with tears.

"I think that's the saddest face in the whole wide world," she said, unable to resist stroking his cheek with her finger.

"And yet nothing is actually wrong," Michael said drily.

They exchanged smiles.

"Let me know if there's anything else I can do."

"I will. Thanks."

She watched as they walked away, Michael's long stride easy despite the fact that Charlie was no lightweight. She was still smiling when she returned to her studio. Having them visit had somehow taken away the worst of her angst over the break-in. What had happened was shitty, but not insurmountable.

As for that awkward flash of sexual awareness... It

had been nothing. A blip. An aberration. Thinking about it now, she felt a little stupid for having been so rattled. With the benefit of hindsight, the moment settled into its rightful place in the big scheme of things: unimportant and insignificant.

The way it should be.

THREE WEEKS LATER, MICHAEL rubbed the back of his neck as he waited at the lights. Life had been crazy lately, filled with interviews with prospective nannies—none of whom had been very impressive—as well as preparations for his first week at work. Today marked his third full day back in the saddle and he was feeling more than a little weary after two complicated client briefings and a series of phone calls that had prevented him from accomplishing anything substantial all afternoon. Just as well he'd arranged with his partners to work from home on Thursdays and Fridays—he was nowhere near match fit after so many months downtime. The lack of distraction in his home office would give him a chance to make up lost ground. Hopefully.

Despite his weariness and even though a part of him felt guilty for cutting short the year he'd intended to spend with the kids, there wasn't a doubt in his mind that returning to work was the best decision he'd made in a long time. It might have only been three days, but it was enough for him to know that Angie had been right—picking up the threads of his career had given him something to hold on to. It forced him to interact with the outside world, and it gave him things to occupy himself with that had nothing to do with Billie.

It gave him a chance to be a person again, and not simply a father and a grieving husband.

He hadn't understood how much he'd needed that until today when he'd finished a phone call with a supplier and noticed that he'd gone a whole four hours without thinking of Billie once. Guilt had come hard on the heels of the realization, of course—but there had been relief, too.

It was exhausting living with the constant weight of grief on his shoulders.

The lights changed and he accelerated through the intersection, very aware of the need to relieve Mrs. Linton. He'd been fortunate enough to get Charlie into day care three days a week, but Mrs. Linton had saved his bacon, agreeing to pick up Eva from school and look after her until he could make a more permanent arrangement. Still, he didn't want to abuse her generosity.

He swung by day care to collect Charlie, then headed home. A familiar green SUV was parked in front of his house when he pulled into the driveway. He smiled as he hit the button for the garage door. Angie had been busy putting her studio back together and they hadn't seen much of her lately. It would be good to catch up with her. Good to assure himself that she was recovering okay from the break-in.

It would also give him a chance to hassle her about the rental listings he'd sent to her, too. He'd touched base with a handful of his real estate contacts and put the feelers out for a suitable studio space for her, determined to get her out of that death trap of a building. So far, her only response had been silence. If she thought that stonewalling him would make him give up, she didn't know him very well.

He released Charlie from his car seat and locked the car. Michael could hear voices and laughter as they en-

tered the house. He walk into the kitchen and found
Angie and Eva putting toppings on three pizza bases.

"Hello," he said.

They looked up with identical surprised expressions,
obviously so involved in their conversation they hadn't
heard his arrival.

"Perfect timing. Dinner is almost ready," Angie said.

Charlie immediately went to Angie, gazing up her
worshipfully.

"Why, hello there, Charlie Bear," she said, tapping
his nose lightly.

She looked different. For a moment Michael was puzzled, then he realized it was because her hair was tucked
high on her head in a ballet dancer's bun. She was wearing her yoga gear, too—tight black leggings and a soft-
looking pale pink top with sleeves that stopped at her
elbows.

"Mrs. Linton left a note for you before she left. Something about having a doctor's appointment next week,"
Angie said.

"Right. Thanks."

"Guess what we're having for dinner, Daddy?" Eva
asked.

"Could it possibly be pizza?"

"Yes! With the lot. I mean *everything.*"

"She's not kidding on that one." Angie cast a significant glance toward the pizza Eva was working on.

It was piled high with salami, cheese, tomato and
mushrooms to the point where it looked more like a pie
than a pizza.

"Check that out. Sure you don't want to throw a chair
or table on top of that thing, too?" he asked Eva, drop-

ping a hand onto the back of her neck and squeezing lightly.

She tilted her head backward so she could look at him upside-down. "Which pizza do you think is the best?"

Michael pretended to consider the options. "I like the simplicity of this cheese-and-tomato one, which I'm guessing is for Charlie. And Angie's is nice and colorful…"

Eva gave him a look, clearly knowing when she was being strung along. "Just admit it. Mine is the best," she said with the unashamed egotism of a six-year-old.

"It does look pretty special."

"Let's put it on the top shelf so all the many, many layers will get a chance to cook through." Angie slid the pizza onto a baking tray and turned toward the oven.

He followed her movements idly, not really paying attention, but when she bent to put the pizza in the oven his gaze slid down her slim spine to her backside, perfectly showcased in black Lycra.

He quickly looked away, but not before he'd noticed that Angie had a very nice ass.

He cleared his throat. "I might go change while those cook."

"Sure," Angie said.

He could feel heat in his face as he headed for the bedroom and he hoped like hell that she hadn't noticed. He kicked his work shoes off with more force than was strictly necessary once he was in his room. He had no business noticing her ass. She was Billie's best friend. Better yet, she was *his* friend. The shape and size of her ass was utterly irrelevant. Certainly it was of no interest to him.

No interest whatsoever.

Even if it was a very fine, very firm-looking ass.

Giving himself a firm mental shake, he concentrated on pulling on his jeans.

ANGIE CHECKED ON THE pizzas, then poured herself a glass of wine. She was glad she'd given in to the impulse to surprise Michael with dinner. Even though she hadn't seen him much recently, she'd been very aware that this first week at work might be hard for him. He'd been on her mind a lot, and she'd wanted to let him know he wasn't alone. Dinner wasn't much, but it was something.

She glanced up when Michael returned wearing a pair of old jeans and a stretched-out T-shirt. He'd put on a bit of weight and it suited him. Made him look more like his old self.

She poured him a glass of wine. "So, how's your first week as a born-again architect been?"

"Not too bad. If I can find a child-care solution that doesn't involve me shamelessly exploiting Mrs. Linton, I think it's doable."

"Still no luck with finding a nanny?"

"Nope. I've got more interviews lined up on Friday, though."

"Well, if you need someone to help relieve Mrs. Linton in the meantime, let me know. I could easily pick up Eva after school a few days if I plan my schedule right."

Michael was already shaking his head. "I can't ask you to do that."

"Why not?"

"Because you do enough for us already."

"No one's keeping a score card, Michael. Besides, I love spending time with the kids."

He shook his head again and she knew from his stubborn expression that there was no point pursuing the subject.

"Fine. Then tell me about work."

"How about we talk about why you haven't responded to my email about those rentals?"

Angie busied herself wiping the counter again. She'd been hoping he wouldn't bring up the matter of her finding a new studio. For a number of reasons.

"Didn't I? Sorry. I've been so busy, getting things on track…" When she risked a glance at him, his gaze was knowing.

"Did you follow up on *any* of those leads?"

"I checked a couple of them out on the internet."

"And?"

She shuffled her feet, feeling for all the world like a kid who'd been called to the principal's office. "One of them was too big. The other one was too far from the city."

"Did you speak to any of the agents, tell them what you're looking for?"

"I'm on it. Relax."

"I'm going to take that as a 'no.'"

She took a big gulp of wine, not liking the disapproving way he was eyeing her. It was a little disconcerting to realize how much his good opinion meant to her.

"Good studios are hard to find. I need the right size, the right price…" She could hear how lame she sounded. She put her wineglass down. "The thing is, I've been at the Stradbroke for eight years." She spread her hands to indicate how entrenched she felt, how much inertia she had to overcome before she could pack up her workspace and rebuild it again somewhere else. "It's my second home."

"I get that, but that place is a disaster waiting to happen, Angie. God knows what you're breathing in every day. As for those bathrooms… And don't even get me started on the lack of security."

"Yeah. I know. I need to move." The knowledge had been crystalizing inside her as she'd scrambled to restore her workspace, stripping paint off her tools and replacing locks and furniture.

"Can I at least keep looking for you?"

"You've got enough on your plate."

"Not so much that I can't look out for a friend." His gaze was warm with affection. Something equally warm unfolded in her chest.

"Let me talk to those agents first," she said. "I'll let you know if I need to call in the cavalry."

He picked up his glass and tilted it toward her. "Deal."

Her mouth twisted wryly as she lifted hers and clinked the rim against his, aware that he'd effectively gotten her to commit to moving.

"You're a hard man to resist."

"The word you're looking for is *persuasive*."

"If you were a woman, it would be *nag,* you know."

He sipped, content to take her jibe on the chin now that he'd won the main point.

"Auntie Angie, I almost forgot to tell you."

They both turned as Eva raced into the room, skidding across the floor in her socks.

"Guess what I learned at school today?"

"How to tame a dragon?" Angie asked.

"No."

"How to burp the alphabet?"

"No one can do that."

"Wanna bet?" Angie said.

"I learned how to do a cartwheel. A proper one, not just a handstand."

"Wow. That's pretty cool."

"Look," Eva said.

She raised her hands over her head, ready to throw herself at the floor.

"Whoa there. No cartwheels inside, please," Michael said.

"Da-aaad."

"There's a perfectly good lawn outside. Show Auntie Angie your circus tricks out there."

"They're not circus tricks. They're gymnastics," Eva said with great dignity. "Come on, Auntie Angie."

Eva took her hand and tugged until Angie followed her to the sliding door and out onto the deck. Angie looked doubtfully at the overly long grass.

"Might be a bit wet, sweetie."

"I don't care. Watch!"

Angie suppressed a smile as Eva bounced down the steps like Tigger.

"Okay. Here I go." Eva hurled herself forward, hands hitting the ground, feet making a wonky, off-balance arc in the sky. She landed and looked at Angie expectantly, her face flushed, her eyes bright.

"Look at you go! That was fantastic."

It was enough to set Eva off again. Each time she completed a cartwheel, she looked to Angie for approval, her small face expectant. Angie showered her with praise and Eva redoubled her efforts.

Angie sipped her wine and laughed at her antics, her gaze drifting around the yard. It occurred to her that she hadn't been out here since the day Billie had died. The lawn needed mowing, and leaves were piled high beneath the two oak trees in the far corner. The bare wood of Billie's studio was weather-stained, the glass and wood door faded to a silvery gray.

Angie considered the small wooden structure. She hesitated a moment, then crossed the deck and peered through the grubby glass.

The space was as she remembered it—concrete floor, bare plaster walls, exposed wooden beams overhead. The boxes containing Billie's pottery wheel and other ceramics supplies were piled in a corner, unopened and untouched. Angie remembered her friend's intense and sudden passion for all things ceramic. Like so many of Billie's crazes, it probably wouldn't have lasted, but that was beside the point.

After a few seconds she walked toward the house. Eva continued to whirl through the air, her skirt up around her ears, underwear shamelessly on display.

"Did you ever get the electricity connected to the studio?" Angie asked as she entered the kitchen.

Michael was taking the pizzas out of the oven. "No. Why?"

She watched as realization dawned. He wiped his hands on a tea towel before crossing to the door. They both considered the studio.

"Would it be weird for you?" Angie asked after a moment. After all, this was Billie's studio.

"Someone should use it. It's not doing anything for anyone the way it is. The question is, is it big enough for you?"

"Absolutely. And it's well ventilated. At least, it will be if I keep the windows open."

"What about being near your suppliers?"

"I'll just have to be more organized. The important

thing is that I could pick Eva up from school three days a week, no worries."

Which would leave Michael to collect Charlie from day care on his way home from the office. The perfect tag-team arrangement.

Michael frowned. She could almost hear the internal debate he was having. Pride versus need, his sense of fairness versus practicality.

"Just say yes. It's a perfect win-win and you know it," she said with a grin.

He met her gaze. "It has to work for both of us. This can't be a roundabout way of you doing me a favor."

He looked very serious standing there, his dark hair touched with gold by the dying sun. She fought the urge to reach out and ruffle the strands like a little boy's to get a rise out of him and loosen him up. This was a great idea. The best she'd had in ages.

"I wouldn't have even brought it up if I didn't think it could work."

He contemplated the studio again. "I'll need a couple of weeks to get it ready for you."

"Oh, good decision, Mr. Robinson. Excellent decision." She clapped her hands together, delighted.

Finally Michael smiled.

CHAPTER FIVE

ANGIE UNPACKED THE LAST of her sanding disks onto the workbench, setting them in a neat row between the polishing mops and drill bits. Satisfied everything was in its rightful place, she turned to survey her new studio.

In the three weeks since they'd struck the deal, the walls had been painted a crisp, warm white, and Michael had installed a bank of lighting overhead. Her equipment had been moved in and set up over the past two days and her gaze slid over familiar things made strange by the unfamiliar setting.

For the first time she admitted that it would take a while to get used to the new space. Not only because it was all so *nice,* but also because it had been intended to be Billie's studio, her secret hidey-hole where she could be creative. Gripped with a momentary sadness, Angie moved to the window, looking out to the green of the backyard.

That was something else she'd have to get used to— instead of the teeming city and the hum of traffic and the clang of trams passing, she had grass and trees and could hear nothing but silence and the occasional dog barking or bird calling.

All in all, it was a huge shift—and not just for her, either. Michael's car had been gone when she arrived this morning, even though it was a Thursday which meant he should be working from home. She'd guessed he was dropping Eva at school and let herself into first the house, then studio. It had felt strange making free with his home, but one of the things they had discussed while hammering out the details of the arrangement was the fact that she needed access to the kitchen and bathroom. At the time, Michael had seemed supremely comfortable with the notion of having his home invaded, but Angie couldn't help wondering how the reality would feel for him. She wasn't sure how she would cope with having a stranger encroach on her personal space—but then maybe she was more of hermit crab than Michael. He'd lived with Billie, after all, and had two small people who invaded his personal space every chance they got.

Satisfied she was as set up as she was ever going to be, Angie crossed to her safe and pulled out the job bag for Dr. Mathews. A successful dermatologist, he was planning to propose to his live-in girlfriend and wanted the engagement ring to be both personal and spectacular. He'd selected a stunning princess-cut Australian sapphire in an unusual green-gold hue to be the centerpiece of the design—now Angie had to decide what, exactly, that design would be.

She sat at her table, pencil in hand. After contemplating the diamond, she started to sketch. An hour later, she eased the crick in her neck, stood and arched her back. She grabbed a mug from the sideboard and headed into the house to make coffee and get a little perspective.

She was spooning grounds into the French press, lost in thought, when a deep voice sounded behind her.

"How's it going?"

She whirled to face Michael. "Bloody hell! You scared the bejesus out of me."

His mouth quirked at the corner and she guessed she'd amused him. "Sorry. No shoes."

She saw that his feet were bare yet again. True to form, he was also wearing faded denim, but instead of his usual sweatshirt he had on a wrinkled white shirt.

"What is it with you and the no-shoes thing?"

"Don't know. I've never really liked them, ever since I was a kid."

"Heathen." She lifted her mug. "Want one?"

"Sure. Why not? It's better than staring at the Watsons' beach house for another hour."

"Problems?"

"Just the usual. They have about ten different ideas and styles they want incorporated into one building, yet they still want it to be coherent, clean and modern."

"Bah, clients. Who needs 'em?"

He smiled. "Yeah. If only we could build houses without them."

"If only."

She passed him a cup and they sat on adjacent stools.

"How about you? How are you finding things?"

"It's been three hours, but so far so good."

"Let me know if there's enough light because I can talk to the electrician again."

"Michael. It's so bright in there I almost need sunglasses."

"If it's too bright, we can do something about that, too."

"It's perfect. Relax. I'm a very happy freeloader."

He frowned. "I wish you'd stop saying that."

"I wish you'd let me pay rent."

"You can pay rent if I can pay you for helping with Eva after school."

"You know I can't let you do that."

"Then you can't pay rent." There was a smile lurking in Michael's gray-green eyes as he waited for her response.

It hit her that he'd been lighter, less grim since starting work.

"You want a cookie? I hid some Tim-Tams from the kids the other day."

"As if I'm going to say no to a Tim-Tam." Chocolate on chocolate with a chocolate filling, they were practically an Australian icon.

He went to rummage in the pantry. She watched as he reached for the highest shelf, the movement tightening his shirt over the muscles of his shoulders and back.

"You realize Eva is only four foot tall, right?"

"You think the top shelf was overkill?"

She held her thumb and forefinger an inch apart. "Just a little."

He dropped the Tim-Tams in front of her. "You can never be too careful with the good stuff."

"True."

She tore open the package and offered him a cookie before taking one herself. She immediately bit off both ends then dunked the exposed parts in her coffee.

"You're a dunker. I never knew that about you," Michael said.

"Isn't everyone when it comes to Tim-Tams?"

"I'm not a fan of the dunk."

Angie blinked, genuinely surprised. "Really? How can you not enjoy a dunk?"

"I don't like it when the biscuit gets all soggy and waterlogged."

"But that's the best part!"

Michael laughed. "There's no need to look so out-raged."

"I feel outraged. Next thing you're going to tell me you don't like *The Sound of Music*."

"I can take it or leave it."

"Get out of here."

He laughed again. He looked so carefree, so much like his old self that she felt a warm sense of achievement.

She wanted him to be happy.

The thought had barely registered when she became aware of two things in rapid succession. The first was that his shoulder was solid and warm against her own, their upper arms touching.

And the second was that they were completely alone in the house.

A strange heat raced down her spine and spread throughout her body. It was the third time it had hap-pened now and she recognized it for what it was straight away—sexual awareness.

Or, more accurately, sexual attraction.

I am not attracted to Michael. No way.

The denial was instant, a knee-jerk response. She shifted on her stool, moving away so that they were no longer touching. The feeling remained. She frowned, shifting her coffee mug unnecessarily on the counter.

"You know what I've always wanted to try? The straw thing. You ever done that?" Michael asked.

"Um, I don't think so."

"Guess there's no time like the present." He bit off both ends of his cookie then stuck one end in his mug. His cheeks hollowed as he attempted to suck coffee through the center of the cookie.

Even though she was more than a little alarmed and

unsettled by her reaction to his closeness, she couldn't help laughing as the makeshift straw dissolved in his fingers and crumbled.

"Now that's what I call waterlogged," she said.

Michael stared into his mug for a second before shrugging. "You win some, you lose some."

He had melted chocolate on his fingers and he licked it off as unconsciously as a child. He should have looked foolish, or at least mildly silly. He didn't. He looked like a grown, sexy man enjoying one of life's little hedonistic pleasures and something warm and heavy settled in the pit of her stomach.

Retreating from her own feelings, she stood, her feet hitting the ground with a thump. "I'd better get back to it. Got lots on at the moment."

She didn't look at him as she gulped the remaining coffee then rinsed her mug. She raised a hand in farewell, saying over her shoulder, "See you later. Thanks for the empty calories."

She didn't stop until she was safely in the studio. Then she stood at her desk and tried to understand what was happening to her.

I am not attracted to Michael. It's not possible.

She wanted that to be true, but there was no denying the surge of heat and awareness when she'd registered how close they were sitting. She didn't even want to begin to think about her reaction when he'd licked chocolate off his fingers.

Then there was that frisson she'd experienced when he'd hugged her in her vandalized studio and she'd become aware of the fact that he was a man...

She'd acknowledged it a number of times—Michael was good-looking. The strong planes of his face, those clear gray-green eyes, the dark, rumpled hair. And his body. Even in his current lean-and-mean state he was still built on heroic lines. She'd have to be blind not to notice so much male beauty.

But he'd always been tall and dark and handsome and he'd always had the body of a god and it had never bothered her for a second before.

Yes, but he belonged to Billie then.

The realization hit in a cold rush.

She'd never been the sort of woman who coveted other women's men. It wasn't part of her makeup. But Billie was dead, and even though Angie would never, ever dream of looking sideways at her best friend's husband, on some subconscious level she was obviously aware of the fact that Michael was now a free agent.

She shook her head, deeply uncomfortable with the direction of her own thoughts. She didn't want to be aware of him in that way. He was her friend. She wanted to help him. She did *not* want to be aware of him on a physical level. She definitely didn't want to feel self-conscious and antsy and stupid around him.

For a moment she teetered on the brink of panic. This was the last way she wanted to be feeling when she'd given up her studio and thrown her lot in with him. She was going to see him every day during the working week. *Every day.*

Anxiety tightened her chest and she glanced toward the pile of flattened boxes in the corner. How hard would it be to find a new studio?

Then reason came calling.

It wasn't as though she would suddenly leap on Michael because she'd tuned into the fact he was a hottie. He was still Billie's husband and she was still Billie's best friend. Angie's awareness that Michael was an attractive man didn't change a thing between them.

Not a single thing.

There had been lots of men in her life whom she'd found attractive who she hadn't so much as sneezed on. It was…*uncomfortable* that Michael now appeared to be one of them, but she could live with that. She *would* live with that, because she wasn't about to give up her friendship with him or her relationship with his children. They were all far, far too important to her.

And no doubt, as with most cases of sexual awareness and attraction, familiarity would quickly wear her unwanted feelings down to nothing. Routine and overexposure would soon return him to the status of platonic friend he'd always occupied.

It was a reassuring thought, enough so that she was able to return to the design she'd abandoned for her coffee break and take up her pencil again.

HE LIKED HAVING ANGIE in the studio. Until today, Michael had only thought about it in terms of helping her out and how handy it was for Eva's after-school care. He hadn't anticipated how much pleasure he'd gain from having Angie close by. She was good company, and he'd enjoyed the sense of comfort he'd had all day, knowing that she was only a few steps away.

Not that he'd abused the privilege. If anything, he'd gone the other way, resisting the urge to go to the studio to see if she wanted another coffee or to share a stupid joke someone had sent via email. He didn't want to cramp her style, and she was here to work, after all.

For the same reason, he waited until she came into the house at the end of the day before asking if she wanted to join them for dinner. He was watching Eva play *Dora the Explorer* when he heard the French doors open, announcing Angie's arrival.

"Whoa, Eva, you are on fire, girl," Angie said as she joined them.

Michael glanced over his shoulder, ready to issue his invitation, but the words died on his tongue. She'd changed out of the utilitarian hoody she'd been wearing earlier in the day into a fitted, fuzzy sweater in a deep blue-teal color that did amazing things for her eyes.

"That's new," he said before he could stop himself.

Angie seemed equally surprised by his comment. "It is. I picked it up on the weekend."

"It looks, um, warm," he said, feeling incredibly stupid now. What was he, the fashion police? Since when did he comment on other people's clothing?

"It's cashmere, so, yeah, it's warm."

He nodded, although he wasn't really sure what he was agreeing to. "Listen, the kids talked me into dinner at the local bistro. Do you want to join us?"

"Sure. Sounds good. When were you thinking?"

He kept his gaze fixed on Angie's face, even though he was very aware of the fact that her new sweater was tight in all the right places. He'd learned his lesson with the yoga pants, and he wasn't going there.

"We're pretty much ready to go now, I think."

They piled into his wagon and drove to the restaurant. He shot Angie an apologetic look as they entered the overly bright, too noisy family section of the pub.

"I have a feeling I'm going to owe you dinner to make up for this dinner."

"What are you talking about? This place is great. It's got a dessert bar *and* a playroom," Angie said. "Not to mention about a million slot machines in the adults' part."

Eva fixed her big, pleading brown gaze on him. "Can I go play? Please?"

She was already starting to edge away and he reached out and caught the collar of her coat and made her pick a meal from the menu before letting her disappear into the playroom. He and Angie settled at a table in the corner and he headed to the counter to order their food, returning with a number in a metal holder and two glasses of beer.

They talked casually and easily, neither of them going out of their way to fill the occasional silence that fell. Another thing to like about Angie—she didn't mind silence. In fact, he suspected, like him, she sometimes preferred it.

Their meals came and Angie went in search of Eva, hauling her to the table long enough to wolf down her burger before racing off again. Charlie wanted to play, too, once he'd eaten a handful of chips and smeared the rest into the table. Michael took him into the rubber-floored toddler playpen and let him loose, watching with a smile as Charlie immediately raced to the roundabout and began pushing it round and around. As far as his son was concerned, there was nothing better in life than being dizzy.

"Here."

Angie nudged his arm with her elbow and he saw she was carrying two more beers.

"Thanks."

"Also, I thought I'd better warn you that a bunch of the women from Billie's mothers' group came in."

Michael glanced over his shoulder and immediately

made eye contact with Gerry, who gave him a little finger wave. She was standing with half a dozen other women he vaguely recognized.

"Whoops. Now you can't pretend you didn't see them," Angie said out of the corner of her mouth.

Gerry started walking toward him, another woman falling in behind her.

"I will pay you a thousand dollars to stay by my side for the next ten minutes," he said quietly to Angie, the smile never leaving his face.

She grinned. "I should so hold you to that."

"Feel free to. Just don't disappear on me."

"Michael. I knew we'd run into you again," Gerry said as she joined them.

"It's a small world."

"You remember Ros, right?"

"Sure. How are you?" Michael said, shaking the other woman's hand.

He introduced Angie and minutes passed torturously as they exchanged pleasantries and talked about the weather. Both women offered to help him out with child care should the need arise, explaining that as single parents they understood the pressures he was under.

"That's very kind of you," Michael said.

It was, too—if only they weren't both looking at him as though he was the last chopper out of Saigon. Angie had joked about him being seen as fair game now that a suitable mourning period had passed, but there was no mistaking the signals both women were sending.

"We've all been there, Michael. Not in exactly the same way, but we understand how it feels," Gerry said.

Ros glanced toward their table and pulled a face. "Looks like they're ready to order."

"Michael, great to see you. Don't be a stranger," Gerry said.

"Great to see you, too. All of you," he said, offering a wave to the rest of the table. He kept the smile on his face as Gerry and Ros rejoined their group.

"Wow. For a minute there I thought they were going to fight to the death over you," Angie said.

He took a huge swallow from his beer. "It's not funny."

"You're right, it isn't. But it also kind of is. I felt as though I was watching a nature special. All we needed was David Attenborough doing a voice-over."

He gave her a look. He really didn't want to talk about this stuff. "Can we change the subject?"

Angie's smile faded. "Sorry. I was just mucking around."

"I know."

He watched Charlie clamber up the stairs of the miniature slide. He could feel Angie watching him and he made an effort to unclench his jaw. He was overreacting and he knew it—he also couldn't do anything to stop it.

"It really bothers you, doesn't it? The idea that those women are interested in you?"

"It's not about them."

"Okay." She didn't sound convinced.

"It isn't. I don't want to be in this position. I don't want to be single. I definitely don't want to even think about replacing Billie. But none of those things has anything to do with those women."

Angie's expression softened with sympathy. "No one will ever replace Billie. She was one of a kind."

He stared into his beer, aware that his throat was suddenly tight.

"But that doesn't mean you won't ever want to be with someone else." Angie said it so softly he almost didn't hear her. His head whipped up and he stared at her.

"I won't," he said unequivocally.

"Billie would never expect you to spend the rest of your life alone. You know that, right?" It seemed Angie was choosing her words very carefully. "She'd want you to be happy."

"I'm not interested. Period. Billie was it for me." The words caught in his throat.

"Okay. Fair enough. What are you going to do about sex, then?" Angie's words were so unexpected she surprised a bark of laughter out of him.

"Wow. That was…to the point."

He could feel his face getting warm. Which was fine, because Angie had a bit of color in her cheeks, too.

"Just pointing out the obvious. You're thirty-five, Michael. Young, healthy. Unless you're planning on developing forearms like Popeye, you're going to want to have sex again."

He couldn't help but smile at her choice of words but his smile quickly faded. Across the playground, Charlie turned and sought him out, his small face anxious as he suddenly remembered that he belonged to someone and that it was important he knew where that someone was. Michael lifted a hand to draw his attention. Charlie's smile was like the sun coming out from behind a cloud—radiant, life-affirming, utterly pure.

"I'm not interested."

Angie let the subject drop then, for which he was eternally grateful. He knew she probably thought he was in denial. Hell, maybe he was. But he didn't want to think about sleeping with a woman who wasn't Billie. That

part of him—his sex-drive, for want of a better term—
had been nonexistent for the past eleven months and if
it stayed that way, he wouldn't be sorry. He'd never been
the kind of guy who slept around, and he'd never had a
problem staying true to his marriage vows. Ever since
he'd met Billie, sex and desire had been uniquely asso-
ciated with her. Her scent, the feel of her skin, the sound
of her laughter, the shape of her body.

He genuinely couldn't imagine wanting another
woman. Not at the moment, anyway.

HE DREAMED ABOUT SEX that night.

Angie headed home once they had returned from the
bistro and Michael put the kids to bed then spent a couple more hours on the Watsons' Frankenstein of a beach
house before hitting the sack.

He didn't know where he was in his dream. It was a
house, but not one he recognized. At first he was alone,
but he caught a glimpse of a woman as she disappeared
through the door into the next room. He started after her.
His first thought was that it was Billie. He'd had many,
many dreams like this, where he pursued her yet never
quite caught her.

But this dream felt different. The faceless woman
turning corners and slipping out of his sight moved dif-
ferently from Billie. The way she walked, the sway of her
hips, the angle of her head. She wasn't Billie. He was still
trying to understand when suddenly he found himself in
a dark room. He reached out and found himself touching bare skin. Warm, smooth skin. A hand closed over
his and guided him to a full, heavy breast. A hard nipple
pressed against his palm, and an arm snaked around his

neck and a soft, fragrant body pressed against him from groin to shoulder.

His lover slid a hand down to caress his burgeoning erection, cupping him, stroking him. Within seconds he was hard, desire a demanding heat in his veins. He cupped his lover's breasts and lowered his head and tongued sweet, tight nipples until she was sighing and shaking in his arms. She lifted a leg and wrapped it around his hips and guided him inside her. She was tight and hot and wet and he buried himself to the hilt. She felt so good, so good. He withdrew and plunged again and again and again. Desire built inside him, tensing his muscles. He was so hard he felt he could burst and there was nothing more important in the world than the place where his body was joined to hers. His climax rose, spreading like heat through his abdomen. He tensed— And woke, sweating and panting in tangled sheets, achingly hard, his heart battering against his ribs. The dream had been so real, so intense, so absorbing that for a few seconds he was disoriented. All he could think about was how good she'd felt. How wet and warm and willing and how much he'd needed the relief of orgasm.

Then his life came back to him and he dropped his forearm across his closed eyes and gritted his teeth against the shame and regret that washed over him.

Billie was dead, and in his head he'd been screwing another woman.

So much for his fine, noble words to Angie. His body and mind hadn't even waited a full twenty-four hours before making a liar of him.

It's not a lie. I don't want anyone else. I love Billie.

There was no denying the fact he'd wanted someone

else in his dream. A naked, sexy siren who'd known exactly what to do.

The heaviness in his groin demanded satisfaction. Without him consciously willing it, his hand slid to his erection. He gripped himself, but instead of stroking his hand and seeking relief, he lay rigid, willing his desire away.

He didn't want this. Didn't want desire and longing. Didn't want to be this fully alive again. It was enough that he was a good provider, a careful, loving parent. He didn't want this part of his life back.

Releasing himself, he swung his feet over the side of the bed and stood. Three steps and he was in the ensuite, another two and he was in the shower, cold water a shock on his skin. He gasped and let the cold leach the need from his body. Images from the dream flashed across his mind's eye. He pushed his face beneath the water.

He was shivering by the time he flicked the tap off, but his body was once again his. Feeling guilty and weary and confused, he returned to bed and spent the rest of the night staring at the ceiling.

CHAPTER SIX

ANGIE MADE SURE SHE WAS at Michael's house early the next day, keen to talk to him before tackling her workload.

She needed to apologize for last night, for making him uncomfortable. She'd been lulled by their mutual teasing and the beer and the us-against-them camaraderie engendered by Gerry and Ros's approach and she'd pushed him in ways she shouldn't have.

Good God, she'd even made a reference to him "taking care of business" and developing forearms like Popeye. Every time she thought of that particular gem her whole body tensed and grew warm with embarrassment.

She and Michael might have become true friends in the past year instead of merely friends-by-association, but they had never ventured into such personal territory before—yet she'd gone rampaging in there with her army boots on last night, taking no prisoners and giving no quarter. She really didn't know why she'd stepped over the line so completely.

He'd looked so sad, so broken as he shut the door on romance and love and sex and companionship. In the immediate aftermath of Billie's death, the thought of Michael living the rest of his life devoted to Billie's memory might have seemed a fitting and worthy tribute to her friend's memory. But after witnessing Michael's pain and grief and, yes, loneliness over the past year, Angie understood what a terrible waste such a sacrifice would be. Billie was dead, after all—she could no longer feel jealousy or betrayal. But Michael was still alive, and he was a loving, generous, good man. He deserved comfort and love and friendship and all the other things a relationship could bring to a person. He deserved to be happy.

Fine, but it's really none of your business. At the end of the day, Michael's grief was his and his alone. If he chose to spend the rest of his days grieving Billie, then it was his choice. Which was why she needed to clear the air and let him know that she wouldn't be stampeding into his private life again in the near future.

Even though she had a key to his house, she knocked rather than let herself in. It felt strange to simply walk in when she knew Michael and the children were home. Eva answered the door, one side of her hair braided into a wonky plait, the other side tangled and loose. The collar on her school uniform was rucked up and Angie reached out to smooth it flat as they walked to the kitchen.

"That's better," she said.

"Can you help me with my hair, Auntie Angie? Daddy usually does it but he's not up yet."

Angie glanced toward the hall that led to the master bedroom, surprised. Michael had always been the early bird in the family.

"Sure, sweetie. Why don't you go grab your brush?"

She ducked her head into Charlie's room and found him still out of it, his small body sprawled with utter abandon across his cot. She slipped into the kitchen where Eva was waiting impatiently, her mouth pressed into a thin line.

"I don't like being late." She handed the brush to Angie. "Being late means that you think you're more important than everyone else."

Angie smiled as she recognized one of Michael's favorite sayings. He and Billie had had a constant battle of wills over punctuality. Billie had been a hopeless case, always running fifteen minutes late, while Michael was a stickler for being everywhere on time.

Except for this morning, apparently.

"Why don't I do this other braid again so they're all nice and even?" Angie suggested.

Eva nodded her assent and Angie pulled the hair tie free and brushed Eva's hair out. She was parting it neatly at the back when Michael barreled into the room wearing nothing but a pair of black boxer briefs and a harried expression. His hair was sleep-tousled, his eyes heavy with fatigue. He pulled up short when he saw Angie.

"Oh. Hi. I was just going to get the kids up."

"I got dressed myself," Eva said.

"I must have slept through the alarm."

Angie took one look at his big, bare chest and snug underwear and quickly fixed her gaze on Eva's hair.

"Charlie's still sleeping," she said, concentrating on what her hands were doing and not on the large, very male body she could see in her peripheral vision.

"Ow, Auntie Angie. That hurts," Eva said, pulling her head away.

"Sorry, sweetie." Angie slid a glance toward Michael in time to catch the ripple of his muscles as he lifted a hand to push his hair from his forehead. She could feel embarrassed, self-conscious heat rising in her face and she ducked her head so severely that her chin was pressed into her chest.

"I can always drop Eva at school. Save you from rushing," she said, willing him to do something about his attire—or lack of it.

"Thanks, but I've got it covered. You had breakfast, squirt?" he asked Eva.

"Not yet."

"Toast or cereal?"

"Toast, please. With Vegemite."

"Angie?"

"Um, no. I'm fine, thanks." She made the mistake of looking at him again as she spoke. He'd turned to the pantry and her gaze slid down his well-muscled back to his tight, muscular backside.

"Ow. You're hurting again," Eva protested.

Angie fastened the last hair tie and dropped a kiss onto her goddaughter's head. "All done. Sorry for the owies."

"It's okay." Eva used her hands to check on her plaits. "You did a good job."

"Plaits are one of my areas of expertise."

Michael moved to the end of the dining table. She heaved a silent sigh of relief when he tugged on a white T-shirt from the laundry folded neatly there. She still had to contend with his long, muscular legs, but at least she could look him in the eye now.

She felt faintly ridiculous. She'd been to the beach with Michael and Billie dozens of times over the years, seen Michael's bare chest more times than she could count. When she was at art school, she'd seen enough naked men in her life-drawing classes to ensure that the male body—Michael's in particular—should hold no mysteries for her. Certainly it shouldn't make her feel oddly skittish, as though she wanted to race for the nearest exit or giggle up her sleeve like a schoolgirl.

And definitely it shouldn't make her palms a little sweaty and her heartbeat ragged.

It's a chemical reaction. A stupid, primitive response to seeing a man in his prime. It doesn't mean anything.

She turned to leave, desperate to get away from Michael's big, hard body and her unwanted reaction to it.

"I should get stuck into it," she murmured.

"Daddy, I keep forgetting to ask. What are we going to buy for Mummy's birthday this year?"

The fridge door closed with a slam. Angie's breath got caught in her throat, her gaze instinctively gravitating to where Michael stood, one hand on the fridge door, the other hanging loosely by his side, his face pale and tight.

"I think Mummy would like some flowers," Eva said, oblivious to the sudden tension in the room as she loaded picture books into her school bag.

Time seemed suspended for a long, still moment.

"I'd forgotten Mummy's birthday was coming up." Michael said it easily, lightly, as though it wasn't a big deal at all.

Angie realized she was clenching her hands. She'd forgotten that Billie's birthday was next week, too. A self-protective mechanism, perhaps, because Billie's birthday was also the anniversary of her death. A cruel irony.

"We can go visit her, can't we? And take her a cake?" Eva asked.

"Sure. We can do whatever you'd like to do," Michael said.

Angie met his gaze. She wondered if she looked as bleak and shaken as he did.

He turned away. "Better get a wriggle on if we're going to make it to school on time."

Angie headed for her studio, fighting an upswell of memories and emotions.

If Billie was alive, next Friday would have been her thirty-third birthday. They would have had a party—Billie always celebrated her birthday, no matter what—and Angie would have made her something to add to her collection of Angela Bartlett originals. A bracelet, perhaps, or earrings to match last year's necklace.

For a moment, longing for her friend was so intense it was an ache in her chest. Then, as always, the grief drained away and she was left feeling merely sad and lonely and empty.

She settled at her desk. It took a while, but her thoughts finally stopped circling. She was using the larger of the ring benders when a tap sounded on the door.

"Come in."

Michael entered, his hair still mussed, wearing the same T-shirt he'd dragged on earlier with a pair of black jeans.

"Hey," she said quietly. "You okay?"

"She caught me off guard, that's all. I knew Billie's birthday was coming up. I just hadn't wanted to think about it."

"Yeah. Me, too."

Michael buried his hands in the pockets of his jeans. A muscle tightened in his jaw. "We talked in the car on the way to school. She wants to go to the cemetery on Friday, visit the grave and leave a present. And she wants to have all of Billie's favorite things for dinner."

There was a lump the size of Texas in Angie's throat. "That sounds nice."

"She wants you to be there, too. I don't know if you have any other plans…."

"I don't. And I'd be honored."

Michael's gaze skittered around the studio. He looked so alone standing there, trying to contain his pain.

"I can pick up some things, if you like. Macaroni and cheese, and hot dogs and Wizz Fizz."

Michael's expression softened. "God, she loved junk food, didn't she?"

"The crappier the better."

"I once saw her eat an entire chocolate cake mix straight from the bowl. She said she liked it better as batter than as cake."

Angie smiled. "I could never work out where she put it all."

"Hollow legs," Michael said.

It was Billie's favorite explanation, closely followed by "vestigial cheek pouch."

"I'll leave you to it."

"Before you go…"

He paused, eyebrows raised.

She took a deep breath. "I wanted to apologize for last night."

"Last night?"

She couldn't believe that he'd forgotten. She'd stared at the ceiling half the night regretting her loose lips.

"The stuff about Gerry and her friend and, you know…" She made a gesture in the air. She could feel her cheeks warming so she forced herself to get the rest out in a rush. "It's none of my business and I shouldn't have pushed you and I want you to know it won't happen again."

To her surprise, Michael's gaze slid away from hers, dropping to the floor. He shuffled his feet. "There's nothing to apologize for. Forget it."

He headed for the door. She was about to stop him again when she realized that she wasn't the only one who was embarrassed—his cheekbones were a dull, brick red, signaling more than words ever could that he was deeply uncomfortable about this topic.

She bit her tongue and let him leave, wishing she hadn't said anything at all.

So much for clearing the air.

That'll teach you to keep your advice and opinions to yourself, smarty pants. Remember this the next time you feel the need to share your point of view with Michael.

Not that she was anticipating that happening anytime soon.

A RISING WIND RUFFLED Michael's hair as he watched his daughter kneel in front of Billie's headstone. He glanced toward the sky, trying to gauge if they would get soaked or not. He hadn't thought to bring an umbrella. There had been too many other things on his mind.

The sky was mottled with dark gray clouds, but none of them looked immediately menacing. With a bit of luck they would be able to pay their respects without getting drenched.

"Hi, Mummy. We made you a cake. Chocolate with sprinkles, the way you like. And we brought you flowers." Eva laid both offerings on the neatly clipped grass. "I want you to know I've been trying to be good. I've been trying to remember to keep my room tidy, because

I know you like it that way. And I've been patient with Charlie because he's only little and he doesn't always know when he's being a pain or ruining things."

Michael tilted his head back, inhaling deeply through his nose. He heard Angie sniff but didn't dare look her way because he knew he'd lose it if he did.

There was a reason he'd avoided coming out here before now. Nowhere was Billie more dead than here, where evidence of her passing was engraved in white marble, utterly incontrovertible.

"School has been okay. I don't like math, and Mrs. Dorrit says that I talk too much but that's because I have so much to say. I've been keeping up my swimming but I didn't want to do ballet anymore because that was always our special thing and it wasn't the same without you."

Michael closed his eyes. He'd thought Eva had simply lost interest in ballet.

"Down. Me down, please," Charlie said.

Michael glanced over as Angie bent to set Charlie on his feet. He walked straight to the headstone and laid his hands on it.

"Careful of the cake," Eva warned.

Michael stepped forward to guide Charlie away from potential disaster. Eva closed her eyes and leaned forward to press a kiss to the headstone.

"I love you, Mummy. I think about you every day." She turned her head and looked at him, her eyes swimming with tears. He held out his hand and helped her to her feet. She wrapped her arms around him and pressed her face into his shirt, her small body shuddering with emotion.

Angie took Eva's place at the graveside. Dropping to her knees, she laid her own tribute on the grass, an intricately woven wreath of fresh flowers. It was too unique to be anything other than her work, and he watched as she bowed her head and closed her eyes. Her hands held each other tightly in her lap and her chest rose and fell sharply as though she was struggling to control tears.

He turned away to give her some privacy, resting his hand on Eva's head, resisting the insistent tug as Charlie strived to free himself.

After a few minutes he heard the rustle of clothing as Angie pushed herself to her feet. She was wiping tears from her cheeks with her fingertips when he looked at her. Her eyelashes were spiky and she gave him a watery smile.

"At least we didn't get soaked."

"No."

"If you want, I can walk the kids to the car."

It took him a second to understand she was offering him some private time at the graveside.

"Thanks."

Angie settled Charlie on her hip before offering Eva her free hand.

"I won't be long," he assured them as they began to walk slowly toward the road that wound its way through the cemetery. He watched them for a few seconds before turning and eyeing Billie's grave. Not for a second could he kid himself that this piece of marble and patch of lawn had anything to do with his wife. She had been life personified, and this place was all about death.

He stared at the date. She'd been so young. Too young. They had only gotten started. He'd had so many plans for them. So many dreams...

Now they were all gone. Today, his dreams were about enduring and surviving and doing everything he could to ensure his kids didn't miss out because life had dealt them a cruel, ugly blow and taken their mother away.

Not exactly inspiring stuff. But he didn't have it in him to aspire to more. Not when his past dreams had been rewarded with a cosmic kick in the teeth.

He laid his hand on the cold marble. He couldn't think of a single thing to say that wouldn't sound like a plea for something that was never going to happen. After a few minutes, he slid his hand from the headstone. His eyes were dry as he started toward the road.

He could see Angie and the kids ahead. Angie's head was tilted to one side as she gave her attention to Eva. Charlie's cheek was pressed against her shoulder, his face turned into her neck. A drop of water landed on his arm and he glanced up. In that split-second the heavens opened, warm dollops of water hitting his face. He heard Eva's squeal of surprise and he broke into a run as Angie hustled the kids toward the parking lot. As he drew closer he could hear Eva protesting.

"We're going to get all wet."

"It's only water. It won't hurt us," Angie said. "It's like having a shower in our clothes."

They were approaching the car. He wondered if Angie realized it was locked and that he had the keys. As he closed the final few meters between them, he drew the keys from his pocket and hit the button to unlock the doors. Angie glanced at him, surprise on her face.

"You caught up fast."

"You walk slow."

She smiled. "That's another way of looking at it."

They reached the car and he opened the rear passenger door so Angie could put Charlie in his car seat. He raced around to the driver's side as she slid into the passenger's seat. The door slammed heavily behind him. He was immediately aware of how wet he was, his jeans soaked through, his hair dripping, his polo shirt glued to his chest. He twisted to check on the kids. Eva looked like a drowned rat, her hair plastered to her skull, her good dress dark with moisture. Beside her, Charlie was equally soaked.

"You guys okay?" he asked.

"This is worse than a shower in our clothes. This is more like a bath." Eva sounded simultaneously disgusted and delighted by the concept.

Beside him, Angie laughed. She was soaked through, as wet as if someone had dunked her in a pool. Suddenly he found himself laughing, too. Then Eva joined in and Charlie, unwilling to be left out, began giggling as though someone had told him the funniest joke in the world. For long seconds the car echoed with their laughter. Part of him was aware that it was as much a release of tension as it was amusement at their soaking, but he figured that was okay. He'd much rather see his daughter laugh like this than witness the sadness in her eyes when she'd addressed her mother's grave.

"All right. Let's go find ourselves some dry clothes," he said as he started the car.

It was a half-hour drive home from the cemetery and the windows kept fogging up as their clothes dried. By the time they pulled into the garage the car was like a sauna.

"Inside and into dry clothes. Off we go," he said, herding the kids toward the house.

It took him a moment to realize Angie wasn't with

them. Instead, she was running through the rain toward her car.

"What are you doing?" he called after her.

"I think I've got some dry clothes in my car."

He unlocked the front door and let the kids in, then grabbed the umbrella from the big Chinese urn inside the door. He jogged down the path, opening the umbrella as he ran, and reached Angie as she extracted a gym bag from the rear of her car.

She laughed at him when he stepped close, sharing the shelter of the umbrella with her.

"It's not like I could get any wetter," she said.

"It's the principle of the thing."

"Very gallant of you."

"No need to sound so surprised."

She grinned at him. She was standing so close he could smell the damp wool of her sweater and see the fine smile lines around her eyes.

They turned as one, her hip bumping his as they fell easily into step.

"Feel free to grab a shower if you want to warm up," he said as they entered the house.

"Why don't you grab a shower and I'll sort Charlie and Eva out?"

"I don't think so. Go get dry."

She started to protest but he grabbed her by the shoulders and turned her toward the main bathroom.

"Quit being so stubborn," he said.

Her shoulders were fine-boned but strong and he felt them flex beneath his fingers in instinctive resistance to his insistence.

"See you in ten," he said, already heading toward the living room where he could hear Charlie and Eva talking.

She didn't say anything more, but he heard the bathroom door close.

He found Eva trying to wrestle Charlie out of his wet sweatshirt and he placed a grateful hand on her head.

"Thanks for that, sweetie. Why don't I take over from here and you can change?"

"Okay. But good luck."

He smiled, amused by her lack of faith in him. Five minutes later, it wasn't so funny. For reasons known only to himself, Charlie fought him every step of the way as Michael stripped him of the wet items and dressed him in his pajamas.

Finally, Michael left Charlie in Eva's care and sought his own shower. It wasn't until the hot water hit the bunched shoulders of his neck and back that he registered how tightly he'd been holding himself. He hadn't been looking forward to today. Had been dreading it, in fact. But it hadn't been too bad. He'd survived, and so had the kids. They had even managed to find a small moment of joy in the experience, albeit peripherally.

So. Maybe he was doing more than simply surviving and enduring. Maybe the dark, dim days of his early grief weren't the only color he had to look forward to.

Maybe.

"I FEEL UTTERLY DISGUSTING. As though I need to scrub the inside of my body with bleach and steel wool." Angie lay on the couch, one hand on her much-abused belly.

Michael was sprawled on the other side of the U-shaped modular piece, his legs clad in faded denim, his hands clasped across his chest as he rested with his eyes closed.

They had feasted on a cornucopia of Billie's favorite foods. Miniature hot dogs, salt-and-vinegar chips, party pies and sausage rolls, macaroni and cheese—the kind with the canned cheese sauce—and a host of sweet treats that they had stirred through softened ice cream. Now, Angie's stomach was rebelling, clearly highly ambivalent about the heady mix of salt, nitrates, sugars and animal fats she'd fed it.

"I bought some antacid, just in case," Michael said.

"Good. I'll let you know if I need it." She eyed her stomach. "Digest, please. Make all the badness go away."

Eva looked up from where she was fiddling with the iPad.

"I don't know what all the fuss is about. I thought dinner was perfect."

"That's because you've inherited your mother's taste buds," Michael said.

"Really?" Eva appeared buoyed by the prospect.

"Definitely," Angie confirmed.

Eva smiled hugely before focusing on the game she'd been playing. Michael cracked open an eye to check on Charlie, who lay curled on his side on the section of couch between him and Angie, dead to the world.

"I should probably put the C monster to bed while he's out to it," he said.

"Excellent plan," she agreed.

Michael didn't move.

"On the other hand, he seems very comfortable where he is," he said.

"For sure."

After a short silence Michael stirred again, sitting up and swinging his feet to the floor.

"Can I get you anything while I'm up?"

"A bucket?"

"Seriously?" He looked alarmed.

"Joke. I think."

"Oh. Good."

He lifted Charlie, carefully tucking him against his shoulder. Angie felt a pang in her chest as she saw the tender, utterly devoted expression in his eyes as he looked at his son's sleeping face.

"He's just about perfect when he's sleeping," he said quietly.

"Yeah. He's not bad when he's awake, either."

Michael walked slowly from the room. Angie lay with her eyes closed, listening to the chirpy music emanating from the iPad. After a few minutes it occurred to her that she couldn't hear Eva playing anymore and she opened her eyes. Sure enough, Eva had succumbed to the sirens' song of a full stomach and was now dozing, her head resting on her loosely clenched fists.

"You have another customer for the sleepyland express," she said when Michael returned to the living room.

"Wow. Maybe I need to reconsider the no junk food rule if it knocks them out like this."

Eva blinked to wakefulness as Michael lifted her. "I don't want to go to bed yet."

"I don't think your body agrees with you, sweetheart."

"No, I want to stay up with you and Angie." Eva pushed at Michael's chest, wanting to be set down.

"Here's a deal for you. You go to bed now, and if you can't sleep or you get up later, you can hang with us. How's that?"

Eva considered for a moment before settling against her father's chest. "Okay."

Michael returned in under five minutes. Angie heard

him moving around in the kitchen and could only shake her head.

"Please tell me you aren't considering eating more food," she called.

"I'm opening a bottle of wine. You want a glass?"

Angie consulted her stomach and discovered it was surprisingly silent on the subject. "You know, I might."

"Just as well, because I'm not getting drunk on my own."

She watched as he strode from the kitchen, two glasses and the wine in hand.

"That bad, huh?"

"Better than I'd thought it would be. But I'm still getting drunk."

She used her elbows to wiggle herself into a more or less upright position and held out a hand for a glass. "The least I can do is ably assist you."

"Good. Because I'm planning on doing this right."

Michael poured the wine and passed a glass over to Angie.

"To Billie," he said.

"To Billie."

Michael dropped his head back and finished his glass in one big, greedy swallow.

Angie hesitated, then followed suit. Apparently it was going to be one of those nights.

CHAPTER SEVEN

"REMEMBER THE TIME Billie got really wasted at her twenty-seventh birthday party?" Angie asked.

"That's the night she slept in the bathtub, right?"

"That's the one."

Billie had been out-of-control funny that night. Angie had laughed so hard her stomach had hurt the next day.

"Yeah. I remember."

"And her doing her Uma Thurman from *Pulp Fiction* impersonation? God, she was good." Angie held out her glass for a refill.

They were onto their third round and the world was getting nicely fuzzy around the edges.

"Yeah. She could move."

"She could. She could boogie like no one else I know."

"Remember when she decided to take up the cello?" Michael said as he filled her glass.

Angie laughed, nodding. "You had to drive to Albury to pick up the one she'd bought on eBay."

"Three hours there and back. And the bloody thing sat in the garage for two years before she admitted she was never going to learn how to play it." Michael's words brimmed with affection and fond frustration.

"To be fair, the cello was almost taller than she was," Angie said.

"The first clue it wasn't going to fly. Like learning

how to surf and French lessons and life drawing and karate…"

Angie sipped her wine, thinking of her crazy, wonderful friend. "She was a ratbag, wasn't she?"

Michael remained silent and she glanced at him. He was staring into his glass, a muscle ticking in his jaw.

She searched for something to say, something to distract him from the pain he was no doubt feeling.

"Did I ever tell you how I met Billie?" She launched into the story, telling him how Billie had arrived at the rural boarding school Angie had just started attending and caused a stir with her posh London accent and cool European clothes and the fact that her parents were assigned to the British High Commission in Canberra. As Angie had hoped, the tight look left his face. One story led to another and, somehow, one bottle of wine became two. Angie sank deeper and deeper into the softness of the couch, pleasantly buzzed and more than a little mellow.

"I never understood what you were doing at that school," Michael said when she finished telling him about the time Billie had scared their biology class to death by rampaging into the room bearing the gardener's huge chainsaw—engine off, fortunately—her own special take on the *The Texas Chainsaw Massacre*. "I got why Billie was there, because her parents were idiots and she was a handful and they didn't want her interfering with their diplomatic duties, but what was your parents' excuse?"

Angie leaned forward to set her glass on the coffee table. "Honestly? I think it was half about wanting the best for me and half about not knowing what to do with me. My mum was forty-six when she had me, my dad fifty. They'd tried for years and given up on kids before I came along. I was this precious unexpected thing, and they loved me to death, but they were also a little scared, I think, that they would mess it up. My mother in particular wanted me to have every opportunity, to think beyond the farm and the town. If she could have, she'd have sent me to a school in the city, but Dad wouldn't have it so New England Girls' School was the compromise."

"What did you want?"

She smiled, recalling the terror with which she'd faced the prospect of leaving everything that she knew and held dear.

"I wanted to cling to them like a limpet on a rock. But my mother told me that she knew I was shy, but I needed to learn to be brave or the world was going to pass me by. I cried myself to sleep for the first two weeks before Billie arrived and was assigned to share a room with me."

"Why do people always think that introverts are afraid? As if all those loudmouths out in the world aren't desperately braying to cover up some inadequacy."

She gave him a knowing look. "I gather you had the 'be brave, little camper' speech, as well?"

"Every time Dad got reassigned and we had to pack up and move. Like a pep talk was going to change who I was and the situation we were in."

Angie rolled onto her side so she was facing him more directly and wedged a cushion under her head.

"Did you hate it? The moving?" She was aware from past conversations that Michael's father had worked for a big multinational corporation and Michael and his family had relocated no less than six times during his school years.

"At first. But after a while it felt like a get-out-of-jail-free card. If things were shit, if I had a bad teacher, if something went wrong at school, I never got too bent of shape because I always knew Dad would come home sooner or later and tell us they wanted him to 'help out' at another office and the packing tape and boxes would be out again. Two years was the longest we ever spent anywhere."

"I don't know how you stood it. I hate moving," Angie said.

"So do I. With a passion."

"In fact, I can't wait until I'm in my forever home. I'm going to fill up the cupboards with crap I don't need and collect knickknacks and become so settled they'll need a bulldozer to dig me out of the place."

"Why aren't you married?"

It was such an out-of-left-field question that she blinked. "Wow. Where did that come from?"

"It's something that's been bugging me for a while. You're hot. You're sane. You're funny and smart. Why aren't you already in your forever house with some lucky bastard, filling it up with knickknacks and kids?"

Angie's alcohol-soaked brain scrambled to keep up with what Michael had thrown at her. Apparently he thought she was hot and smart and funny. And he couldn't understand why she was still single. "Thanks. I think."

"It's a compliment." He swallowed a mouthful then looked bemused when he discovered the glass was now empty.

"I happen to quite like being single."

"You don't get lonely?"

"Of course. But there are other pluses. Doing what I want when I want it. Not having to compromise."

Michael pushed to his feet. "See, those things don't even come close to counterbalancing the pluses of a good relationship in my book."

He headed for the kitchen and Angie twisted her neck so she could follow him with her gaze.

"They look pretty good when you measure them against a bad one, though."

He glanced at her before pulling another bottle from the pantry. "I take it you're referring to the infamous Finn?"

She subsided onto the couch as he returned.

"Why does everything always come back to Finn?"

"Because he was the great love of your life?" Michael suggested.

She held out her glass for a top-up. "He was my first serious boyfriend. Or partner. Or lover. Whatever you want to call it. It was intense. It ended badly. But he was *not* the love of my life."

"Billie seemed to think so."

"Billie liked the drama of that idea. She liked Finn, too. I'm sure she secretly hoped we would one day get back together. Fated lovers reunited blah, blah, blah. But I refuse to believe that he was as good as it's going to get for me. There's something better out there. There has to be."

"Ouch. I'm feeling a little sorry for Finn now."

"Don't be. He was incapable of fidelity, as well as possessive, demanding and moody."

"God, no wonder Billie liked him. He sounds like Heathcliff."

Angie smiled. "I knew there was a reason I could never finish that book."

Michael set the bottle on the floor, presumably so he

wouldn't have to reach too far to pour himself more. He settled into the cushions, legs stretched out in front of him, ankles crossed, his glass resting on his flat belly as he gazed at the ceiling. They were both silent for a long moment.

"I miss sex, though," Angie mused. "I will admit that. Not just the sticking tab A into slot B bit, but being naked with someone and trusting them enough to make stupid orgasm faces and noises and lying in bed afterward talking about nothing and everything…"

There was no response. Belated heat flowed up her neck and into her face. Should have edited herself. She glanced toward him.

"Too much information? Sorry."

The hand gripping his glass was white-knuckle tight. She was about to apologize again, sure she'd offended or embarrassed him, when he took an abrupt, noisy swallow of his wine as though bracing himself for something arduous or awful.

"I had a dream last week. A sex dream." The words sounded as though they had been dragged from him, a reluctant confession. Yet clearly he wanted to talk about this or he wouldn't have brought it up.

"What sort of sex dream? About Billie, you mean?" she asked cautiously. Their friendship may have deepened in recent months, but this sort of intimacy was a whole new ball game.

"No." He seemed on the verge of saying more but lapsed into silence.

Angie couldn't decide if she should push or not.

"Was it about someone else?" she finally ventured.

"It was dark. I couldn't see her face. I could only feel her body, her skin…"

Unbidden, an image popped into her mind: Michael's hands on a woman's body, shaping her curves, caressing her. Angie immediately pushed it from her mind, but it was too late, her body was flooding with unwanted, illicit heat.

She squeezed her thighs together, willing the desire away, profoundly aware of what a betrayal her reaction was—of both Billie and Michael.

"This is going to sound stupid, but I honestly thought that part of me was dead. You made that crack about Popeye the other day, but I haven't so much as looked down with intent in all these months... And then suddenly there's this dream and it felt so real, as though she was there and we were really having sex—" Michael ran a hand over his face. "Sorry. That's definitely too much information."

Angie tried to push past her own discomfort and embarrassment to respond to what he was telling her. She could deal with her own reaction later. Much later. Michael was sharing this because he'd clearly been troubled by the dream. She owed it to him, to their growing friendship, to be worthy of his trust.

"You feel guilty because you were turned on in your dream?"

"Yes."

"You shouldn't. Like I said to you the other day at the pub, you're thirty-five years old. No one in their right mind would expect you to live the rest of your life like a monk now that Billie is gone."

"I don't want it."

She frowned, confused. "Sorry?"

"I don't want to want someone else. I don't want any of it."

She smiled sadly. "Ever heard the saying 'life goes on'? You can't stop the world from turning, Michael. Even if a part of you wants to."

"Jesus." He rested his forearm across his eyes, obscuring his face.

"I'm sorry. I know it's hard."

Her voice seemed to echo in the room and after a few seconds it occurred to her that given the subject of their discussion, she could have chosen her words more carefully. She snuck a glance at Michael and saw that the corner of his mouth was a little crooked. As though he was trying to suppress a smile.

"Bad choice of words. Sorry," she said.

"You think?"

She could hear the amusement in his voice but there was something she wanted to say before they both happily swept this conversation under the carpet.

"Don't punish yourself for being human, Michael. Billie is the last person who'd want you to lock yourself away from life."

He let out a heavy sigh. "I know. Doesn't make any of it any easier, though."

"I know."

Michael reached for the bottle. "More?"

"I think I'm done. Actually, I think I was done a while ago. Now I'm well done. Time to call a cab."

Michael looked surprised. "I thought you were staying the night."

"Oh. I hadn't thought about it…."

It was something she used to do when Billie was alive, on the rare occasions when she'd had too much to drink to drive home safely.

"You're always welcome. You know that."

She knew she should go, especially given her reaction to his sexy dream confession but it was an expensive cab ride and she didn't want the hassle of having to deal with collecting her car tomorrow.

"All right. If it's cool with you."

"I'll grab you a pillow and blanket."

She sat up as he went off for the bedding. Her head swam as she collected the glasses and bottle and ferried them all to the kitchen. Even though she knew she was way too tanked to totally ward off a hangover, she poured herself a glass of water and gulped it.

"I brought you a quilt as well as a blanket, in case it gets cold," Michael said as he entered, his arms full.

He dumped his burden on the couch before joining her. She filled her glass again and offered it to him wordlessly.

"Like that's going to make a difference," he said drily.

"It's worth a shot."

He swallowed the water in one long gulp then handed the glass to her. "Thanks."

Her gaze fell to the strong column of his throat and she remembered the defined planes of his bare chest and belly.

"Bed for me." She took a jerky step backward, away from him and her own reactions. She misjudged how close she was to the sink and Michael reached out to stop her as she collided with the counter. "Ow."

His hand gripped her shoulder a second too late. "Duffer."

"It's not my fault someone moved your house around while I wasn't looking."

"Idiot. Did you hurt yourself?"

"I'll survive."

He wasn't prepared to take her at her word, however, drawing her forward and then sliding his hand from her shoulder down her back to her hip.

"Was it here?" he said, his hand rubbing gently but firmly against her hip through the soft fabric of her yoga pants.

"Yes. It's fine. Really."

She kept her gaze focused over his shoulder as his palm rubbed heat into her skin, telling herself all the while that he'd do exactly the same if Eva had hurt herself and pretending that her whole body wasn't lighting up like a flare at his touch. Awful, confused panic rose inside her, mixing with desire. She didn't understand why this was happening, why she'd suddenly lost control of her own body.

"Better?" he asked.

"Thanks." This time she stepped to the side as she moved past him. "See you in the morning." She made her way toward the living area, not looking back.

"Turn the heating on if it gets too cold out here, okay?"

"I will."

She concentrated on unfolding the quilt and spreading it just-so along the couch until she heard him leave. She pulled cushions out of the way and replaced them with the pillow, then reached around to unclasp her bra. She wriggled until she was able to pull her bra free from inside her left sleeve, then flicked off the overhead light and slid beneath the quilt.

Her head spun dizzily for a few seconds and she took a couple of deep breaths before it settled. Then it was just her and the dark quiet and her very unquiet thoughts.

Because it was one thing to recognize on some instinctive level that Michael was a technically available male in his prime and another thing entirely to "enjoy" a full body flush of lust because he outlined in barest detail the content of an erotic dream.

As for what had happened to her body when he'd rubbed her hip...

She squeezed her eyes shut tightly, but it didn't protect her from the realization bearing down on her as inexorably as a freight train.

She was attracted to Michael. And not in a general, admiring-a-handsome-man kind of a way. Her attraction was very specific, very targeted. It was about Michael. About how he looked and who he was and what he said and did.

The awareness made her feel sick with guilt and discomfort. He was Billie's husband. Her lover. The father of her children. He was off-limits—and yet when he'd talked about touching a woman, Angie's head filled with images of him touching *her,* not some faceless dream woman. And then he *had* touched her and she'd had to step away from him before the tumult he'd triggered in her body became obvious.

God, Billie, I'm so sorry. So sorry.

She pressed her fingers to her lips, overwhelmed by confusion and dismay. This was so wrong, on so many levels. Michael trusted her—witness him confessing, looking to her for advice—and his kids trusted her. She was their Auntie Angie, and Michael was becoming her dear friend.

Yet her body desired his. When he was close, she noticed things about him that she shouldn't. Like how he smelled and how the warm, sleek muscles of his body moved beneath his clothes.

I don't want this. I don't. I didn't come looking for it, and I don't want it.

Yet she still felt this way. The knowledge pulled her knees tightly to her body and made her press her fingers even more firmly against her lips. She could feel the hard edges of her teeth against the tender skin of her mouth but she didn't reduce the pressure, happy on some level to be feeling physical pain when she was so confused and disgusted with herself. She deserved to hurt. What she'd been thinking tonight, what she'd wanted was wrong, a horrible betrayal of the many years of her friendship with Billie.

This stops now. *Right this second. Not another thought. Nothing. Because this is not happening. This will never, ever happen. I do not want to be this person and I refuse to be.*

The taste of iron filled her mouth. She'd pressed her mouth so hard she'd broken the skin inside her lip. She dropped her hand and ran her tongue over the tender spot as resolve hardened inside her. She'd recognized the problem, stared it in the eye and now she would deal with it. No one except herself would ever know how far her thoughts had slipped.

Definitely Michael never would.

She drifted into sleep with her hands clenched into determined fists. She woke to the dull light of dawn coming through the window. The first thought she had was that something terrible had happened. It wasn't an unfamiliar feeling—she'd woken that way for weeks after Billie's death—but this morning the feeling of dread wasn't about Billie's absence but about her own thoughts and feelings.

In the cold light of day, with a queasy stomach and

a headache looming, last night's realization was even more appalling. Angie wanted to pull the quilt over her head and retreat into sleep, to pretend that it had all been a horrible nightmare. But she was lying on Michael's couch in Michael's house and any minute now he would shuffle into the kitchen and she would have to deal with him while carrying the full weight of her own guilt and attraction.

She mouthed a four-letter word and rolled off the couch. Moving silently and quickly, she folded the bedding. She placed the pillow on top of the pile before tiptoeing to the bathroom to collect her wet clothes. She waited until she was outside on the porch before putting on her shoes.

She drove straight home. The moment she was in the door she shed her clothes and walked straight into the shower. Standing beneath the stinging heat of the water, her thoughts slowed and she was able to see beyond last night's drunken disgust and self-recrimination for the first time.

Michael was a good man. He was a great father, and he was smart and self-aware and he had a wicked sense of humor. As she'd noted a number of times, he was also easy on the eyes. She liked him very much as a person in his own right, not simply because of his connection to Billie. Angie cared for him and wanted the best for him.

Given all of the above, it wasn't exactly a miracle that she'd crossed the line. Not that that made it any more acceptable, but maybe it wasn't quite so unforgivable. Maybe.

She was toweling herself dry when her phone rang. One glance at the display told her it was Michael. She guessed he was calling to check on her, to make sure she'd gotten home okay. She hesitated about taking the call, her thumb hovering over the button. After a few seconds the phone stopped ringing. A few seconds after that, her phone beeped indicating she had voice mail.

She ignored it. She didn't want to hear his voice right now. In fact, it might be good to arrange next week's schedule so that she didn't have to see him except when strictly necessary. A little built-in safety measure until she had a grip on this unwanted thing that had sprung to life inside her.

It wasn't much, as far as strategies went. In fact, it felt a little as though she was heading off to fight a dragon with a toothpick as her weapon. But it was all she had—that and her determination to remain true to her friend. It would have to be enough.

MICHAEL WOKE WITH GRITTY eyes and a dry mouth. He staggered to the bathroom and drank a glass of water before swallowing some aspirin. It had been a while since he'd written himself off so emphatically and when he returned to the bedroom he sank onto the edge of the bed and allowed himself a few seconds of head-in-hands self-pity.

The urge to roll beneath the quilt and sleep off the worst of his self-inflicted discomfort was almost irresistible, but it was a Saturday and Eva and Charlie had swimming lessons at ten. Plus Angie was on the couch, and he should make sure she had some aspirin before the kids started making a ruckus.

He'd stripped to his boxer briefs last night and he tugged on a robe before making his way to the kitchen. Even though it was nearly seven the room was still dim. He flicked on the kettle before crossing to the living room to check on Angie. If she felt up to it, he'd make her and the kids pancakes for breakfast. She might even want to come swimming with them.

He stopped sharply when he saw the couch was empty, the bedding folded neatly at one end.

She'd left already. He confirmed his suspicion by walking to the door and stepping onto the porch. Sure enough, her car was gone.

The cold morning air blew under his robe and he stepped into the house and shut the door. They'd had a lot to drink last night—mostly at his behest—and he hoped she'd been sober by the time she got behind the wheel. Worry niggling at him, he grabbed his phone to call her. The line rang and rang before finally going to voice mail.

"Hey, it's me. Hope you're not feeling too rough. Thanks for being my wingwoman last night. Just so you know, you're missing out on pancakes for breakfast." He hesitated, tempted to ask her to call to let him know she'd gotten home okay. He reminded himself he wasn't her mother and disconnected.

He moved to the other side of the counter. Pancakes were the kids' favorite treat and he knew the recipe from heart. He grabbed flour and milk and eggs, and once he'd mixed the batter, set the bowl aside for ten minutes and crossed to the couch to collect the bedding. He knew from experience that if he didn't put it away today, it would haunt the living room for the rest of the week.

He lifted the blankets, then paused when something caught his eye. A scrap of black lace and coffee-colored silk peeking out from between the seat cushions. He set down the blankets to pull the scrap free and found him-

self holding an elegant, sexy bra, a confection of caffe-
latte silk and sheer black lace.

It had been so long since he'd seen a woman's bra
that he simply stared at it, dumbfounded, for a few seconds. It was Angie's, of course. She must have taken
it off last night and then forgotten it this morning. He
rubbed his fingers together, testing the fineness of the
silk. It felt cool and softer than liquid against his skin.
Then he registered what he was doing—feeling up Angie's bra—and dropped it as though it was a hot potato.

The last thing he needed or wanted was to know what
Angie's underwear looked or felt like.

"Daddy, I can't find my swimsuit." Eva's voice preceded her as she made her way toward the kitchen.

Michael's gaze shot to the bra abandoned on the
couch. He snatched it, folded it and was stuffing it awkwardly into his pocket when Eva entered.

"Have you checked the laundry basket?" he asked,
feeling ridiculously furtive and juvenile and caught out
as he faced his daughter.

There was no reason in the world for him to feel self-
conscious about the fact that Angie had left a piece of
clothing behind, even if that piece of clothing was a bra.
Yet his first impulse upon hearing Eva's voice had been
to hide it. As though it was a dirty secret he needed to
conceal.

"Does that mean it hasn't been washed since last
week?" Eva asked, already pouting.

For a little girl with a very messy room, she had an
obsession with clean laundry that Michael found hard
to fathom. "Let's go check. There's no reason we can't
run it through the washer and dry it before your lesson,
so don't freak out."

"I wasn't freaking out. If I was freaking out, I'd have gone like this." Eva jumped up and down on the spot, her hands flailing, her face screwed into a comic representation of panic.

"My apologies. I stand corrected."

Together they went into the laundry room and sorted through a pile of clothes. As he'd predicted, her swimsuit was there and he put on a load of washing and lifted her so she could be the one to measure out the detergent.

"Can we have pancakes for breakfast?" Eva asked as he set her on the floor.

"As a matter of fact, you can. I've already got the batter ready to go."

Eva's eyes got big with excitement. "Really? Fair dinkum?"

Michael laughed at his daughter's use of the Australianism, even though a significant part of his brain was preoccupied with the scrap of silk and lace he'd pushed into his pocket. He was burningly aware of it, keen to remove it from his person in case Eva somehow discovered it. Having to explain why he was carrying Angie's bra around in his pocket would be far, far worse than having to explain why it had been left abandoned on the couch this morning.

"Where did you pick that up?" he asked as he ushered Eva into the kitchen.

"At school. We're learning about Australia at the moment. We talked about bush tucker, and a whole bunch of other stuff." She told him more about her classes as he cooked pancakes, but every time he glanced down he caught sight of the black lace and felt uncomfortable all over again. Once he'd served their meal he made an excuse and escaped to his bedroom. As soon as he was alone he pulled the bra from his pocket and opened the nearest drawer, dropping it in with his socks. He turned away, then stilled, thinking how it would look if, by some completely unimaginable series of events, someone happened to open his drawer and found Angie's bra stashed there. It would look as though he was saving it, like a keepsake. Or a fetish.

Shaking his head, he yanked the drawer open and pulled the bra out. He stood, the bra dangling from one hand, his gaze bouncing around the room as he tried to work out what to do with damned thing.

Dude, it's a bra. A piece of clothing. Unclench, find a shopping bag and leave it in the studio for Angie. Problem solved.

The moment the thought occurred he felt calmer. He found a bag in the closet and dropped the bra into it, then left it on his chest of drawers. Later, he would take it out to the studio. Right now, he had pancakes to eat and two children to prepare for swimming lessons.

Send For
2 FREE BOOKS
Today!

I accept your offer!

Please send me two
free Harlequin® Superromance®
novels and two mystery
gifts (gifts worth about $10).
I understand that these books
are completely free—even
the shipping and handling will
be paid—and I am under no
obligation to purchase anything, ever,
as explained on the back of this card.

❏ I prefer the regular-print edition
135/336 HDL FNNG

❏ I prefer the larger-print edition
139/339 HDL FNNG

Please Print

FIRST NAME

LAST NAME

ADDRESS

APT.#   CITY

STATE/PROV.   ZIP/POSTAL CODE

Visit us online at
www.ReaderService.com

CHAPTER EIGHT

By the time Michael was sitting beside the toddlers' pool watching Charlie splash around with the other children, the bra incident had resumed its rightful place in his mind and he felt more than a little foolish.

He'd overreacted. Big-time. And he had no idea why.

He frowned as he watched Charlie smack the surface of the water with his palms, his squeals of delight carrying clearly.

Michael wasn't in the habit of lying to himself—a pointless exercise if ever there was one—and he figured he wasn't about to start now. He had *some* idea why he'd wigged out. Last night, they had exchanged intimate confidences. He'd told her about his dream, about the fact that he'd been thinking about sex again. And she'd told him that she thought about sex, too.

Mind, her confession had come first, which probably explained why he'd felt the urge to come clean about his dream. He gazed at the scuff mark on the toe of his sneaker as he remembered what she'd said.

I miss sex... Not just the sticking tab A into slot B bit, but being naked with someone and trusting them enough to make stupid orgasm faces and noises and lying in bed afterward talking about nothing and everything...

There had been a wistfulness, a wishfulness to her words that had hit him in the gut. She'd made him think of the empty space in the bed and the cold sheets and how long it had been since he'd felt the warmth of skin on skin. She'd made him achingly aware of the absolute aloneness he felt whenever the kids weren't around and he found himself in a moment of quiet. The sex-dream confession had emerged in an impulsive, ill-thought-out blurt.

Angie had said all the right things about his right to be human and Billie wanting him to be happy, but it was one thing to know something rationally and another to convince the unknown, subterranean parts of his mind it was okay that he still had desires now that Billie was gone. But perhaps this was yet one more thing that would be dealt with by time. Perhaps when he'd had his fiftieth erotic dream he'd be cool with it and wouldn't have to retreat to the shower to wash away the guilt.

His thoughts drifted—again—to what Angie had said. He'd been so wrapped up in his fuzzy, confused, internal monologue that he hadn't really considered what her words meant for her. In the bright light of a new day, with a clear head, it was impossible to stop himself from parsing over them.

She'd been incredibly generous with her time and affection with him and the kids. Although she was un-stinting with her hugs and kisses for them, she'd always been a little standoffish with adults. Not that she was cold—far from it—more that she was careful about who she allowed close. He couldn't help but wonder how that reserve would translate into the bedroom. Would Angie be shy? Would she need to be coaxed? Or would she make love the way she worked, with a single-minded, passionate intensity?

An image slipped into his mind: Angie's lean, supple

body clad in coffee-colored silk and black lace. Her dark hair slipping over her shoulder, her blue eyes smoky with need and desire—

A high-pitched scream drew his attention to the pool. He was on his feet before he saw that it wasn't Charlie. His son was oblivious to the drama at the other side of the shallow pool. One glance at the author of the scream assured him that she was simply excited, not hurt or in danger. Michael made eye contact with the lifeguard, who gave him a reassuring nod. After a moment's hesitation, Michael sank into his seat.

He was uncomfortably aware that there was a heaviness between his thighs, the result of having allowed himself to cast Angie in his own private peepshow.

Angie, his friend. The woman who had almost single-handedly stopped him from slipping under in the past twelve months. Billie's closest, most beloved confidant.

What is wrong with you?

It was a good question. He'd gone from being dead below the waist to latching onto the first available woman and fantasizing about her like a horny fifteen-year-old.

He crossed his arms over his chest, squeezing them so tightly against his body that his shoulders ached. A wave of anger washed over him. Didn't he have enough on his plate? Didn't his life suck enough already without adding this extra bowl full of wrong into the mix? Was it really too much to ask for a few moments of normality and peace and contentment without guilt or grief or pain intruding?

He wallowed in self-pity before something Angie had said recently popped into his head.

"Normal is a setting on the washing machine. I don't know what it is in real life."

At the time he'd laughed and now, a week later, he smiled and all the anger and frustration leached away. Last night, Angie told him not to punish himself for being human. Not bad advice. He wasn't a saint, after all. And he'd never given himself a hard time about looking at or thinking about other women when Billie was alive. Not that he'd made a practice of it, but he had eyes in his head and being married hadn't made the world less full of attractive women. He'd figured it was an ordinary part of life that he might occasionally look at another woman and wonder. He knew Billie had looked at other men because she'd always made a point of teasing him about it. It had never even crossed his mind to do more than wonder, however.

He'd never looked at Angie in that way, though. She had always been off-limits, an absolute no-go zone. Clearly, that had changed recently. But that didn't mean anything was about to happen. It wasn't as though he would suddenly lose control and start humping her leg. He wasn't some oversexed monkey in the jungle. He was just a guy who had found himself single against his will, trying to navigate his way through a new world.

He knew it was all true and he applauded the rational part of his brain for trotting out so many convincing arguments. Still, he felt like a crummy asshole by the time Charlie was finished. He collected Eva from outside the girls' change room where she was giggling with her friends and went home via the supermarket.

By evening, the asshole feeling had subsided somewhat and he was more inclined to give himself a break. That didn't mean he wouldn't be stomping all over any thoughts that strayed into forbidden territory where Angie was concerned. He simply wasn't prepared to go there. End of story.

He did feel honor bound to check in with her after their boozy evening. When she hadn't responded to his earlier message by dinnertime he called her again. The phone rang and rang and he was beginning to think he'd be talking to her voice mail again when she picked up.

"Hi."

"Hi yourself. I wanted to make sure you didn't spend the whole day hugging the toilet bowl courtesy of my bad idea."

"I'm fine. Nothing a few painkillers didn't fix, anyway."

"Good. Glad to hear it."

"How's your day been?"

Michael frowned. Was it just him, or was there a certain…coolness to Angie's tone? A polite, arm's-length distance?

"Pretty low-key. Swimming with the kids then some grocery shopping. With a bit of luck, they'll both crash early and I can sneak some work in."

"Sounds good. Listen, I need to get going. I'm due somewhere. But I'll see you Monday, okay?"

"Sure. Have a good night."

He disconnected, an uneasy feeling in his gut. He hoped like hell he'd been imagining the coolness, that it was merely a figment of his guilty imagination. Because if he'd put her off-side with something he'd said last night, if he'd somehow jeopardized their friendship by confessing too much…he would kick himself from here until next Tuesday.

She's going out. Since when did you turn into such an old nana that you had to overanalyze every little thing?

He chose to believe the voice in his head but the next few days didn't do much to allay his fears. On Monday night, Angie was packing to leave the second he arrived home from work, barely stopping to exchange greetings. He'd left her bra in her studio for her, neatly folded in the shopping bag, but she didn't so much as glance sideways at him to acknowledge its return as she headed for the door. Tuesday night was the same. Wednesday night was what had become "her" night to cook and she honored the tradition by making a huge shepherd's pie—enough to feed him and the kids and the neighbors for the next week. He barely had a chance to comment on how good it smelled when she started gathering her things.

"You're not staying?" he asked, surprised. He'd just walked in the door from work.

"I can't. I've got a thing." She slipped the strap of her handbag over her shoulder and avoided looking him in the eye.

She was a terrible liar. He figured it was a credit to her, really, but at that moment he wished she was a more accomplished bullshit artist because the unease that had been sitting in his belly since Saturday night was rapidly solidifying into out-and-out worry.

Baffled and tense, he stood with his hands stuffed into his trouser pockets while she kissed Charlie and Eva goodbye.

"I'll see you crazy cats tomorrow, okay?" she said, straightening and tossing her hair over her shoulder. She risked a glance his way before turning toward the door. "Remember, don't take the pie out of the oven till the potato's crunchy on top."

He followed her to the door, which earned him a startled look.

"Well. I guess I'll see you tomorrow, too," she said, flashing a quick smile as she exited to the porch.

Michael caught the screen door before it could swing closed between them. "Are we okay?"

It was a hard question to ask, but he didn't want to lose her friendship because he'd let something fester between them.

"Of course." Her voice was higher than usual. Unconvincing.

"Listen, if I said something the other night… I didn't mean to make you uncomfortable. I promise that from now on this will be a confession-free zone. No exceptions."

Her forehead puckered. "No. You don't need to apologize. You didn't make me uncomfortable."

He wanted to believe her, but he wasn't stupid. Something was going on.

"So why do you keep bolting the second I get home?"

"I've got some stuff going on, that's all. I'm trying to get on top of it.…"

He waited for her to elaborate, then realized she wasn't going to. Whatever was going on in her life, she didn't want to share it with him.

"Okay. Well, you know our door is always open. If you need to talk or whatever."

"I know. You've always been great. You and the kids." She smiled, the first real smile he'd had from her all week.

He stepped into the house. "Let me know if there's anything I can do."

"Michael—" He waited for her to keep talking but

she pressed her lips together and shook her head. "Just ignore me, okay? I'm a moody artist type. This is nothing to do with you. It's all me and my craziness. Okay? You're great."

She reached out and caught his wrist, her fingers sliding against his skin until she was gripping his hand with her long, strong fingers. He returned the pressure, letting her know she was important to him.

"I'll see you tomorrow, okay?" There was warmth and absolute sincerity in her deep blue eyes.

"Okay."

She slipped her hand free and strode toward her car.

He hoped she'd been speaking the truth. He hoped he hadn't stuffed things up between them. He didn't want his life without Angie in it. Even the thought of it made his belly tight. He needed very badly for them to be okay.

Angie had to blink away tears as she drove home. She'd been trying to do the right thing, and instead she'd made Michael uncomfortable and guilty.

Way to go, Bartlett. Well done.

The way he'd stood there, telling her he wouldn't bother her with any unwanted confessions again... It had about killed her. She didn't want him thinking that she disapproved of him or judged him in some way. He had every right to the way he felt—it was her own emotions she didn't approve of.

What a mess—and she didn't know how to fix it, apart from sucking up her own discomfort in order to alleviate Michael's. No more dashing out the door. No more avoiding the fun, witty chats they often enjoyed at the end of the day. No more keeping her distance until she had a grip on her hormones or misplaced grief or misplaced sympathy or whatever it was that was fueling her unwanted attraction to him.

A part of her was stupid enough to feel happy that her self-imposed isolation was about to end. She liked spending time with Michael and the kids. She liked feeling part of the bustle and warmth of their home. It had been a wrench to make herself leave the moment he came home. Which went a long way to showing exactly how screwed up this whole situation was, really.

All thanks to you, stupid head.

She made a point of arriving fifteen minutes early the next morning, to make sure that she and Michael would have time to chat and to reassure him that she'd been as good as her word and that they really were okay.

She found him wiping Vegemite off Charlie's face, looking elegant and almost shockingly handsome in a single-breasted charcoal suit and a crisp white shirt. His hair was damp, starting to curl, and she could see the marks from where he'd run a comb through it to tame it into business mode.

"Who are you trying to impress today?" she asked lightly.

"That obvious, is it? I've got a client meeting in Sydney. I need to be at the airport by ten."

They both glanced toward the clock. It was eight-thirty already, and the traffic to the airport could be hellish in the mornings.

"Come on, Eva, get your skates on. We need to leave on time today," Michael called.

"I can drop her at school if you like."

"Thanks, but I've booked extra day care for Charlie and I need to get him off, too."

"I can do that. That way you can head straight for the airport now."

Michael paused for a moment, then shook his head. "It won't work. He needs his car seat and by the time we've taken it out and put it in yours I might as well deliver them myself."

"Easily fixed—we swap cars for the day. You get my heap of crap, and I get your lovely Audi."

She offered her keys along with a cheeky smile.

"Are you sure? I don't want to ruin your day."

"It's fine. I'm ahead on everything for once. Half an hour to drop off the kids is neither here nor there."

The tight expression left Michael's face. "Thanks, Angie."

She waved off his gratitude. Michael grabbed his briefcase as Eva entered, socks in one hand, shoes in the other.

"Almost ready," she said. "Have you made my lunch yet?"

"Damn," Michael said.

Angie shooed him toward the door. "Go. I've got it covered."

He shot her a grateful look and stooped to kiss Eva and Charlie goodbye. "I'll see you tonight, okay?" Then he turned toward her. "I owe you."

"You don't."

"I do. Big-time."

He surprised her then by stepping close and dropping a kiss on her cheek. His lips were warm and firm against her skin and she sucked in a big lungful of his leather-and-sandalwood aftershave before he moved away from her.

"Have a good one," he said as he left.

Angie fought the absurd, teenage urge to press her fingers to her cheek where he had kissed her. No way was she indulging herself like that. No way.

A few seconds later she gave herself a mental shake and surveyed her two charges.

"Okay. One of you has to go to school today. Remind me again which one of you that is?"

Eva giggled. "You're silly, Auntie Angie."

"Indeed I am. Now, what shall we pack you for lunch?"

She dropped Eva at school and Charlie at day care and dived into the day's work. She was locking up the house to collect Eva and Charlie at the other end of the day when Michael called.

"Hey, there," she said. "Have you schmoozed your clients into submission?"

"I have no idea if I sold them the project or not."

"Bummer."

"Yeah. Listen, Angie, there's a problem. My flight has been delayed."

"By how long?"

"At the moment, they're saying half an hour. But they're also not saying what the issue is."

"Ah. I love it when they do that."

"Tell me about it. I'm really sorry, Angie."

"What for? So you'll be half an hour later than you were supposed to be. It's no skin off my nose."

"I'll keep you posted. Hopefully it won't be a big deal."

But it was.

Michael called again at four-thirty to tell her that the airline was still being cagey about the status of his flight. At five he let her know the flight had finally been offi-

cially cancelled and passengers were being redirected as
availability allowed. Given that Michael's plane had been
full, as were most of the other Sydney-to-Melbourne
flights, he had been warned it might take some time.

She told him not to worry and made the kids nachos
for dinner. She was washing the dishes afterward when
Michael called to say he'd been shuffled onto the last
plane of the day at eleven o'clock. He was understand-
ably furious and frustrated and Angie did her best to
keep things light once he'd finished updating her.

"Look on the bright side—there's all that fantastic
airport food to keep you going," she said.

"Remind me never to fly again."

"I'll put a note on the fridge."

"Angie—"

"Michael, if you say you owe me one more time, I'm
going to punch you in the face when I see you. It's not
a problem. Okay? It's not like I had other plans for the
evening, and in case you hadn't noticed, I like your kids."

"I know." He sounded troubled and weary.

"Here's a deal for you—if I ever feel as though you're
treating me like your bitch, I'll let you know, okay?"

"Okay, deal." She could hear the smile in his voice.
"Will you put Eva on so I can tell her what's going on?"

"Sure thing."

Angie handed the phone to Eva and listened as she
peppered her father with questions before holding the
receiver to Charlie's ear so he could say good-night.

By nine o'clock the children were both fast asleep.
Angie cleaned up the kitchen and folded some laundry
and then dropped onto the couch to watch TV. There was
nothing on that interested her and she stood and went
in search of a book. Billie had never been a big reader,

something Angie had never been able to fathom. Books had been her closest friends when she was growing up, a secret portal through which she escaped to magical worlds and far-off places. As an adult, she read for entertainment and inspiration, leaning toward biographies and fantasy.

Feeling a little as though she was invading Michael's private space, she ducked her head into his study. She'd never spent a lot of time in here, since it had always been very much a working study rather than the kind that simply housed a computer and a few household files. Her gaze ran over the deep, wide desk made from a piece of highly figured timber—Blackwood Box, if she had to guess—and the angled lines of a drafting table. One wall was lined with shelves filled with books, while the wall beside the door was home to an old, squishy-looking leather couch. It was a very masculine space, dark wood and chocolate-brown leather dominating, with a red-toned Turkish rug providing a counterpoint. It was very Michael, too—understated, comfortable, serious yet not unwelcoming.

She crossed to the bookshelf and was pleased to discover that as well as a wide selection of architecture and design books and manuals, Michael had also devoted a couple of shelves to biographies and crime thrillers.

Five minutes later, she had three books in her arms as she turned to go. Her gaze slid across Michael's desk and got caught on the small framed photograph he kept there. It had been hidden by the computer monitor when she first entered, but she had a clear view from here.

It was of Billie, naturally. A candid shot taken at the beach. It had clearly been a very windy day and Billie's hair was flying around her face, her dress billowing.

She held her hair back with one hand, while the other fought to keep her skirt down. Far from being dismayed by her dilemma, she was delighted, her mouth wide with laughter, her eyes sparkling with energy.

Angie hadn't seen the picture before but judging by the length of Billie's hair it had been taken about three years ago. She smiled at her friend's exuberance, but the picture made her sad, too. All that life was gone now. Buried six feet under.

And now you're making goo-goo eyes at her husband, like the very *best of friends.*

She didn't know what nasty, vindictive corner of her mind the thought came from but it made her take an instinctive, jerky step backward.

She wasn't making goo-goo eyes at Michael. She never had. She'd become aware of him lately, and she'd been honest enough to admit she was attracted to him. But she would never even consider acting on that attraction.

She glanced at the books in her arms. She shouldn't have come in here. This was Michael's space, and she shouldn't be helping herself as though she had a right. Guilt gnawing at her, she reshelved the books.

The ring of her phone interrupted her retreat from the room.

"Guess who?" Michael said as she took the call. He sounded resigned and more than a little tired.

"Don't tell me you've been delayed again?"

"Electrical storm. They've grounded everything until it passes through, but things are going to be backed up. Am I the luckiest guy alive or what?"

"You definitely shouldn't waste money on a lottery ticket today."

"So my ETA is now sometime after midnight, which means I won't be home till the small hours."

"No worries. The kids are in bed here so I'll bunk on the couch again."

"At the risk of inviting a punch in the nose, I have to say you're a godsend."

"Have you had something to eat?"

"I'm about to grab something now."

"Hang tough. By hook or by crook you'll get home."

"So they keep telling me. I'll see you later, okay?"

"Sure."

She made her way to the living room. Even though the television was offering nothing but pap, she turned it on and settled in for the duration. A couple of hours later she collected the bedding from the hall cupboard and set herself up for the night. Her skinny jeans were too tight to sleep in so she stripped down to her tank top and panties and slid beneath the quilt and let the late-night TV drowse her to sleep.

And every time her thoughts turned to Michael, she sent them somewhere else. Because she was not going to be that woman. She refused to be.

MICHAEL WAS BONE TIRED by the time he pulled into the garage at one-thirty in the morning. The moment his flight had hit the ground he'd headed for the short-term parking lot, thoroughly pissed at the world. He was so tired he'd walked past Angie's green SUV three times looking for his Audi before he remembered that they had swapped cars. He'd driven home with the windows open in order to keep himself awake.

Now he grabbed his briefcase and headed for the house. The kids' rooms were adjacent the entrance and he tried to keep the noise to a minimum as he let himself in. He could hear the faint sound of the TV from the living room meaning Angie must still be up.

He set down his briefcase and went to check on the kids, tugging Charlie's blanket a little higher on his shoulders and easing a book from Eva's lax hand. Trust his little night owl to fight off sleep for as long as she could.

He made his way to the main area. He expected to see Angie pop up from the couch but the only action was on the TV where a sockless Don Johnson was chasing a criminal down a pastel-tinted Miami street.

He moved closer and saw that Angie was out, her body curled into the couch, her dark hair fanned across the pillow and her shoulder. Like Eva, she'd fallen asleep with the remote control in her hand. Smiling, he leaned down and gently slid the remote from her grasp. She didn't stir as he clicked off the TV and tiptoed out of the room.

He would have to do something nice for her. Maybe shout her to a facial or massage or one of those other day-spa type activities that women always seemed to relish. Or maybe he could take her out for dinner, somewhere fancy to let her know how much he appreciated her. It would be nice to eat at a plush and lush place for a change and talk without interruption.

He brushed his teeth on autopilot and was about to undress and crawl into bed when he remembered that he'd promised he'd email some figures to his clients. He knew absolutely that if he didn't do it now, he'd forget in the morning. Rubbing his eyes, he headed for the study where a five-minute job became a twenty-minute job when he saw that he had two new emails from other clients.

Finally he switched the computer off and headed for bed. It was a testament to how weary he was that he didn't register the light from the open refrigerator door until he was halfway across the kitchen. Then the door swung shut and he found himself staring at Angie.

"Oh! You're back. I didn't realize," she said, eyes wide in the dim half light.

He opened his mouth to reply but nothing came out. She was wearing only a pair of black panties and a pale pink tank top. A little patch of belly was visible between the two and her legs were long and bare and seemed to go on forever. The pink fabric of her tank top stretched over her full, round breasts, the color pale enough that he could see the dark shadow of her nipples.

She looked soft and warm and leggy and utterly feminine and the male instincts that had lain dormant within him for the past year came roaring to life with a vengeance.

Heat rushed south, his pulse picked up, every muscle went tense and within seconds he was hard, his body making ready for an act that was never going to happen. Appalled at himself and the shocking insistence of his body's reaction, he lashed out.

"What do you think you're doing? What will the kids think if they catch you running around the house like that?"

The smile froze on Angie's face. She blinked, then color flowed up her chest and neck and onto her face.

"I was thirsty," she said. "Anyway, I doubt the kids would even notice. They see a million times more on the beach every summer."

"We're not at the beach. This is my home. I don't want people getting ideas."

Again she blinked at his harsh tone. He knew he was out of line—way out of line, off the planet—but he was hanging on to his self-control by the slenderest of threads.

He'd slept alone for over a year. He hadn't so much as smelled another woman's perfume and suddenly Angie was standing here, sexy as hell, nearly naked, and his body was making a lie of his pretense that he could spend the rest of his life denying himself to preserve his memories of Billie.

This was Billie's best friend. He should not be feeling this way about her. It was wrong on every level.

Without saying another word, Angie stalked toward the living room. He told himself not to look after her but his gaze was already locked onto her ass and thighs. He stared long enough to imprint the image on his mind before dragging his gaze away and fixing it on the fruit basket on the counter. A few seconds later he heard the unmistakable sound of jeans being zipped, then the sound of Angie's booted feet as she stood.

"I need my car keys," she said.

He could hear the shock and hurt in her voice. He told himself to apologize but he was too afraid of what might happen, of how his body might betray him if he looked at her again.

So instead, he placed the keys on the kitchen counter. She moved close enough to scoop them up before heading for the door.

Jesus, he was an asshole. An out-of-control, sleazy, desperate, guilt-ridden asshole.

"Angie," he called, but either he didn't speak loudly

enough or she chose not to hear him because the next sound he heard was the front door closing.

He swore. He couldn't believe what had just happened—that she'd looked so good to him, that he'd reacted so vehemently, that he'd said the things that he'd said. God only knew what she was thinking right now. She'd given up her whole day to help him. She'd been patient and kind and incredibly generous for months on end. And he'd repaid her by behaving like an outraged family morals campaigner.

And like some morals campaigners, he was a raging hypocrite because even now he had a hard-on that wouldn't quit. For his dead wife's best friend.

He swore again and headed for his bedroom. He dragged his clothes off angrily, carelessly, furious with himself, with his body, and, yes, with Angie, even though he knew she was the only one who was blameless in this situation.

He got into bed and punched his pillow and steadfastly ignored the demands of his body. He wasn't a kid, after all. He might not be able to control who he desired, but he could damn well control what he did about it.

Even though he was gritty-eyed with tiredness, it took him a long time to fall asleep. He kept hearing his words echoing in his head and seeing the shock in her face. And he had to keep wiping the image of her wearing next to nothing from his mind's eye. Her long, lean legs. The plush, full roundness of her breasts. That enticing glimpse of belly...

He must have eventually fallen asleep because he woke to find daylight streaming in his window. He stared at the triangle of bright white light on his ceiling and knew that his only priority for the day was to make things right with Angie.

Somehow.

He had no idea how he would achieve that. He only knew that anything else wasn't an option.

CHAPTER NINE

ANGIE DROVE AROUND THE block twice before parking in front of Michael's house the next morning. Her first instinct on waking had been to not go to work at all. She didn't want to see him. Not yet. Not until she'd gotten past the hurt and anger she felt at his baffling, unwarranted attack. But she had clients coming midmorning to brief her on a new commission and she needed to prepare.

She didn't understand what had happened, why he'd spoken so harshly. As she'd said to him at the time, Eva and Charlie had seen far more at the beach. Nothing that shouldn't have been on show had been on show. She'd been perfectly decent, even if she had felt more than a little exposed, given the circumstances.

The only conclusion she could come to was that it had been about a lot more than the fact that he'd busted her in her underwear. Michael's reaction had been so strong, so visceral, and responses like that didn't come out of nowhere.

She sat in her car long after she'd turned off the engine, hands tight on the steering wheel. She felt absurdly wounded by what had passed between them. Which went to show how much she'd invested in Michael and Eva and Charlie.

Given that, and given her...*issues* around Michael,

maybe her first instinct to retreat had been the right one.
Maybe she needed to start putting a bit more distance
between them. She'd allowed herself to become so absorbed with Michael and the kids that she'd let her own
life slide. Maybe she needed to address that.

The engine ticked, cooling in the morning air. She
grabbed her bag and got out. For the first time since
she'd moved into Billie's studio, she used the side gate
to access the backyard, walking the long way around.
Feeling more than a little cowardly and furtive, she let
herself into the studio. She didn't relax until the door
was closed behind her, then she let out a heavy sigh.
Pushing her hair off her forehead, she dropped her bag
onto the table and shed her jacket and prepared to very
deliberately lose herself in her work.

She was using the flexi-drive drill, buffing work
marks from an almost completed ring when a short,
sharp rap sounded on the door. She glanced at the
clock. It was a little past nine, which meant Michael
had dropped Eva off at school already.

She let the drill fall silent and pushed her chair back
from her desk. She took a deep breath, let it out, then
swiveled to face the door, bracing her legs and resting
her hands on her knees. "Come in."

The door opened and Michael filled the frame. His
gray-green gaze was troubled when it met hers. He
looked tired, his face pale and tight.

"Have you got a minute?"

"Of course."

He entered, his body stiff with tension. She clenched
her fingers and forced herself to maintain eye contact
with him. She might feel awkward as hell right now,
she might be hurt and confused by what had happened,

but this man was her friend. She wanted to hear what he had to say. She wanted to find a way to put last night behind them.

He was wearing a pair of black dress pants and a finely striped shirt and his dark hair was rumpled. His hands fisted and relaxed at his sides, as though he didn't quite know what to do with them.

"I'm sorry about last night. I was totally out of line. I was tired and you surprised me and before I knew it a bunch of crap was spilling out my mouth—" He shook his head. "Sorry. Let me start again, without the excuses. I should never have spoken to you like that. Period. You mean a lot to me and the kids and I hope that you can forgive me."

There was no doubting the sincerity of his words. Angie loosened her grip on her knees.

"It's not a matter of me forgiving you, Michael. I guess I don't really understand what happened. Like I told you, I had no idea you were even in the house."

"It wasn't about you, Angie, I swear."

"If I've been coming around too much, hanging around too long after I finished each day, let me know. Because I would totally understand. This is your house, after all."

It was one explanation for his extreme reaction. An unpleasant one from her point of view because it meant she'd worn out her welcome, but an explanation nonetheless.

He took a step toward her, one hand raised as if to erase her words from the air. "Angie, no. We love having you around. You know that."

"Okay." She knew she sounded unconvinced, probably because she was.

"Please believe me—this is all on me. You've done nothing but be generous and gracious and kind."

"Okay," she said again.

He made a frustrated sound. "I don't know what to say to make this go away."

"Tell me the truth."

Because if she'd said or done something, if he was feeling that strongly about something to do with her, she wanted—she needed—to know. To be able to fix it if she could.

Michael stared at her. A muscle leaped in his jaw. After a long beat, he looked away.

"It was a stupid reaction. I-It's been a while since I've been in the same room with an almost-naked woman."

For a long moment she simply stared at him, her brain refusing to process what he'd said. Then she registered the color in his cheeks and the nervous, boyish bob of his Adam's apple and comprehension washed over her.

"Oh," she said. Heat rushed into her own face. "Right. I—I didn't realize."

"Relax. You're not in any danger. I'm not going to leap on you or anything." Michael's laugh was nervous, awkward. "I guess I'm not as ready to become a monk as maybe I thought I was."

She nodded, unable to think of a single thing to say. He glanced toward the door, the desire to escape writ large on his face. He didn't make a run for it, though. He stood his ground and waited until she looked him in the eye again.

"Like I said, it was me, not you. And I'm sorry for being such a dick about it."

"You don't need to apologize."

"I do, Angie. I definitely do, on both counts. I've been

a shit friend and an even shittier husband." He offered her a small, tight smile and turned to leave.

She didn't say anything to stop him. Instead, she watched him exit and listened to his slow, deliberate tread as he crossed the deck to the house.

She stared at the patch of concrete where he'd been standing and tried to get a grip on what he'd revealed.

Michael had seen her in her underwear and been turned on. Despite what he'd said about not being interested in sex. Despite his lack of interest in other women.

And he hated himself for it. She'd seen it in his eyes as he confessed—guilt and self-loathing and shame. That was why he'd lashed out at her—because he'd been shocked at himself. Because he'd been so bloody determined to deny that part of himself.

She closed her eyes, reliving the way he'd faced her and confessed his "crime," inviting her censure and judgment.

I've been a shit friend and an even shittier husband.

It was the absolute opposite of reality. Michael wasn't a shit friend or a shit husband. He was loyal and generous and loving and gentle. And he was human—very human. Something he didn't seem ready to accept.

Yet she'd let him walk away without correcting the record. She'd let him walk away carrying all that guilt and confusion and self-disgust, as though he was the only person who had been wrestling with an unwanted, uncomfortable attraction in the past few weeks. As though he was utterly alone and wrong and disloyal and all the horrible things she'd been hurling at her own head since the weekend.

A sudden, urgent certainty gripped her. She strode for the door, not daring to give herself a chance to think or second-guess. The French doors to the kitchen swung open with too much force, their glass panels rattling as they hit the side of the house. She didn't stop until she was standing on the threshold of Michael's study.

He was at his desk, his shoulders hunched and tight as he gazed at the blueprints spread in front of him.

"It's not just you," she said. Her voice sounded too high, the pitch all wrong.

He swung to face her, an uncomprehending frown on his face. She gathered her courage. After all, he'd been brave and honest enough to tell her the truth—the very least she could do was return the favor.

"Last Friday, when you told me about your dream, I couldn't stop thinking about it. About you. That's why I haven't been hanging around as much. That's why I didn't stay for dinner the other night."

Her face was on fire. Her armpits prickled with embarrassed sweat. She felt as though she'd stripped naked and run onto a crowded football field.

"Right." He looked shocked. As though the possibility of her returning his feelings—of their attraction being mutual—hadn't even occurred to him. She knew how that felt—she'd experienced the exact same feeling not five minutes ago.

"When you think about it, it's not exactly a miracle. I mean, we're both single. We spend a lot of time together. We like each other. It was probably inevitable. But it doesn't mean anything. It definitely doesn't mean you're a shitty husband, and it doesn't mean I'm about to betray Billie. Believe me, I've been thinking about this a lot lately. It simply means that we're mortal and flawed and human. Nothing more, nothing less. Because it's not as though you're going to suddenly jump my bones or I'm going to jump yours. It's just a thing that has happened, and we've acknowledged it, and now we can move on and get past it and life can continue as usual." Angie paused for breath, aware that her speech had been closer to a stream of consciousness blurt than a rational statement.

A frown formed between his eyebrows. She could see him grappling with his guilt and trying to work out how her confession fit with his own culpability.

"It's just a thing, Michael," she said quietly. "It doesn't mean anything."

"It still happened."

"If you're going to punish yourself for every less-than-noble thought you have, you might as well knit yourself a hair shirt and start sleeping on a bed of nails."

He shifted in the chair, uneasy. "If it was anyone else. One of those women from the mothers' group. Someone at work... But you and Billie—"

"I know. Same here. But a thought is only a thought. It's not an action. We haven't hurt anyone. And before you know it, this weirdness will pass and I'll be about as attractive to you as a lump of wood and vice versa. Hell, we'll probably laugh our heads off over how ridiculous it all was."

Michael's gaze swept down her body. His frown intensified as one hand lifted to pinch the bridge of his nose. He swore, the single word pithy and heartfelt.

Maybe it had been a mistake coming in here, being honest with him. Maybe she'd made things worse, not better. She'd been driven by the need to show him that he wasn't alone, that they were both struggling with the same thing. But maybe she'd only confused the issue.

"I'm sorry," she said helplessly.

Michael immediately shook his head. "Don't apologize."

"Why not? You apologized to me."

They stared at each other, the silence loaded.

"I don't want this to mess things up between us," he said. "There's no way we could have gotten through the last year without you. I refuse to screw that up, Angie."

"You think I want that? You and the kids mean the world to me. The world."

"So, what? We wait this out?"

"You got a better idea?"

He dropped his head back and stared at the ceiling. "No."

"Okay. Well, I need to get back to work. And you're probably swamped, too." She took a step away. "I'll see you later."

"Sure."

She glanced over her shoulder as she left. Michael had already swiveled to face the desk. If anything, his shoulders looked even more tight and hunched.

Good one. Way to go.

What else should she have done? Let him fester in his misguided guilt? Let him go on thinking that he was some kind of freak for having a perfectly understandable response to a difficult, tragic situation?

She stopped in the hallway and pressed her palms to her face, trying to clear her head of the many confusing thoughts and feelings whirling through it. It was useless, however, and she was just as confused and unsettled when she returned to her studio.

She picked up the ring she'd been working on, but her mind kept throwing up the image of Michael's tense posture. If only there was something she could do to help him…

You can. Stay away from him. Keep your distance. Let this thing die a quick, painless death.

It was the right answer, the only answer—and she hated herself for the little stab of disappointment she felt at the idea of having to distance herself from him.

Which proved that the voice in her head was right.

MICHAEL WROTE A NOTE on the blueprint. The balance between the two wings of the Watsons' beach house was all wrong. He needed to chat with them and—

Who was he kidding? Approximately ten percent of his brain was focused on the plans in front of him. The other ninety percent was reviewing what Angie had told him.

She was attracted to him, too. She'd been turned on by his sexy dream. She refused to feel guilty about something she viewed as almost inevitable, given their proximity and involvement in each other's lives. She firmly believed that this, too, would pass and that their friendship would endure.

He hoped like hell she was right, because the part that was stuck in his imagination like peanut butter was the turned-on part. Not the part about their friendship enduring. Not the part about him feeling guilty or not guilty—to his shame. All he could think about was Angie wanting him. Angie being aroused by the notion that he'd dreamed about sex. Angie looking at him and thinking the same things he'd been thinking about her.

Bloody hell.

He rested his head in his hands. When it came to sex, what turned him on had always been pretty vanilla by today's standards—sex with a willing woman who meant something to him. He'd never felt guilty or conflicted about his own needs and desires, even when he was married. Until now.

He didn't want to want Angie. He didn't want his wife's best friend to be the object of his sexual attraction. But there Angie was, lodged in his brain in the slot marked *sex*. He'd seen her in her underwear. He'd held the delicate silk of her bra in his hand. He'd listened to her talk about sex. He'd imagined her naked, looking at him with smoky, knowing eyes. He'd gotten hard over her. He was hard now, thinking about the dangerous, dangerous possibility her confession laid before him.

Because if she wanted him, and he wanted her, and they were both consenting adults, what was to stop them from acting on their needs, wants and desires?

Because you both love Billie. Because it would make a lie of everything you shared with her if you rushed into her best friend's arms. Because you have never been the kind of asshole who was led around by his dick.

The tension leaked out of his body as he answered his own question. Nothing would happen between him and Angie. He wasn't that guy, and she wasn't that woman. They both loved and respected Billie too much to betray her with some muddy, grubby affair.

It was a relief to have drawn the line so clearly in his own mind. It didn't stop him from feeling guilty at having gone there in the first place, but it helped. It helped a lot.

He stood and went to check on Charlie, aware that it had been twenty minutes and his son had been ominously silent. He found him where he'd left him—in his room, still playing with his train set. Charlie's expression was one of rapt attention as he guided an engine over a suspension bridge, his small, chubby fingers clenched tightly around the diecast metal.

"You okay in here, matey?" Michael asked.

Charlie glanced at him distractedly. "Train go choo-choo."

"I know. Pretty cool, hey?"

Charlie nodded, his mouth curving into a grin that was pure Billie. Guilt and grief tangled in a hard knot in Michael's chest.

How could he even think of himself when he had Charlie and Eva to look after? How could Michael even consider being with another woman the way he'd been with Billie? Even if that person was Angie? *Especially* if that person was Angie?

He dropped to his knees and reached for one of the many carriages that lay abandoned beside the track.

"How about we take things up a notch?" he suggested.

ANGIE WORKED HARD TO AVOID being with Michael as much as possible over the next two weeks. It wasn't too difficult, since it was obvious he was doing the same with her. When the kids were in the room, she had no trouble meeting his eyes or responding to his jokes— being normal, in other words. But the moment it was only the two of them the conversation they'd had in his study took center stage and she could barely look at him without thinking about all the things she'd banished from her mind.

Like how good he smelled.

And the way he filled out his suit.

And the way his mouth kicked up at the corner when he was trying not to smile.

Every time they were alone, she headed for her studio or her car or the bathroom and gave herself a severe talking-to. He never tried to stop her, never addressed the elephant in the room. They had said all that needed to be said. They were enduring now. Waiting for normal services to resume.

Even though she tried like hell to ensure that their new distance didn't affect the children, Eva picked up on the fact that Angie was spending less and less time around the house.

"You're never here anymore," she complained as Angie prepared to leave on Friday night.

Angie couldn't help herself—her gaze darted from Eva's confused, hurt expression to Michael's face before coming back to her godchild again. "Sure I am," she said after a slightly too long pause. "I'm here every day."

"But you never have dinner with us. And the other night when I asked you to watch the movie with us you said you had to go. And on the weekend when I asked Daddy if you could come roller skating with us he said you were too busy and that I couldn't bother you."

Michael moved forward, almost as though he was going to physically intervene in the conversation in some way.

"Sweetheart, it's a busy time, that's all." Angie slid an arm around Eva's shoulders. "But maybe you and I could go shopping again soon. Or go check out a movie?"

Eva looked at her, her eyes still clouded with concern. "Is that a promise?"

"Absolutely. We can make a date right now, if you like." Angie looked to Michael, raising her eyebrows in question. "When would suit you?"

He glanced at the calendar on the fridge. "We're going

to the beach tomorrow with one of Eva's friends. But there's nothing booked for Sunday. And all of next week is free."

"Then how does Sunday sound?" Angie suggested.

"Good."

"Then it's a date. I'll pick you up at two, okay?"

"Okay. Awesome, Auntie Angie." Eva beamed at her, throwing her arms around Angie's waist.

Angie bent to drop a kiss on the top of her head. "It will be awesome." She very carefully didn't look at Michael as Eva ended their embrace. "I'll see you all later."

Angie half expected him to follow her to the door, but he didn't. She paused on the porch.

She missed the easiness and comfort of their old relationship. She missed *him*.

Well, suck it up. Maybe it's a good thing that you're realizing how much you've relied on him. He's got his own life and you've got yours. And that's the way it should be.

She drove home and spent the evening cleaning out her closet. She slept heavily and woke to the phone ringing the next morning. She saw with some astonishment that it was past ten—way past her usual waking time—and she groped on her bedside table for the receiver.

"Hello?"

"It's me. Michael."

She fell back onto her pillows. "Hi." Her voice caught and she cleared her throat. "Let me try that again. Hi."

"Did I wake you?" He sounded surprised.

"Sort of. But I needed to get up."

"You're busy, then?"

His voice always sounded deeper over the phone. Richer, the bass more pronounced.

"What, today, you mean?"

"Yes."

Where was this conversation going? "I have a few things I should probably do. Like washing and cleaning and whatnot. Why?"

"We're going to the beach today, and Eva asked me if you could come, too."

She waited for him to say more but he didn't. As invitations went, it wasn't the most enthusiastic she'd received. But she knew why that was the case. A part of her didn't like it, but most of her knew that Michael's reluctance to spend a day with her was wise.

"It's probably not a great idea. Right?"

She could hear the thread of hope in her own voice and she winced. Could she be any more conflicted and torn and pathetic?

"It's up to you. I know the kids would be happy to have you along."

"It's not just up to me. You know that."

"What do you want me to say? That I want you to come, too?"

Yes.

"No."

He sighed, the sound loud down the line. "This is so messed up."

"No kidding."

"Come to the beach, Angie. I miss you. The kids miss you. Like you said the other day, it's not as though we'll leap on each other like sex-crazed maniacs. We're both rational adults. We can handle this."

She didn't give herself time to think. She wanted to go. She wanted a day with Michael and the kids.

Maybe that made her a bad, weak-willed, evil person, but so be it.

"Okay. Should I come to you or do you want to swing by and pick me up?"

"We were thinking of going to Edithvale," Michael said, naming a suburban beach halfway around the curve of Port Philip Bay.

"Then I'll come to you, otherwise you'll have to double back. Give me forty minutes or so and I'll be there."

She ended the call and lay for a moment, thinking about the day ahead. Sun, surf, Michael, the kids… It would be good, and it would also be a chance for her and Michael to prove they could handle this…situation without having to resort to almost-estrangement.

A little voice in the back of her mind spoke up pointing out that all her justifications were exactly that— excuses for doing what she wanted and spending time with Michael.

Nothing is going to happen. I won't let it. But surely there's no harm in us spending a day together at the beach?

She didn't let the voice resurface with more arguments—she rolled out of bed and hit the shower and pawed through her chest of drawers until she reached the tangled pile of her swimsuits. Because she wasn't a fool or a tease, she chose her most conservative suit, a black two-piece with a boy-leg bottom and a halter-neck tankini top. It wasn't exactly Victorian, but it wasn't a little bitty bikini, either.

She slathered sunscreen on all the bits she could reach, grabbed a hat and pulled on a pair of black capri pants. A change of clothes, her sunglasses, sunscreen, her beach towel and a book went into her bag and she headed for the door.

Michael's Audi was in the driveway, all four doors open when she arrived. Eva bounced out of the house as Angie made her way up the drive.

"I told Daddy you'd come if he asked," she said triumphantly.

"You were right."

"I'm helping pack the car."

"Good girl."

Eva turned and headed into the house, while Angie walked to the car. The rear cargo section was already piled with a stack of beach towels, a beach ball, blow-up water wings, a baby change bag and a folding beach shade. Angie added her own bag, wedging it into the farthest corner. When she stepped back Michael was approaching with a blue plastic cooler.

"That looks heavy."

"So it should. It has enough food and drink in it to feed a small army." He was wearing a pair of colorful board shorts, his strong shoulders and arms on display thanks to a black tank top. His biceps flexed, bulging impressively as he hefted the cooler and slid it into the remaining empty space.

For the first time it hit her that today might be more complicated than she'd imagined. Somehow, she'd glossed over the fact that Michael would most likely be bare-chested for the bulk of the day when she'd weighed up her options.

Not something that was easy to ignore with him standing in front of her, six foot one of strapping, muscular man in his prime.

"Right. That's it for supplies. Now we just need to

buckle the kids in, pick up Greta and we're away," Michael said, hands on his hips as he considered the rear of the car.

"I'll get the kids." She headed for the house, pleased to have a task. Especially one that wouldn't involve her having to look at Michael's muscular, lightly haired calves.

She hustled the kids to the car. Michael locked up and they hit the road, detouring to pick up Eva's friend Greta before heading for the beach.

Angie kept her gaze front and center as they drove, one ear on the girls' chatter, the rest of her resolutely refusing to notice the way Michael's thigh muscles flexed every time he hit the brake. They were lucky enough to find a parking spot near the beach. Angie herded the kids onto the sand while Michael made three trips to the car to transfer their gear.

"Right. Let's set up the shelter," he said once he'd dumped the last load.

Angie followed his lead, mimicking his moves to set up her side of the sunshade frame before they attached the cloth. Eva and Greta immediately claimed the prime spots, stripping down to their bikini bottoms and Lycra sun protection shirts.

"We're going for a swim," Eva announced, ready to run for the water.

"A few rules first." Michael told the girls they were to only swim where he could see them and that they were not to go deeper than their waists. Then he made them put on their hats and smeared zinc cream onto their noses and across their cheeks. Angie did the same for Charlie, tying his floppy terry-cloth hat beneath his chin as the girls scampered to the water.

"I don't like the chances of that staying on long," Angie said doubtfully as Charlie immediately began pulling at the ties.

"We can but try."

Angie handed Charlie a spade and bucket before popping the stud on her capri pants and shedding them. She was very aware of Michael in her peripheral vision and she knew the exact moment he looked away. She told herself it was a good thing and plonked her own hat on then led Charlie down to the wet sand to help him build castles.

The day slipped by beneath a clear blue sky. The girls swam, dried off and then swam again. Angie built castles and dug moats with Charlie and watched fondly as he destroyed them all like a pint-size Godzilla. Michael called them all to the sunshade for sandwiches, fruit and juice boxes and more sunscreen, then the girls hit the water yet again.

Charlie was tired after a morning of wreaking havoc on his self-made sand metropolis and he lay down on Angie's towel and fell asleep with his thumb in his mouth.

With the girls gone and Charlie asleep, it was the first time she and Michael had been alone all day. Angie looped her arms around her knees and gazed at the shimmering ocean. All around them were families and couples basking in the hot Australian sun. The sound of laughter and conversation and the smell of suntan lotion drifted along the breeze. Beside her, Michael stirred restlessly.

"I might take a dip," he said after a long, uncomfortable silence.

"Okay."

He stood. She made the mistake of glancing at him

as he pulled up his tank top. He'd put on a bit of the weight he'd lost but he was still lean and his belly and chest muscles rippled invitingly as he dragged the top over his head. Angie swallowed audibly and dragged her gaze away.

Was it hot on the beach or was it just her?

It shouldn't be you. And you know it.

As always, guilt came hard on the heels of desire, a one-two punch that was becoming only too familiar.

"Won't be too long," Michael said.

She murmured something noncommittal, then made a big deal of checking on Charlie as Michael walked to the water's edge. She couldn't stop herself from watching him wade into the water, however. His board shorts got progressively darker as he went deeper, clinging damply to his hips and backside before he dived beneath an incoming wave and momentarily disappeared from sight. When he surfaced, his chest and shoulders gleamed in the bright sun. He wiped water from his eyes and pushed his hair off his forehead. Then, as though he could feel her avid, intent gaze, his head turned toward shore and they locked eyes across fifteen meters of sand and surf.

For a heartbeat she stared and knew that he knew exactly what she'd been thinking. What she'd been wanting. He was the one who looked away, breaking their connection, something which only increased the guilt weighing on her shoulders.

Sick of herself, she rolled onto her belly and reached for her book. If she couldn't be trusted to behave on her own, then clearly she needed some serious distraction.

A few minutes later, Eva's delighted squeals made Angie prop herself up on her elbow. Michael was horsing around with the two girls, taking turns lifting them up and tossing them into the water. It was a lovely moment, a perfect family snapshot—except Billie wasn't here to complete the picture and Angie couldn't seem to take her eyes off the way Michael's muscles bunched and flexed each time he lifted and threw Greta or Eva.

She shifted to rest her forehead against the open pages of her book. She inhaled the scent of paper and ink and took refuge in the only comfort she could find—that soon this day would be over and she would know never to say yes to this kind of excursion again. Or at least until she could safely look at Michael and see her friend rather than a man who made her aware that she was a woman. A woman who hadn't had sex for more than six months.

And counting.

CHAPTER TEN

MICHAEL BRUSHED THE stinging salt water out of his eyes as Eva and Greta cavorted around him.

"Easy on your old man. You don't want to break him," he said as Eva tried to climb his back like a little monkey.

"You won't break. You're too strong," she said.

Michael waited till she was dangling off his arm before grabbing her and tossing her into the water for the third time. She landed with a huge splash, her face a picture of delight. He couldn't help laughing, too.

It was good to know she could still feel this kind of joy. Good to know he could, too.

Greta giggled by his side and he swooped on her and lobbed her through the air in a gentle arc. She landed beside Eva and they both collapsed into fits of laughter again. Thirty seconds after that, they were clamoring for a repeat performance.

Twenty minutes later, he was officially over being the human play-gym and he left the girls to their own devices and waded toward shore. The sand was warm underfoot as he headed for the silver dome of the sunshade. Angie was lying on her belly, her torso propped on her elbows as she read her book. Without his permission, his gaze raked down her long, athletic legs before he got a grip on himself and focused on Charlie.

His son was still out to it, his cheeks rosy from the

heat, one hand curled over his heart. Michael leaned down to adjust the awkward angle of his hat, being careful not to drip on him. Then and only then did he sink onto his towel and glance at Angie.

She gave him a small, neutral smile. "How was the water?"

"Wet and cold and full of screaming little girls."

"You looked like you were holding your own."

"Barely."

She returned her attention to her book. He sought Eva's bright pink sunshirt in the water, satisfied that she and Greta were okay, and told himself he would not look at Angie's legs again. He'd barely framed the thought before his gaze was running up the lean length of her body, settling on the firm roundness of her backside. Out of nowhere the memory of the time he'd embraced her after the break-in came calling—the way her body had fit so well against his. The way everything had matched up so naturally.

He reached for his sunglasses and forced himself to focus on anything except Angie. After a few seconds she stirred. He watched out of the corners of his eyes as she rose to her knees and tossed the book into her beach bag.

"I might go see how cold the water really is," she said.

"Sure thing."

He didn't even fool himself that he wouldn't watch her walk to the water's edge. Her stride was long and easy as she navigated past family groups and sandcastles and clusters of teens. Her butt bounced, her hair swayed against the smooth skin of her back, her hips swung ever-so-slightly from side to side.

He could feel himself getting hard and he swore under his breath. He didn't take his eyes off her, though, as she strode into the shallows. When the water was lapping around her thighs, she lifted her hands in the air and took a hesitant step backward, a sure sign that the coldness of the water had registered in earnest. She hovered uncertainly for a moment, then pinched her nose and sank beneath the water in one determined move.

A second later she shot to her feet, body streaming, her long dark hair plastered to her head and neck and shoulders and breasts. She looked like a siren, unknowable and desirable and utterly female, more than capable of luring a man to his ruin.

Not that he needed much encouragement. Apparently not even the great love he'd had for Billie was enough to stop him from wanting something he could never have.

He turned away, disgusted with himself. Of all the women in the world, why did he have to have the hots for Angie?

Charlie made a mewling sound and when Michael glanced over he was blinking, his expression uncertain as he tried to work out where he was.

"It's okay, mate. Daddy's here. We're at the beach, remember?"

It took Charlie a moment to fully wake, but once he registered their surroundings he was on his feet, a big smile on his face.

"Water. Me go for swim."

Charlie protested, but Michael insisted on fitting him with the inflatable wings before leading him to the water's edge. Eva looked up from where she and Greta were hunkered collecting shells, giving him a quick wave. Michael waved and eased Charlie into the shallows. There was nothing his son liked better than the water and soon he was kicking and splashing to his heart's content.

"Someone's having fun."

Angie joined them, and Michael was glad he wore his sunglasses because for the life of him he couldn't stop his gaze from dipping to her breasts. The cold water had turned her nipples hard, and two small points pressed against the wet fabric of her swimsuit top.

His body surged in reaction, as responsive and out of control as a teenager's. He lifted his gaze to her face and reminded himself that she was his friend—and, more important, that she'd been Billie's friend.

It was enough to kill the buzz of desire running through his body and he didn't let his gaze slip again as Angie took Charlie's free hand. Between the two of them they swung Charlie to and fro, dipping him into the water then pulling him out again. It was a game Charlie would have been happy to play all day, but Michael could feel the intense heat of the sun bearing down on them. He glanced at Angie and saw that her nose was a little pink, as well as the back of her neck and shoulders.

He'd slathered the kids with sunscreen and they had their SPF 40+ tops on, but nothing was proof against so much relentless UV.

"Time to head home?" Angie asked, having noticed his assessing glance at the sky.

"I think so. Before we all turn into lobsters."

"I'll round up the little ladies."

Eva was predictably sulky about having her fun cut short, but he averted disaster with the promise of ice cream on the way home, a piece of domestic bribery that generated so much goodwill that the girls even helped carry some of the gear to the car. They found an ice-cream parlor and sat beneath the shade of a giant ghost gum in the adjacent nature reserve to eat their bounty.

By the time they made their way across town it was nearly five. He opted for fish and chips for dinner and they ate them off the paper, picnic style, sitting cross-legged on the deck.

The moment Angie had polished off the last of her chips she brushed her hands together decisively. "Right. That's me. I'd better get going."

"No. Not yet. I wanted to show you my art assignment for school. I drew the life cycle of a tree and Mr. Parker said it was really, really good," Eva said.

Michael busied himself folding up the paper from their meal. He knew why Angie was going so early. He didn't like it, but he understood, and a part of him—the part that had been on edge all day—was grateful.

But there was another part, too, that wanted her to stay, to wait while he put the kids to bed and hang out with him in the warm night air and maybe share a cold beer or two.

He would never ask her to do that, though, because today had already offered more than enough temptation. As it was he'd be lying awake for hours, berating himself for every second of desire he'd felt.

The doorbell echoed through the house before Angie could respond to Eva's cajoling. It was Greta's parents, come to take her home, and somehow Angie got roped into bathing Eva and Charlie instead of leaving. Eva then insisted Angie come inspect her assignment, and Michael got Charlie into his pajamas and tucked him in.

Michael was loading the dishwasher when Angie appeared in the doorway. She was still in her swimsuit, having simply pulled her capri pants on when they left the beach, and her nose was shiny and pink, her hair rumpled and slightly messy.

"Eva's out for the count. She hasn't brushed her teeth but she's so tired I figured you wouldn't mind."

"She'll survive one night."

"That's what I thought."

He saw that she'd already collected her bag, and her car keys glinted in her hand.

Nothing like a quick escape.

"I'll see you tomorrow, then," she said.

"Tomorrow?" He was wiping down the sink but he paused, momentarily confused.

"I'm taking Eva to the movies. Remember?"

"Oh. Right. Of course."

Angie bit her lip and shifted her weight from one foot to the other. "I can make it another day, if it's too much. After today, I mean. I'm sure Eva won't mind."

"No, no. It slipped my mind. That's all."

Her smile was tight. Uncomfortable. "Okay."

"I mean it, Angie. It's not too much."

Although that was the problem, really. It was never too much with Angie.

"I'll see you tomorrow. Good night, Michael." She gave him an awkward little wave before disappearing through the doorway. He stared at the empty space, regret clashing with relief inside him.

He knew it was smart for her to go, for them to limit their time together until this thing blew over. But he hated what it was doing to their friendship. To the warm ease that had always existed between them.

Before he could think too much about it, he took off after her. He caught up with her as she was about to walk through the door and he reached out to grasp her arm to stop her from leaving.

"Angie…"

She stilled, looking at him with wary, uncertain eyes, her slender arm slipping through his fingers. He tightened his grip, anchoring her.

"Stay and have a beer with me."

The wary look in her eyes softened and he knew without asking that she missed their old ease, too.

"I'd love to. But I won't. Thanks for asking, though. Believe it or not, it means a lot."

She tugged on her arm, an unspoken request to be released. He didn't let her go.

"It wasn't that bad today, was it?" he asked.

The judge and jury in the back of his head told him to let her go and step away and leave well enough alone. He didn't move, his gaze glued to her face.

"Compared to what? Water boarding?" Angie's smile was wry.

His gaze dropped to the trace of salt that had dried on her collarbone. His focus shifted minutely to the right, finding the telltale flutter beneath her skin where her pulse was beating wildly at the base of her neck.

Racing. Out of control.

His own pulse was racing, too, because he was holding her arm, touching her, and they were alone, truly alone, for the first time in weeks.

He raised his gaze to her face again and her blue eyes looked into his, full to the brim with the same frustration and need that had been doing battle within him for too long now.

All the want and lust and desire that he'd pushed down, down, down came rushing up, rocketing through him. Moments from the day flashed across his mind's eye: Angie, wet and glistening from the sea, her hair slicked back, her nipples beaded from the cold. Angie stretched out in the sun, her body loose and relaxed.

"Jesus, Angie…" he whispered.

What self-control he had blew away like dust on the wind. All he could think about was touching her. Tasting her. Satisfying the many, many questions he had about what she liked and how she would respond and how it would feel to be inside her.

He wasn't sure who moved first, her or him. There was the thunk of her bag sliding down her arm to hit the floor, followed by the muted clank of her keys a split-second later, then he was pulling her into his arms and she was lifting her face to kiss him.

She tasted of salt and fresh air and life and he spread his hands across the small of her back and pulled her closer, need an urgent tattoo drumming through his blood. She felt so good, so strong and supple, and they fit together perfectly.

He stroked her tongue with his and she made an approving sound and he needed to be a whole lot closer. He slid his hands onto her ass, palms curving over her greedily, drawing her hips closer to his. He was hard as a rock and she must have felt it because she rolled her hips forward, pressing her mound against his erection. He retaliated by walking her two steps backward until she hit the wall. He pinned her there with his body weight, devouring her mouth, inhaling the scent of beach and hot woman.

Her hands slid beneath his shirt, gliding up his belly before cupping his pecs. She thumbed one of his nipples and he lifted her more firmly against him, thrusting his hips against her. She smoothed her hands down his belly and over the front of his board shorts and gripped the hard length of him through the thin fabric.

It had been so long and she felt so good, he was afraid he would embarrass himself. When she stroked her hand up the length of him the top of his head about came off. He reached for the tie on her halter top, tugging it free with one urgent pull and yanking it down. Her breasts spilled out, creamy and full, her light brown nipples already beaded with desire.

He ducked his head, tonguing her right nipple, tasting more salt as well as a sweetness that could only be Angie. Her hands grasped his head and for a moment he thought she was going to push him away. Then her fingers burrowed into his hair and she pulled him closer, her whole body was trembling with need.

His hands found the opening of her pants. He fumbled with the button. She pushed her hips forward, encouraging him. The button slipped free and he slid his hand down her belly, past the waistband of her swimsuit bottoms. His fingers found silky hair before moving into slick, hot heat, and then he was sliding a finger inside her, feeling the tightening of her body around him.

"Michael. Please…"

The words were a whisper, a plea, an exhalation. They blew his mind, tipping him over the edge. He wanted everything. Right now.

He started pushing her pants and swimsuit down, intent on only one thing—being inside her, making her come, feeling those long legs around his hips.

He lifted his mouth from her breasts and found her mouth again, kissing her avidly. Her hands tightened on his hips and she tilted her head back. It took him long seconds to register that she was trying to break their kiss. He eased away a bare few inches, chest heaving, his pulse a roar in his head.

Surely she wasn't going to call a halt? Because he needed this, needed it so badly.

"Not here," Angie said. "The children…"

Reality slammed into him. He became painfully aware of exactly where they were, of the fact that his sleeping children were meters away and that he'd been about to push Angie to the wooden floor and plunge inside her.

He tensed, stunned at his own recklessness. Angie's hands found his face, framing his jaw, and she pressed a fierce, almost violent kiss to his lips.

"Don't," she said, and he knew that she meant "don't think, don't regret this before it's even over."

Her hand grasped his and she led him to his office. The door closed behind them with a solid thunk. Angie pressed his palm to her belly. She squeezed his hand tightly, a silent order for him to keep touching her, then she stuck her thumbs into the sides of her pants and shed them and her swimsuit bottom in one efficient move. The sight of her long legs and the neat patch of dark, silky-looking hair between them drowned out the recriminations already circling his mind. Need once again took over, undeniable, demanding.

She took a step backward and shimmied the rest of the way out of her tankini top, and then she was in front of him, naked and aroused and ready. Without a word he pulled his tank top over his head, then he shucked his board shorts. His erection pulsed against his belly so hard it ached. He closed the distance between them, kissing her, his hands traveling down her slim back to her ass, one hand delving farther, into the hot, wet place between her thighs. Her hand found his erection, stroking him, her movements jerky and urgent.

Her legs started to tremble and together they went down to the rug. Angie lay spread before him like an impossible offering and every thought, every memory, every consideration dissolved and there was only the need to be inside her, to lose himself in the slick warmth of her, to feel alive and to feel pleasure.

He stretched on top of her and her legs spread to accept him. He gripped himself and found her entrance. He slid inside her, into tight, wet heat. And then he really did lose his mind.

ANGIE GRIPPED MICHAEL'S big shoulders and bit her lip as he slid inside her, filling her, stretching her. It felt so good she sobbed, her fingers digging into his skin.

This. This was exactly what she'd needed. What she'd craved.

She looked into Michael's face, straight into stormy gray-green eyes. They stared at one another for a long, long moment, then he lowered his head to kiss her and his hips flexed and he started to pump into her, each stroke more intense than the last.

Her hands found his ass and she held on for dear life as he set a punishing, desperate pace. He kissed her neck, passionate, openmouthed kisses, blazing a trail to her breasts. The pull of his mouth on her nipples was almost too good, too much. She lifted her hips, wrapping her legs around him, panting his name as desire tightened inside her.

His body became even more tense, his movements more urgent, their bodies slamming together. His hand found her hips, angling them just-so, and he stroked into her and all of a sudden she was arching off the floor, her climax rippling through her. It seemed to go on and on, Michael coaxing more and more from her, and then he tensed, his muscles turning to granite beneath her hands. He pressed his face into her neck and she felt his breath rush out as he came, his body shuddering for long moments before it became loose and heavy on hers.

Angie blinked dazedly, her palms flat against his back, feeling the dampness of sweat, the sensitive fullness between her thighs where he was still inside her. Tiny aftershocks ricocheted through her as she stared at the overhead light, her breathing harsh, waiting for guilt and regret and self-recrimination to descend.

After all, this was Michael inside her. Billie's beloved husband. Michael, her friend. Michael, who loved Billie more than he could bear.

Michael who had made love to her with so much desperate intensity that he'd literally taken her breath away.

His face was still pressed against her neck. She could feel his chest expanding and contracting as his breathing slowed. She could also feel the tension creeping into his body, and she knew that he was already regretting what they had done, giving himself a hard time for seeking warmth and comfort and life.

Tentative, she slid her hand to the nape of his neck. She rested it there, wanting to say something or do something to make everything all right for him but unable to find the words.

It was a mistake. He shifted, withdrawing from her and rolling to one side. She braced herself to look into his face but he was already on his knees, his back to her as he reached for his clothes. He stood, his body impossibly big and strong as he towered above her, his muscles standing out as he yanked on his board shorts. He left the room without a word, without looking back.

She lifted her hands to her face, pressing her fingers against her eyelids until she saw bursts of light amongst the blackness.

They had done something awful. They had betrayed Billie, the woman who had been like a sister to her for more than half her life. They had jumped on each other and taken comfort and pleasure despite having agreed that this would never, ever happen.

She was a bad friend. A terrible, disloyal, faithless person.

Are you, really? Billie is dead. And this would have never happened if she was alive. You would have never even looked sideways at Michael, or he at you. This is not an affair. This is something different.

It was such a self-serving thought she instinctively rejected it, but a second thought came hard on its heels: Michael had needed this.

Angie didn't know how she knew that, but she did— she'd felt it in him, in the desperate thrusting of his body inside hers, in the way he'd kissed her, in the way he'd pulled her body so tightly against his.

He'd needed the comfort, the visceral confirmation of being alive. He'd needed it very badly.

Tears pressed as she remembered the way he'd shuddered into her. Whatever else happened, right now, right this minute, she didn't have it in her to regret that she'd been the one to give him what he'd needed tonight.

Which made her sound like some kind of sexual martyr, lying back and enduring one of the most explosive orgasms of her life in the name of all that was good and kind and nurturing, but it hadn't been anything like that.

She'd needed him, too. On some deep, unspoken level, she'd needed the closeness and the passion and the life-affirming intimacy of sex.

She sighed heavily and sat up. Her clothes lay in a tangled heap, her swimsuit twisted with her capris. It took her a minute to separate them, then she dressed. She left the study in search of Michael. He wasn't in the kitchen, but she hadn't really expected him to be. She walked toward the master suite.

He was sitting on the edge of the bed, his head in his hands. He looked so broken she had to stop herself from going to him and pulling him into her arms. He wouldn't let himself accept that kind of comfort from her.

After a long beat he lifted his head and looked at her. "I'm sorry."

She shook her head, her chest aching for him, tears once again threatening. She cared for him so much. Hated seeing him so unhappy and conflicted.

"You don't owe me an apology. We both knew what we were doing."

"I didn't even think about a condom—"

"It's okay, neither did I. But I'm on the Pill."

And, more important, she trusted him.

Michael looked at the floor. He radiated hurt and confusion and regret. She tried to find something to say, but every sentence she framed in her mind felt false and thin.

"Do you want me to go?" she finally asked.

There was a long pause. She knew what he wanted to say—*yes*—but she also knew he was too nice a man to do so.

"I'll go," she said, saving him the trouble of being the bad guy.

"Okay." He forced himself to meet her eyes. "Thanks."

She smiled sadly. This was such a messed-up situation—and yet ten minutes ago, she had felt as though she was in exactly the right place with exactly the right person.

She left. Every step of the way to the door she expected him to come after her, but he didn't. She understood why, but a part of her still smarted.

Maybe there was something wrong with her moral compass, maybe she was, at heart, a self-interested opportunist, but she couldn't regret what had happened. It had been too real, too powerful, too instinctive.

Too necessary.

She collected her bag and keys and headed for her car. She drove home with the windows down, fresh air blowing her hair around her shoulders. She let herself into her apartment, leaving her bag just inside the door, dropping her keys on the little table she kept there. She felt oddly detached, as though some part of her was still at Michael's lying on the study floor recovering from the intensity of what had happened between them. She stood in the center of her open-plan living space, completely at a loss. Then, suddenly, she knew what she wanted. She crossed to her bookcase and pulled her tattered old photo album from among her art books. Holding it against her chest, she sat on the end of her bed.

The first few pages held pictures of her parents and the homestead where she'd grown up and her old dog, Woofy. She flicked past them until she found what she was looking for.

The picture had been taken in the first year of her friendship with Billie. She couldn't remember who the photographer had been—one of their teachers, perhaps, or one of their fellow students. She and Billie were standing on the green grass of New England Girls' School's sport field, both of them dressed in their P.E. uniforms. Angie's left leg was bound at the ankle to Billie's right, ready to run the three-legged race. Billie had compounded their intimacy by hooking her arm around Angie's neck and smooshing her cheek against Angie's for the picture. Billie was grinning fit to bust, absolutely delighted. In her own eyes, Angie could see a more quiet but no less sincere joy. Even in those very early days she had adored Billie.

"You know I would never have looked twice at him. You know that," she told her friend quietly.

Billie stared at her, captured forever in a moment of love and friendship. A warm tear trickled down Angie's face. Suddenly she couldn't bear to look at Billie. She shut the book and pushed it away.

Sobs tightened her throat. She went into the bathroom and shed her clothes. Standing under the stinging heat of the shower, she washed away the evidence of those wild, crazy minutes in Michael's arms, her tears mixing with the water as she leaned against the tile.

All the certainty she'd felt in the immediate aftermath disappeared down the drain. The bleak unhappiness of Michael's expression wouldn't leave her mind and a terrible fear gripped her.

It was possible the sex had ruined everything, that by taking comfort in one another they had poisoned their friendship and made it impossible for things to ever be the same. Their easy relationship, her closeness with the children—it might all be gone.

Please, God... If she lost Michael and the children over this...

CHAPTER ELEVEN

MICHAEL SAT ON THE END of the bed for a long time. He felt heavy with the weight of his thoughts and feelings. Heavier than at any other point since Billie's death.

Despite having told himself over and over that he would never lay a finger on Angie, the moment temptation had come knocking he'd folded like a house of cards. There had been no restraint, no thought of anyone or anything apart from him and her and what he wanted.

No thought of Eva and Charlie.

No thought of Billie.

He pinched the bridge of his nose so hard it hurt.

His wife had been dead a year. He'd mourned her, sitting through long days in a haze, desperately clinging to his memories, alternating between fury that she was gone and a bone-deep sense of loss and futility. He'd told himself he'd love her forever, that no one would ever replace her, that the rest of his life would be about the kids and only the kids.

Then this thing with Angie had reared its ugly head and tonight he'd pushed her to the study floor and pushed himself inside her and abandoned everything he thought he knew about himself as a man and a husband.

Even in his teens he'd never been so out of control, so turned on that he'd had no thought of where he was or the consequences of his actions. He'd never gotten carried away like that. Ever.

And yet tonight he'd been nuts. Absolutely nuts. He'd wanted Angie, hadn't been able to think beyond having her, so he'd reached out and taken what he wanted.

And it had been…mind-blowing. That was the worst part of it. Even sitting here in the dark, awash with remorse, he couldn't deny the intensity of the experience. She'd been so silken and responsive and abandoned. Their bodies had fit so well, as though they were made for each other. For those few minutes when he'd been inside her, the world had ceased to exist.

Completely different from sex with Billie.

He shot to his feet, acid burning in his gut as everything in him resiled from the thought. He had loved Billie. With every fiber of his being. He had adored and admired and enjoyed and desired her.

Because he didn't know what else to do, he went into his study to work. It wasn't until he paused on the threshold that he realized he was, effectively, returning to the scene of the crime. He set his jaw and crossed to his desk, hitting the button to bring his computer to life. He didn't so much as glance at the rug where he'd made love with his friend and betrayed his dead wife. He called up his design program and started working, forcing himself to concentrate until the thoughts circling his head faded to a background buzz.

He was dry-eyed and stiff by the time he pushed back his chair. A glance at the clock told him it was nearly one in the morning. He went to bed and woke early. Somehow he got the kids breakfast and managed to fake his way through the morning. He made sure he was out in the yard mowing the lawn when Angie arrived to pick

Eva up at two. He waved to her and offered her a tight smile and she offered him one in return before returning to the house.

Two hours later, he opened the front door and found Eva on the doorstep. He glanced to where Angie's car idled in the drive. For the second time that day their gazes locked, but this time neither of them bothered to force a smile.

"I asked Auntie Angie to come in but she said she has lots and lots of stuff to do. I couldn't even bribe her with pizza."

"I'm sure we can bribe her with pizza another time."

If she ever wanted to speak to him again. If they could ever get past the mess they had made of everything.

The rest of the day passed in a blur of housework and homework and he once again worked himself into a stupor before rolling into bed in the small hours.

Monday morning brought thunderstorms and no Angie. He was both grateful and worried as he hustled the kids out the door. Between the two of them they had decided his studio was the perfect place for her workshop. He didn't want what had happened to interfere with her work. It was enough that it had potentially ruined their friendship.

Which was why he found himself pulling into the driveway at two that afternoon. He'd had a site visit nearby and wasn't due at the office until later.

He and Angie needed to clear the air. Somehow. At the very minimum he needed to apologize for shutting her out so abruptly the other night. This was important. He really didn't want to screw it up.

He made his way to the kitchen. He saw Angie the moment he entered—she was outside, sitting on the deck steps, her profile to the house, her hands curled around a mug. Her hair was pulled into a ponytail and her expression was pensive, her gaze distant.

Her head whipped around as he opened the French doors, her eyes widening with surprise. "Michael. Is everything okay?"

"I had a meeting nearby."

The startled, worried look left her face. "Oh. Good. For a moment I thought something was wrong with Eva or Charlie."

The fact that her first thought was for his children made something tighten in his chest.

"I wanted to talk to you. If that's okay...?"

She didn't say a word, simply shuffled along the step, making room for him, and he crossed the deck and sat beside her to contemplate the grass.

"In case you're wondering, I'm trying to find the words to excuse the inexcusable," he finally said. "What happened the other night, the way it happened, the way I was afterward... You deserve better, Angie. And so does Billie."

A small crease appeared between Angie's eyebrows. "You think I didn't want it? That I didn't enjoy it?"

He couldn't hold her gaze. "I think it should never have happened."

"But it did. And we both wanted it, exactly the way it happened. I was the one who led you into the study, remember? I was the one who lay down on the rug."

He was powerless to stop the memory—Angie, naked, her hair a dark halo around her head, her skin creamy against the rug's ruby tones.

He pushed the visual away, along with the flash of desire that followed hard on its heels.

"Tell me something—you think this would have happened if Billie was still around?" Angie asked.

He flinched. "No."

"I never looked at you as a man when Billie was alive. Not once. You were her husband, utterly off-limits. And I'm willing to bet it was the same for you with me."

"You know it was. I loved Billie."

"I know. So did I. But she's gone, Michael." Angie's voice was soft and sad. Resigned. "What we did... That was just something that happened. Neither of us planned it. God, I don't know, maybe it even needed to happen, to get it out of the way..." She shrugged, the gesture revealing her own confusion. "But you giving yourself a hard time over it is crazy. Especially if part of that is because you feel you hurt me or used me in some way."

He honestly had no idea how to separate out all the different ways he was messed up, but part of it was definitely the way it had happened, how out of control he'd felt and how he'd freaked out afterward.

"I can't tell you how to feel," Angie said. "All I know is Billie knew that we both loved her. She knew that in her bones. What we did doesn't take that away from her. Not for a second. Maybe that's me trying to let myself off the hook, but I don't think so. I think you're allowed to be a man every now and then, Michael, and not just a widower and a father."

His mouth twisted. Rationally, logically, he knew Angie was right. He'd been a good husband to Billie when she was alive. It was only now that she was dead that he was leaking at the seams. Even though he'd been utterly miserable during the darkest days of his grief, there'd been a certain comfort in living a half life, cloaking himself in his loss. Hanging on to his pain was the last sure connection he'd had to her. Letting go of that over recent months had been hard, almost impossible, but it wasn't as though he'd had a choice. Life hadn't stopped because Billie died, after all.

But it was one thing to step into the land of the living and another thing entirely to find himself feeling the kinds of emotions he'd been experiencing lately. Lust and liking and happiness and—very occasionally—joy.

He wasn't ready for that kind of full-color, high-definition living again.

"We might have to agree to disagree on that one," he said. His phone chirruped and he glanced at it. It was a message from work, a problem with some engineered beams he'd specified. "I have to go."

They both stood, Angie dusting off the seat of her jeans. He scanned her face, registering the shadows beneath her eyes and the sad tilt to her mouth. She was so damn gorgeous and wonderful. His chest ached when he thought of everything he'd risked when he'd let his worst impulses drive him on Saturday night.

"I don't want this to screw things up between us, Angie."

He needed her in his life. It wasn't until this moment that he'd realized how much. Not only for the kids, but for himself.

"Ditto. Big-time." Her blue eyes were shiny with emotion as they stared at one another. The need to hold her, to reassure himself that she was okay, that they were okay, was undeniable. She must have been prey to the same instinct, because she stepped toward him at the same moment he stepped toward her. They met in the middle, arms coming around each other in a fierce, intense embrace. Michael pressed his cheek against her hair and squeezed her tightly. She was no slouch in the ferocity department, either, her arms a strong band across his shoulders. After a long beat they parted.

A tear traced down Angie's cheek and Michael caught it on his thumb. He hated the thought that he'd made her unhappy. They had both had more than enough of that over the past year.

"I'm okay," she reassured him.

"If you say so."

"I do. Thanks for dropping by."

"Thanks for listening."

She gestured with her chin. "Go. You don't want to be late for your thing."

He took a step backward. A part of him wanted to go, wanted to walk away from all of this and put it behind him, chalking it up as a foolish, reckless one-off. The other part of him wanted to stay. To keep talking to Angie. To assure himself that she was okay, that they were okay.

"All right," he said. "I'll see you later."

"Yeah, you will." Her smile was faint but unmistakable and it did a lot to ease the remaining tension from his chest.

He headed into the house, relieved beyond measure that they had had this conversation and that they were both on the same page. A thought occurred as he was about to close the French doors. He pivoted to face her. The words he'd been about to say stalled in his throat as he watched Angie bend to collect her cup from the deck. Her jeans tightened across her ass and thighs. He tried to remember what he'd been about to say but he was too busy watching the long, elegant lines of her body as she straightened and remembering how goddamned good she'd felt beneath him.

Her skin had been soft and warm and salty from the sea and when she'd come, her whole body had arched against his and she'd sobbed his name, her knees tightening around his body....

Without saying a word he left, heading for his car, away from Angie and all the feelings and memories that he didn't want to have. Somehow, through a minor miracle, they had managed to navigate the treacherous waters of having slept with each other and still been able to look each other in the eye and like one another.

There was no place for continuing lust and desire in their recent conversation. None at all.

ANGIE WALKED INTO THE kitchen to rinse her coffee cup after Michael left. She felt oddly shaky, as though she might cry at any second. Which was...unnecessary. After forty-eight hours of feeling like crap, marinating in her own guilt and confusion, she'd finally looked him in the eye and listened to him talk and said her own piece.

They were going to be okay. She wasn't sure how she knew that—it was still very early days—but she did. The worst had happened and they had survived and now they were cleaning up the aftermath and moving on, concentrating on the important stuff—the kids and their friendship.

The fact that they'd had fierce, desperate, deeply intense sex on his study floor was now a historical artifact—one they would wrap in tissue paper and pack safely away for the rest of their lives, never again to see the light of day.

A fitting end for a wildly reckless act—and a hugely

fortunate one. Because this conversation could very easily have gone another way. He could have told her he didn't want her hanging around as much, that he thought it would be best for all of them if they took a break from each other. He could have been angry with her for the way she'd taken him by the hand and stripped her clothes for him. He was more honest than that, a far better man, but it could have happened.

Even though she'd just had coffee, she made herself a cup of tea, taking comfort from the simple act of wrapping her hands around the warm mug. She took it to the studio and sat at her desk and stared unseeingly at the wall, reviewing their conversation again, reassuring herself that the crisis really was over. She'd been living on adrenaline for the past two days, freaking out, lashing herself with guilt and regret—but they had survived.

Which was why she steadfastly refused to dwell on the moment when Michael's shoulder had brushed hers while they were sitting on the step. And why she would not allow herself to even contemplate sniffing the neck of her shirt to see if any of his aftershave had transferred to her during their embrace. And why she was not going to sit staring into space for another second.

That night in the study was going to remain there—safely under lock and key.

She finished her tea in a couple of big gulps, then picked up her flexi-drill and resumed the task of cutting out reveals from what would eventually become a three-layered wedding ring. She worked on it until it was time to pick up Eva from school, then she did some long overdue banking and tax paperwork on her laptop, sitting at the kitchen counter while Eva watched one of her after-school shows.

Angie was aware of a certain tension inside herself as it drew closer and closer to Michael's usual time to get home from work. Then she heard his car in the driveway, followed by the telltale rumble of the roller door on the garage. A minute later his footsteps sounded in the hall and her heart did a strange little shimmy in her chest. He walked into the room, rumpled and worn out by the day, his curly hair tousled. He was holding Charlie under one arm, his son wriggling and protesting, and something warm and hot and primitive thumped in the pit of Angie's stomach.

"Hey," he said, offering her a faint smile.

She nodded an acknowledgment, appalled by the wash of sexual heat that was flushing through her body, flooding through her torso, up into her chest and neck, making her breasts tingle and triggering a faint, needy ache between her thighs. She'd been so miserable and confused all weekend. All she'd wanted was to know that Michael was still talking to her, that they were going to be okay. She'd had that assurance this afternoon—and now her body was ambushing her, reminding her in no uncertain terms that she had slept with the tall, dark-haired man standing not four feet away from her.

He'd been inside her body. He'd kissed and licked and bitten her breasts and slid his hand into her pants. He'd made her come, his name on her lips. She'd slid her hand along the silken steel of his erection and gripped the firm, rounded muscle of his ass as he thrust into her. She'd—

Angie shut her laptop with a snap. "I should get going," she said, sliding off the stool so quickly she knocked it off balance.

"You don't want to stay for dinner?"

She knew he was simply being polite, trying to get things back onto an even keel, but right now she needed to be someplace he was not.

"I've got yoga," she lied.

Michael frowned. She waited for him to point out that she usually had yoga on Tuesday nights, but he didn't say anything. Instead, he put Charlie down and walked across to kiss Eva hello.

"I've got a surprise for you," he said. "You want to turn that off for a second?"

Eva muted the TV but kept both eyes on the screen in a blatant attempt to have her cake and eat it, too. "Yeah...?"

"Grandma Faye is coming to town. She's arriving tomorrow morning and she wants to make sure she gets a chance to see you."

That got Eva's attention. Angie's, too. He hadn't mentioned that his mother was coming to town.

"Is she staying with us?" Eva asked, bouncing on the couch. "Because she can have my bedroom if you like and I can sleep in with Charlie."

"I was thinking she could have my room and I would crash on the couch," Michael said.

"Oh. Okay. That sounds good, too," Eva said, her gaze drifting to the television.

Angie was hovering, halfway to the door, caught mid-exit by Michael's news. "Did you know she was coming?"

His expression was wry. "Nope. Mum won a mystery flight in a raffle at bingo night and it turned out it was to Melbourne. She's got two nights in town."

"It's a long way to come for only two nights," Angie

said, frowning. Michael's parents lived in Perth, a three-and-a-half-hour flight away.

"I know. But apparently the tickets are non-transferable and Dad won't spring for a one-way ticket home because he says it's highway robbery and Mum never argues with him when it comes to money, so..."

Angie knew he wasn't hugely close to his parents, but she couldn't help thinking it was a shame his mother wouldn't be staying longer. Still, it was none of her business.

"I'll see you tomorrow."

"Yeah, you will," Michael said.

She smiled, recognizing the echo of her earlier words. The smile held until she was in her car.

She didn't understand how she could feel sick with regret all weekend and yet still want to do it all over again the moment he walked in the door. It was crazy, absolutely counterintuitive and more than a little self-destructive.

She scrubbed her face with her hands. She didn't know what to do. What move to make next. She'd tried business-as-usual and failed spectacularly. She'd tried keeping her distance, which had not exactly been a big winner, either. She was all out of strategies.

How about you stop being an idiot? Michael is not some hot guy you had great sex with. He's Michael, and right now you're the biggest regret on his horizon. The sex doesn't matter. He matters. Get with the program.

Such good advice. So sane and rational.

She started her car, throwing it into gear with a little too much punch before heading home to yet another night of giving herself a hard time for feelings that she couldn't seem to control.

"MICHAEL. YOU'RE SO SKINNY. Haven't you been eating?"

Michael kissed his mother's cheek. If he'd thought about it, he could have guessed this would be her opening gambit. Even before Billie's death she'd always been on about him putting some "meat on his bones," something he'd always found ironic since both she and his father were lean and tall.

"I've been eating."

"More than frozen meals, I hope," his mother said, her gaze scanning the kitchen as though searching for giveaway cardboard boxes and plastic containers. She was dressed neatly in a pair of tailored trousers and a peacock-blue twinset, her steel-gray hair sitting in a smooth chin-length bob.

"I *can* cook, you know, Mum."

"Yeah, Daddy cooks all the time. Spaghetti and more spaghetti. Luckily Auntie Angie cooks for us on Wednesday nights or me and Charlie would be spaghetti-shaped by now," Eva piped up.

"Thanks for the vote of confidence, Eva. I know I can always count on you," he said.

"No worries, Daddy," Eva said, the heavy irony in his tone going over her head.

"Angie. She's Billie's friend, isn't she?" his mother asked.

"That's right."

"The tall, dark-haired one. The pretty one."

His mother's gaze remained fixed to his face as she waited for his confirmation.

Michael picked up her overnight bag. "That's her. I've put you in my room." He headed for his bedroom, very aware that his stilted response had made his mother curious, but he hadn't trusted himself to say anything else. He wasn't ready to talk about Angie, even in the most innocuous way.

He dropped his mother's bag beside the bed. "There's a fresh towel for you there. Let me know if there's anything else you need."

"You don't have to give up your bed for me, Michael. Don't be silly. I can bunk in with Eva or sleep on the couch."

Michael's shoulders relaxed as he realized his mother wasn't going to pursue more talk of Angie.

"You're not sleeping on the couch," he said firmly. "Now, do you want to eat in or go out?"

"Which would you prefer? What's easiest?"

They went out, back to the family bistro where he'd used Angie as a shield to protect himself from Gerry and her friend. He listened to his mother detailing the cruise to Canada and Alaska they had planned for next year and answered her questions about being back at work and the children.

"And what about you?" she asked when Eva took Charlie to inspect the dessert bar. "How are you?"

He slid his empty drink coaster half an inch to the right. "I'm getting there."

"Are you going out? Doing anything?"

He was uncomfortable with the conversation for more than one reason. He'd never had a confiding-type relationship with either of his parents, and he wasn't about to start now. Plus the only thing he'd "done" lately was Angie. He could barely let himself think about it, let alone talk about it. He could imagine how shocked his mother would be if she learned he'd slept with another woman already, and that that woman was Billie's best friend.

He shifted in his seat. "The kids keep me busy. And work."

To his surprise, his mother reached out and rested one of her hands on his. She gave his hand a squeeze, her eyes sympathetic.

"I think you're a wonderful father, Michael. But don't let that become everything for you."

"What's that supposed to mean?"

"That you're allowed to have a life, too."

"I have a life."

His mother simply patted his hand again. They went home not long after, and once the kids were in bed and he'd won yet another tussle with his mother over who was sleeping on the couch, he stretched out across the cushions and stared at the darkened TV screen. For the first time since Billie's death, he tried to think about the future in terms of what he wanted and not what he had to simply endure.

Some of it was easy. No-brainer stuff, really. He wanted Eva and Charlie to be happy and healthy and safe. He wanted to be enough for them. Despite the fact that his interest in the firm had died to next to nothing in the early days of his grief, there was still a tickle of professional ambition itching at him. There were things he wanted to achieve, projects he'd like to land.

Which left only his personal life—the empty side of the bed. Not so long ago, he'd honestly believed he could spend the rest of his life living off memories of Billie. The incident with Angie was proof positive that that had been nothing but a noble, naive fantasy. He was a man. He enjoyed sex, and he enjoyed women—apparently that part of him hadn't died with Billie.

But that didn't mean he wanted to do the whole

falling-in-love-and-marriage thing again. He was almost certain he didn't have it in him to love like that a second time. More important, he didn't want to. He wasn't sure he could survive the loss of someone who meant so much to him again. Maybe that made him a coward, but so be it. It was too much, the hurt too profound.

No, he was done with that kind of love.

He rolled onto his side, yanking the quilt with him. A faint waft of perfume drifted to him and he inhaled, chasing the scent. Citrus and flowers.

Angie. She was the last person who'd used this quilt, of course.

He tucked a hand beneath his head and closed his eyes, refusing to think about Angie or the other night in any detail. It had been a mistake. Something he wanted to put behind him. Something he would regret till his dying day.

Except for the part where you slid inside her. Except for the fact that you now know how soft and firm her breasts are. What her nipples taste like. How tight she feels. What she sounds like when she comes. Be honest and admit you don't regret knowing any and all of the above.

He swore, the sound muffled by the couch. He rolled onto his back again. The quilt was a tangle around his legs and guilt an acid burn in his gut, a perfect counterpoint to the throbbing of his hard-on.

Could you be any more messed up?

He didn't think so. The truth was, he had no idea what he wanted anymore. He needed his friendship with Angie, relied on it to get him through, yet he couldn't stop thinking about the other night. Couldn't stop the guilt, either, that accompanied those thoughts—it was too early for him to want what he wanted from Angie, especially because of who she was and what she'd been to Billie.

It took him a long time to fall asleep.

THE NEXT MORNING, HIS mother insisted on taking Charlie for the day, something Michael was more than happy to agree to. Angie arrived as he was leaving and he realized from his mother's baffled expression that he hadn't explained about Angie taking over the studio, an oversight he honestly couldn't explain.

There was nothing to feel ashamed about there, after all. Just one friend helping out another.

"It sounds like an excellent arrangement," his mother said crisply when he'd finished outlining Angie's problems with the Stradbroke and his difficulty finding someone to collect Eva from school.

"It's worked out well," Angie said with a small smile.

She was uncomfortable. He could see it in her eyes and the way she held her body.

"I've always admired your work, Angie. Billie was always wearing one of your pieces," his mother said.

"She was my biggest fan," Angie said.

"I think Eva's your second biggest. She's been raving about you. Apparently you make a terrific chicken curry."

"Oh. Yes. It's not *my* curry, as such. I got the recipe from the paper. But the kids seem to like it." Angie was blushing now. She took a step toward the French doors. "It was nice to see you again, Mrs. Robinson."

"It's Faye. And it's lovely to see you, too, Angie."

Michael busied himself gathering his things as Angie exited to the deck.

"I'd forgotten how warm she is. Quiet, but she has a lovely presence, doesn't she?" his mother said.

"Yes. I'll see you later, okay? Call if you need anything."

Like last night, his words sounded stiff and unnatural, and, like last night, his mother didn't comment on it, simply tilting her cheek for his kiss. "Have a nice day."

"You, too."

He didn't have a nice day, he had a shitty day. Temperamental clients, wayward contractors, a huge blowout on the budget for a project he was trying to convince a client to commit to—he was more than happy to draw a line under it when he left the office that evening.

Angie's car was gone when he arrived home. Not really surprising, given how uncomfortable she'd been with his mother this morning.

"Something smells good," he said as he entered the house.

"Homemade chicken nuggets and chips," his mother announced. "Charlie and Eva's choice."

She was watching a DVD with the children on the couch, her feet stretched in front of her.

"Sounds good. When are we eating?"

"*We're* eating in half an hour. I'm not sure when *you're* eating," his mother said.

"Sorry?"

"I'm giving you the night off. Go out, see a movie, catch up with a friend. Whatever." She made a shooing motion with her hand. "Have some fun."

He blinked. How like his mother to make plans for him without consulting him.

"It's a nice idea, Mum, but I've had a crappy day. I'm more than happy to be here with you and the kids."

"Tough luck. There's only enough for the three of us."

"Then I'll have an egg on toast or something."

He headed for the kitchen. He heard the rustle of clothing and knew his mother followed him.

"I'm not going to take no for an answer, Michael."

"Mum, it's a lovely gesture, but I'm fine. I don't want to go out."

"Which is exactly my point. When was the last time you did something on your own? Something for you?"

He sighed. She sounded like one of those women's magazine self-help articles.

"I'm fine. I don't need 'me time.'"

"Everyone needs me time, Michael. Especially men who are trying to establish a new identity after the loss of a spouse."

Her words were like a slap in the face. Dear old Mum, always the diplomat.

"My identity is fine."

"Great. Take it out for the night, give it some exercise."

She had a martial glint in her eye, and he could see Eva watching from the couch. Not wanting to make a bigger deal out of it than necessary, he shook his head.

"Fine. If you're so determined. I'll go out."

"Good man."

Twenty minutes later, he'd showered and changed into a pair of jeans and was driving away from the house with no idea what he would do for the next two to three hours. After a moment's thought he aimed the car toward the nearest multiplex. He didn't really want to see a movie, but given the options available to a single guy at seven-thirty on a Wednesday night, he figured he didn't have much choice.

As he'd half suspected, the movies on offer weren't really his speed, but he dutifully bought a ticket to a movie that promised lots of special effects and noises and grabbed a rear seat so he could make a quick exit if need be.

He'd never been a movie alone before. He knew people did it all the time, but he felt ridiculously self-conscious as packs of teens and couples filed into the cinema. He imagined what they would think if they knew he was only here because his mother had made him come.

Beyond pathetic, really.

He endured the movie as long as he could before boredom and growing frustration forced him to his feet. This was not how he wanted to spend his time. He emerged into the neon-lit foyer, digging for his keys in his pocket. Then he caught sight of the time. No way could he go home yet. He'd barely been gone an hour.

He looked around helplessly, utterly clueless. There was a sticky-looking coffee shop next door to the cinemas. He could sit there and nurse a coffee for another hour or so. Next to that was an arcade. He could empty his wallet into a coin slot and play pinball and shoot 'em ups with a bunch of sweaty teenagers.

He wound up in the car, driving toward the city and the hip and happening streets of Fitzroy. A parking spot appeared on his left so he took it and walked into the first likely establishment, a huge barn of a bar with a distressed industrial sign that declared it was Naked for Satan. Inside, he discovered dozens of different varieties of vodkas, too much noise and a clientele that was so young they made him feel older than God.

He ordered a straight vodka and sat at the bar and

fiddled with his phone in an attempt to make it seem like he had something to do. Sound whirled around him, laughter rising and falling above the general hubbub. Girls flirted with boys. Boys flirted with boys. The bar staff handed out disdainful looks and overpriced novelty vodkas.

Michael had never felt more alone. Not simply because he *was* alone, but because he didn't fit into any of this. He wasn't a bar kind of guy, the same as he wasn't a blockbuster movie kind of guy. He was a father, and he'd been a husband. He liked days at the beach with his kids and bad bistro food in the suburbs. He liked talking and laughing with Angie, watching the emotions move across her face.

He went very still, suddenly understanding why he was sitting in this bar in this suburb. Angie's apartment was around the corner. Only a few hundred very dangerous meters away.

You freakin' idiot.

He headed for the door, leaving his untouched vodka on the bar. He emerged onto the street to find it had started raining. He started walking in search of his car, determined to go home.

Because no way could he even contemplate the alternative: going to Angie's place. Knocking on the door. Telling her that he couldn't stop thinking about her.

No way.

CHAPTER TWELVE

ANGIE WAS DOZING ON the couch when a sharp rap woke her. A few muzzy seconds later she realized someone was knocking at her door. At—her gaze found the clock on her DVD player—at ten at night.

She'd stripped to her panties and a tank top when she got home from dinner out with a group of her Stradbroke friends, and she diverted to her bed to grab her silk kimono-style robe before approaching the door. Hands busy tying the sash at her waist, she squinted through the spyhole.

Michael stood on the other side of the door, his head downturned, his expression unreadable.

"Michael," she said out loud, stunned to see him there. She twisted the lock and swung the door open.

Without the distortion of the spyhole lens she saw that he was wet, his hair half plastered to his head, his T-shirt clinging to his chest and shoulders. His gaze lifted to her face. He didn't say a word, but she knew instantly why he was here.

Because, like her, he hadn't been able to forget what had happened between them.

Even though they had both agreed it was a mistake. Even though neither of them wanted to endanger their friendship.

Common sense said she should offer him a towel and

then send him on his way. If she let him into her apartment, she knew what would happen. It was a foregone conclusion.

She stepped backward, opening the door wider. Michael's gaze held hers, questioning. She took another step. He walked in.

She shut the door, heat already building between her thighs, excitement licking along her veins.

Michael stood in the middle of her space, his gaze bouncing from the kitchen to the couch to her bed. She grabbed a towel from the bathroom, passing it to him. Then she walked to the bed and untied the sash on her robe. The silk slid down her arms, a whisper against her skin. She didn't dare look at Michael as she pulled her top over her head. Her panties followed. She tugged back the corner of the quilt and climbed into bed.

She watched as Michael stripped and walked toward the bed, his erection standing proud. The bed dipped as he got in the other side. She rolled toward him, and he pulled her into his arms. His skin was cool against hers, making her nipples bead. She wrapped her arms around him and pressed herself against him, offering him her heat.

Offering him everything.

His lips found hers, his tongue sliding into her mouth. His hand caressed her hip, tracing the curve, moving onto her thigh and then up again before curling around to cup her ass. As though he couldn't get enough of her. As though he'd been thinking of touching her ever since he'd stopped.

She smoothed her hands over his shoulders and down his back. His mouth left hers, kissing a trail to her ear. He pressed an openmouthed kiss to the sensitive skin

there, sending sensation ricocheting through her body.
She pressed her hips forward, seeking the hard length
of him, needing more.

His hand found her knee, encouraging it over his hip,
exposing her to his touch. His hand smoothed down her
ass and between her legs. She knew exactly when he discovered how wet she was because his erection surged
against her belly, hard and hot. He started to stroke her,
his other hand teasing her breasts. She slid a hand between their bodies, curling her fingers around his shaft,
and stroked him in return, learning him, savoring the
strength of him.

He slid a finger inside her and she whispered his
name. He responded with a kiss that took her breath
away before pushing her onto her back. She blinked at
him, dazed and painfully aroused. His gaze swept her
body, lingering on her breasts, her belly, her thighs. Seeing the naked desire in his eyes only excited her further.
He moved on top of her and she reached for his shoulders, already anticipating the hard heat of his penetra-
tion. He surprised her by shifting farther down in the
bed, his hands smoothing down her body in a leisurely
caress. He kissed her breasts, pulling her nipple into his
mouth and alternating between suckling it and teasing
her with the tip of his tongue before switching his attention to her other breast. She shifted on the pillows,
her bones turning to liquid.

After long, torturous minutes, his hand traced a path
up her thigh until he was delving into her folds, stroking
her. She lifted her hips, asking wordlessly for him to give
her what she wanted. He smiled against her breasts and
shifted farther down again, his mouth blazing a hot trail
down her belly. She forgot to breathe as he kissed his

way across her hip, shifting so that his shoulders were between her thighs now. He glanced at her, his gray-green eyes heavy-lidded with carnal intent. Then he lowered his head and pressed an openmouthed kiss to her, his tongue tracing and teasing, his hands stroking the sensitive, pale skin of her inner thighs. She shuddered and twisted her hands in the sheets and started to pant.

He picked up the pace, his hands sliding beneath her backside, lifting her toward him. She was helpless, lost in a world of spiraling desire and sensation. Unable to stop herself, she slid her fingers into his hair, anchoring herself.

She was on the verge, literally seconds away from an explosive climax, when he broke contact with her. Before she could protest, his weight came on top of her and she felt the hard press of him at her entrance. She lifted her hips greedily, eagerly, and he slid inside to the hilt. It was all she needed, her climax rushing over her, arching her back and stealing her breath.

Michael remained still inside her until she'd stopped shuddering, then he started to move. He kissed her, drugging, languorous kisses that only made her want more. His hands skimmed her hips and breasts and belly before he finally slid a hand between their bodies and found her with his fingers.

Stroke by stroke, caress by caress, he built the need within her again. She wrapped a leg around his hips and moved with him, reveling in the slide of his body inside hers and the slow build of sensation. She was so wet, he was so hard, it felt so good....

Her second climax lasted longer, a long, warm pulse of pleasure that went on and on. Michael lost it halfway through, burying himself inside her and grinding his hips against hers as he found his own release. He withdrew immediately this time, rolling to one side. She'd barely registered the loss when he pulled her close, encouraging her onto her side so he could tuck his body in behind hers spoon style.

His arm circled her waist, one hand cupping her breast. She could feel his heart rate normalize, the hectic heat of his body cooling. He pressed a kiss to the nape of her neck. She reached back and rested her hand on his hip.

He didn't say a word, and neither did she. They simply lay in the dark, their bodies warm and sated. After a few minutes, Michael's breathing evened out and she realized he was asleep. She let her heavy lids drop closed. He felt so good snuggled up behind her, the hair on his legs deliciously rough on the backs of hers, his arm a welcome weight across her body.

In a distant part of her mind, she was aware that this had raised far more questions than it had answered, but worry would have to wait for when she was feeling less drowsy and cozy and safe....

MICHAEL DRIFTED TOWARD wakefulness as Billie stirred in his arms. He nuzzled his face closer to her neck, inhaling the smell of oranges and flowers. He smiled to himself. She was such a restless sleeper, just as she was restless in life, too, constantly flitting from one thing to the next.

She moved again, her long legs tangling with his.

And suddenly he was wide awake, his brain telling him that it was Angie in his arms, Angie's long legs that were tangled with his and whose perfume he was inhaling.

Angie—not Billie.

He slid his arm free and rolled away from her, sick with himself for having confused the two women. It had only been for a few seconds, but it had been enough. Angie wasn't Billie. She was her own person. And Billie… Billie was gone.

He threw off the quilt and swung his legs over the edge of the bed. His clothes were scattered on the floor, a sodden mess. He dressed with urgent hands. All he could think about was getting out of here, getting some air and some space to sort through his feelings.

Angie stirred. He was aware of her pushing her hair out of her eyes and blinking as he did up the fly on his jeans.

"What time is it?" she asked as he sat to pull on his shoes.

"Just past twelve. Sorry, I didn't mean to wake you."

"Your clothes are probably still wet."

"It's fine."

"I can put them in the dryer. They'll only take twenty minutes—"

"Thanks, but it's not a problem." He stood, focused on the door.

"Okay."

Angie's face was a pale oval in the dark. He couldn't see her eyes very well but he didn't need to to know that she was trying to work out what was going on. Trying to understand why he was scrambling to leave her bed when only a couple of hours ago he'd been panting to get into it.

"I have to go."

She turned on the bedside lamp. Golden light spilled across the sheets, gilding her bare breasts. He looked away, but not before a lick of need raced through him.

It only made him want to escape more because he couldn't handle it, couldn't reconcile his feelings for her with his feelings for Billie. He felt as though he was at war with himself—and the really great thing was that the person who was copping the worst of it was Angie. First he'd abandoned her in the study, now he was about to bolt for the door. All because he hadn't been able to walk away when he'd found himself on her doorstep this evening.

She rose and reached for her robe. He clenched his fist around the keys in his pocket and forced himself to wait for her to tie the sash and pull her hair out of the collar. His throat tightened as he watched her. She was upset but trying not to show it. Trying to let him go without making a fuss.

"There's a red button beside the street exit in the foyer," she said as she led him to the door. "Hit it and it will let you out."

"Thanks." He hovered, even though she hadn't said a word to stop him from leaving.

"It's okay, Michael, I get it. I know you need to go," she said, her eyes understanding.

He leaned forward and kissed her cheek. "You're the best."

It was a trite, impersonal thing to say, utterly unequal to who she was, to her generosity of spirit and big heart and the experience they had shared, and he regretted it the moment the words were out of his mouth.

"Drive carefully," she said, then the door was swinging shut between them and he was on one side and she the other.

He didn't move for a long moment, trying to understand himself. No answers came, and it was getting late. He needed to get home to his children.

He could deal with the fallout from tonight tomorrow.

ANGIE RETURNED TO SHEETS that smelled of sex and Michael. She pulled the quilt around her shoulders and lay in the darkness, aware of the traffic noises outside and the plumbing noises from within the building and the heaviness of her own feelings.

Right now Michael was making his way to his car in his damp clothes. No doubt he was giving himself a hard time for what had happened, for the fact that he'd come to her. No doubt he regretted giving in to his desire for her.

She should probably be regretting her part in it, too, but she'd made her decision when she invited Michael into her apartment. She'd known then the sequence of events, and she didn't regret it, not for a second, even though all the usual recriminations were circling her mind.

That Michael was Billie's. That Angie was selfish and a hypocrite, proclaiming her great love for her friend while welcoming Billie's husband into her bed. That there was no excuse for her betrayal.

But tonight hadn't been about Billie. It had been about Michael and Angie. Nothing else. The first time, it had been so fiery and impulsive and urgent, she hadn't been able to sort out what she'd wanted from what he'd needed. She'd told herself it was about comfort and loneliness and grief, that they had been acting on the spur of the moment.

This second time hadn't been about any of those things. Michael had come to her door because he couldn't stay away, and she'd let him in because she hadn't stopped thinking about him, one way or another, since Saturday night.

And the sex… A rush of warmth washed through her as she remembered the way he'd looked at her, the way he'd smoothed his hands over her breasts and belly, the way he'd driven her crazy with his mouth. When he'd entered her, his serious gray-green gaze had been fixed on her face, taking in every nuance of her response.

None of that had been about Billie.

Angie could see that now, was starting to understand that what was happening between the two of them was more than propinquity and convenience. They liked each other. They got each other. They cared for each other. And their bodies were ridiculously compatible. All he had to do was look at her and hers fired up, ready for anything he was offering.

None of that matters, because he was Billie's first. He'll always be Billie's, in your mind and his. So don't go getting any ideas. Don't even think about it.

More good advice. Angie did her best to follow it, closing her eyes and willing herself to sleep. She pushed away the memories that threatened to swamp her—the roughness of Michael's stubble against the tender flesh of her inner thighs; the feel of his skin beneath her hands, warm and firm; the passion of his kisses, so intense and demanding—and instead concentrated on the work she needed to achieve tomorrow in order to make the delivery date on her current commissions.

It was no good, though—she couldn't stop her brain from thinking. Worrying about how Michael was feeling, if he was again lashing himself for having slept with her. Wondering what was going to happen tomorrow, how they were going to get past tonight. They had already affirmed to each other that their friendship was special and important, that neither of them wanted to endanger that. Yet it hadn't stopped them from sleeping with each other again.

Desire was a powerful, powerful force. Angie wasn't quite sure she'd ever realized how powerful before—but then she'd never been so drawn to a man and so conflicted about her own feelings at the same time.

She fell asleep with her thoughts still whirring and woke with a faint headache. She had errands to run in the morning, and it was nearly midday before she arrived at Michael's house. She hesitated over which route to take to the studio—around the house or through it— then shook her head at her own foolishness. She would use the front door, the way she usually did, because she wasn't ashamed of what they had done and she wasn't afraid to face Michael again.

Just the opposite, actually. She was aware of a little spurt of adrenaline exploding like a firecracker in her belly as she let herself into the house and heard his deep voice on the phone in the study. She pressed a hand to her torso, then shut the door quietly behind her and walked up the hallway. Her steps slowed as she approached the study door. She glanced in, straight into Michael's eyes. He was sitting at his desk, his chair swiveled to face the door, the phone pressed to his ear. She wondered if he'd turned the chair when he heard her key in the door, or if he'd been facing that way already. She very much hoped that it was the former, because suddenly she was fiercely, intensely glad to see him.

His hair was rumpled, and he hadn't shaved this morning. His gray T-shirt made his eyes seem stormier and more serious than ever. And, of course, his feet were bare.

They looked at each other for a long, drawn-out beat. She raised her hand in greeting. Offered him a small smile. He didn't smile, but warmth flared in his eyes. Warmth that was quickly tamped down, as though he'd just caught himself doing something he shouldn't.

She forced her legs to keep moving, walking into the kitchen and straight to the French doors. She took a deep breath of the warm summer air as she walked onto the deck, hoping it would calm the tremulous excitement that was buzzing through her body.

All because he'd looked at her and been pleased to see her, despite what had happened last night.

She unlocked the studio and transferred the diamonds and rubies she'd just picked up to her safe. She glanced toward the door, wondering if Michael would come see her to clear the air once he'd finished his call.

She tried to anticipate what he might say, tried to decide what she might say in return. Something about the fact that she didn't regret last night, maybe. And that she'd had a good time.

She didn't let herself get beyond that, which was just as well because Michael didn't come calling. Instead, she ran into him in the house in the early afternoon when she went inside to use the bathroom. He was in the kitchen making coffee. There was no way he couldn't have been aware that she was in the house—he'd have heard the French doors opening and closing, her footsteps on the wooden floor, the flush of the toilet—which meant he'd chosen to be in the kitchen so they would run into each other. He gave her a carefully neutral smile when she entered.

"Coffee?" he asked, lifting his mug in inquiry.

"Sure."

He poured a second mug. She crossed to the fridge for the milk, tension making her shoulders stiff. She slid the milk onto the counter and watched as Michael added some to each mug, waiting for him to say something.

"You got home okay?" she finally asked. He wasn't the only one who could initiate a conversation, after all.

"Yeah. Thanks."

"And your mum got away okay?"

"I dropped her at the airport this morning."

"Good. Good."

She accepted her coffee and wrapped her fingers around the warm porcelain. "Do you want to talk?"

Michael's gaze dropped from her face to the counter. She watched his chest rise and fall as he took a deep breath. Then his gaze found hers again.

"Can I say 'not yet'? Is that okay? I'm still trying to get my head together. To understand…"

"Of course," she said quickly. "I'm not going anywhere."

"But that's okay with you? I know it was weird, me leaving so quickly last night… I lay awake half the night kicking myself for being such an asshole."

She reached across and touched his arm, unable to stop herself. "You're not an asshole, Michael. Far from it."

His arm was warm beneath her hand. She wanted to hang on to him so badly, but she forced herself to withdraw.

"Well, I've been doing a pretty good impersonation of one lately."

She wanted to keep talking but he'd said he wasn't

ready so she backed off and picked up her mug. "You do a really bad impersonation of an asshole, actually. Believe me, I've met the real thing."

She left him standing at the counter and returned to her studio. She was distracted as she resumed work, worrying about him, about them. Thinking about Billie and how she fit into all of this. She forgot about her coffee and when she remembered it was stone cold. She zapped it in her microwave and gave herself a mental shake. Her chewing over the situation endlessly wasn't going to change what it was. It was only going to drive her crazy.

She turned on her flexi-drive drill and began the delicate task of creating rivet points to join the three sleeves of the ring she was working on together. She was working close to the edge, using her free hand to augment the vice's grip when a loud bang made her head jerk up. Pain bit into her hand and she looked down and realized that the drill had slipped across the surface of the ring and into the index finger of her left hand, leaving behind a nasty cut that was already welling blood.

"Shit."

She straightened, switching off the drill and letting it drop to the surface of her workbench. She leaned across and grabbed a wad of tissues from the box on the windowsill and put pressure on the wound. The prickling discomfort in her finger confirmed her suspicion—there was metal in the wound, tiny filings from the drill.

Awesome.

All because a stupid bird had flown into the window. She'd recognized what the bang was a split second after she'd registered it, but that hadn't stopped her startle reflex.

With the wound under control, she inspected the ring. The drill had gouged a line across its surface, but she could polish it out. Time-consuming, but doable. At least that was a small silver lining to hold on to.

Blood had soaked through the tissues and she grabbed some more and added them to the first lot before elevating her hand and standing to go collect her first-aid kit. She'd injured herself enough over the years to have a pretty comprehensive kit and she hoisted it by its handle and took it into the house so she would have access to running water.

It was awkward to work one-handed, but she managed to tear the top off some gauze and she used it to clean away the worst of the blood. The cut was a centimeter long and only a few millimeters deep. Nothing major. She used a pair of tweezers to hold it open, trying to sight the fragments of metal. She glimpsed a sliver and reached for a sachet of sterile saline, tearing the top off with her teeth.

She tried three times to flush the wound, but it was impossible for her to hold the tweezers and flush the cut with the saline at the same time. After five futile minutes she gave up and applied pressure with the tissues again. Feeling foolish, she made her way to the study. Michael was tapping away at the computer and she cleared her throat to get his attention.

"Don't freak, but I had a little accident and I need some help flushing out a metal sliver," she said.

Michael's surprised gaze went from her face to her hand. He was on his feet like a shot.

"Are you okay? Do you need a doctor? Damn, there's a lot of blood."

He reached for her hand, pulling it away from where she had it elevated against her shoulder.

"It looks a million times worse than it is. It's a tiny little cut, but it's got a bit of gold in it that needs to come out before I can wrap it up."

"You're sure?"

His hand was warm on hers, his face creased with worry. She couldn't help but be touched by his concern.

"Very. Can I borrow your hands for five minutes?"

"You can even have the rest of me, for as long as you need me."

She wasn't going to touch that one with a ten-foot barge pole, so she simply led the way to the kitchen and explained what she was trying to do. Michael looked at the abandoned gauze and the empty saline sachet and frowned.

"Why didn't you come get me straight away?"

"Because I'm a grown-up?"

"You're too independent, that's what it is. Too used to doing things on your own."

"That's because I am on my own most of the time," she said, amused by his stern demeanor.

"Not today, you're not."

He pulled out more gauze and used the scissors in the kit to open a second sachet of saline. Then he moved closer and took her hand in his.

"Let me know if it hurts, okay?"

"Oh, you'll know."

He took off the tissues and used the gauze and some of the saline to clean the wound. Then he picked up the tweezers and parted the cut.

"I can see it. You want me to try to pull it out with the tweezers or flush it out?"

This close, she could see how long his eyelashes were and the way his laugh lines formed a friendly bracket around his mouth. He smelled good, too, like warm skin and fresh laundry detergent and soap. Her gaze gravitated to his lips, remembering the way he'd kissed her last night, and not just on the mouth.

"Angie?"

She realized he'd asked her something and was waiting for a response. She lifted her gaze from his mouth and saw understanding dawn in his eyes. He knew what she was thinking about. He knew exactly.

"Sorry," she said.

"Don't be." His voice was gruff. He shifted his weight slightly. "You want me to try to pull it out with the tweezers? It might hurt, but at least we'll know we got it."

"Sure."

"I'll be gentle."

"I know."

She looked away from what he was doing, not trusting herself not to flinch at the key moment. What she didn't know wouldn't hurt her, right?

She focused instead on his chest, on the clean lines of his collarbone and the handful of dark curls visible at the dip in his V-neck T-shirt. She knew how those hairs felt against her breasts, rough and silky at the same time. She knew how powerful and heavy his weight felt as it settled over her....

She could feel Michael probing for the fragment and she closed her eyes, trying to be brave.

"You okay?" His voice was soft, concerned.

"Yep."

"Almost there."

She felt him flush the cut with saline, then pressure

as he pressed a pad of gauze to the wound. She opened her eyes and watched as he found a bandage, sticking it to her finger with precise care.

"You're good at this," she said.

"Lots of practice. You've met Charlie, right?"

She smiled. Charlie had never met a dangerous object he didn't want to get better acquainted with. She'd steered him away from certain death more times than she could count.

Michael used the last of the gauze to wipe away the dried blood on her hand. Her back was pressed up against the counter, and he was still standing very close. If she wanted to, she could slide to the left or right to put some space between them. She didn't move, and neither did Michael as he started collecting the various wrappers and sachets they had used. He kept his gaze resolutely on what he was doing, but Angie was aware of every shift of his body as he leaned past her to reach the counter, every breath he took, every flicker of his eye, and instinct told her it was the same for him. Finally he moved away, turning to drop the rubbish in the bin. When he turned, her gaze was drawn to the front of his jeans where a not insubstantial bulge signaled his arousal. His expression was half sheepish, half frustrated when she lifted her gaze back to his face.

"Sorry. Apparently I'm experiencing a second teenagerhood at the moment."

"Is that what it is? It must be contagious, then."

She held his gaze, refusing to look away. Letting him see how much it excited her that simply standing close to her was enough to give him a hard-on. His expression darkened and he took a step toward her, the movement so jerky it couldn't be anything but involuntary.

He reached for her, his hand curving around her waist, but he didn't pull her any closer. Instead, he stilled, his eyes dark with confusion.

"Angie…is it really this crazy for you, too?"

"Yes."

Maybe she was imagining it, but he looked marginally relieved.

"This is new territory for me… I don't really know how to handle it," he said, his voice so low she almost couldn't hear him.

"It's not exactly my area of expertise, either." Because this was new for her, too. None of her previous lovers had pushed her buttons quite like Michael did.

"Everything I said the other day still stands. I don't want to lose your friendship."

"Me, either. You all mean too much to me."

"But I'm not sure I can keep my hands off you."

Her pulse leaped at his words, heat rushing to her thighs.

"Then maybe you shouldn't."

But he still didn't close the distance between them.

"I don't want to hurt you, Angie." He was frowning now, and she understood exactly what he was saying.

That anything that happened between them would only be about sex and friendship because his heart belonged to Billie.

"I understand, Michael." And she did. She knew that this thing between them wasn't something he'd come looking for and that he didn't need or want another relationship. It was too soon, he was too raw.

And yet they were both standing here, thrumming with arousal, ready to jump each other.

"As long as we're both on the same page, it'll be

okay," she said. "You keep talking to me, and I'll keep talking to you. And if this—" she indicated the few inches of space between them "—becomes a problem, then we do something about it."

She was making it up as she went along, but it made sense to her. Or perhaps it only made sense because all she could think about right now was getting Michael naked and inside her as quickly as possible.

As though he could read her mind, he finally closed the distance between them. His hips pressed against hers and his arms slid around her. She drew back slightly as one last rational thought intruded.

"Charlie..."

"He's in day care. I swapped out yesterday for today because Mum wanted to stay with him."

She didn't say another word, simply fisted her hand in his T-shirt and dragged him closer.

CHAPTER THIRTEEN

THEY KISSED, HANDS QUICKLY sliding beneath clothes. He cupped her breasts, his thumb sliding over silk and lace. She slid her hands up his torso, reveling in the hard planes of his body. One of his hands found the stud on her jeans and he popped it and slid her fly down. Then he was sliding beneath her panties, his fingers delving between her folds. Her breathing quickened as he found her with his middle finger.

"There?" he asked against her mouth.

"Yes. There."

He bit her lip gently and started to stroke her. She held her breath, shocked by the intensity of it. But it was like this every time with him—electric, and so damned hot she could barely form a thought.

Her knees started to tremble. "Michael..."

She needed to be naked. Needed him inside her.

But he ignored her plea, deepening their kiss, one hand at her breasts, pinching and teasing and soothing her nipples through the silk of her bra, the other down her pants, sending her crazy. Soon she was trembling so much she had to grip his shoulders to stay upright. He slipped his finger down farther, sliding inside her, using his thumb to tease her. She started to pant, closing her eyes. Michael licked her neck and pulled her earlobe into his mouth and she came, her hips rolling forward, seeking the pressure of his hand, her body tightening around his invading finger. She shuddered for long seconds, utterly lost.

When she opened her eyes, Michael was watching her, a small, slightly smug smile on his lips.

"What?" she said, suddenly feeling shy.

Had he been watching her when she climaxed? Watching her goofy orgasm face, listening to her inarticulate, needy sounds?

"I like watching you come." There was something so knowing in the way he said it, so earthy.

"Yeah?"

"Yeah. I like it so much I want to make it happen all over again."

She gave him her best challenging look. "Then you'd better get cracking, hadn't you?"

He took her at her word, reaching for the waistband of her jeans. She helped him peel them off and she tore at his jeans, yanking them down his hips along with his boxer-briefs, breathing in the smell of warm skin and male arousal as she pushed them past his knees.

"You smell good," she said, reaching for him.

She was already on her knees and he closed his eyes for a long beat as she drew him into her mouth. Then his eyes opened and he reached for her, trying to encourage her to her feet.

"Angie…"

"Shut up and take it like a man."

She circled his tip with her tongue, then took all of him into her mouth. After a moment's hesitation his hands slid into her hair. She started to work him in earnest, teasing the smooth head of his erection, working his shaft with her hand. He groaned in the back of his throat and pushed his hips forward. She moved closer, wanting more. She'd always enjoyed this, but doing it for Michael was a huge turn-on, so much so that she had to squeeze her thighs together to try to keep a lid on her own arousal.

Finally she couldn't stand it any longer and she slid a hand down her stomach and between her own thighs.

Michael swore under his breath when he saw what she was doing and the next thing she knew he was on his knees as well, pushing her back onto the tiles. He reared over her, his cheekbones flushed, stomach muscles tense, his hard-on glistening from her ministrations. She lifted her hips and he thrust inside her in one smooth move.

"Yes," she breathed.

He started to pump into her, every thrust making her crazier. She smoothed her hands over his shoulders and back and ass and panted his name until a second climax took her. She clung to him, grinding her hips into him, feeling his rising excitement, the new tension in his body.

She pressed her fingers into the firm muscles of his ass, urging him on. His mouth found hers and he kissed her, his tongue stroking hers. Then he pressed his cheek to hers and buried himself deep inside her as he came, every muscle tense as pleasure took him.

He was dead weight on her for a moment afterward, his breath coming fast. Then he lifted his head and looked at her. Behind him she could see the refrigerator and the microwave. Beneath her the tiles were cold, a fact she hadn't noticed in the heat of the moment.

They hadn't even made it to the couch.

The corner of Michael's mouth kicked up. She found herself smiling in response.

"And all this time I thought spaghetti was your signature dish," she said.

His smile widened into a grin. "I'm extending my repertoire."

"You certainly are."

He gazed at her body, reaching out to smooth a hand over her breast. His expression sobered as he met her eyes again.

"You really think we can do this?"

"At this point, it's kind of academic, isn't it? Since we can't seem to keep our hands off each other."

Given that they were lying on the cold tile of the kitchen floor, it was something of an understatement.

Michael's gaze scanned her face, serious and intent. He kissed her, then smoothed a strand of hair back from her forehead. There was so much tenderness and affection in the gesture her throat got tight.

He shifted his weight, sliding back until he could sit back on his haunches. He held out a hand to her.

"Come on."

"Where are we going?" she asked, even as she slid her hand into his.

"To the couch. I don't have to pick Eva up for another hour."

"Oh. When you put it that way..."

She watched his muscular ass flex and contract as he towed her into the living room, but even the sight of so much impressive masculinity couldn't quell the little voice that piped up in the back of her mind.

The couch, not the bedroom?

But she knew why it was the couch and not the bedroom. She knew exactly why—and she'd signed up for this regardless.

Which either made her very foolish or very game. Or, perhaps, a bit of both.

TWO AND A HALF WEEKS LATER, Michael side-stepped a crack in the pavement, aware of the burn in his lungs and legs but unwilling to slow his pace. Eva was at a sleepover and Mrs. Linton was minding Charlie and Michael was taking advantage of a rare hour to himself to blow the cobwebs from his brain.

The road continued to climb and he put his head down and dug in. After doggedly putting one foot in front of the other for what felt like too long, he finally reached the high point of the road and slowed to a halt. One hand on his hip, he sucked in air and soaked up the view. Below him, the city of Melbourne rose up out of the sea of trees that was Studley Park, the buildings glinting in the late-afternoon sun.

Michael breathed in eucalyptus-scented air and used his forearm to wipe the sweat off his forehead. For a moment his mind was blessedly blank, empty of all thought except an appreciation of the view and the warmth of the sun on his face and the pleasing looseness of his muscles after strenuous exercise.

A bird flew high overhead, soaring on the wind. A car drove past behind him, engine laboring as it tackled the incline. A bead of sweat trickled down the side of his neck.

He let his head drop back, drew a deep breath into his lungs…

And suddenly his head was full again, teeming with the many thoughts and concerns that occupied his days. Eva and Charlie and the practice.

And, of course, Angie.

They had been sleeping with each other for three weeks now. Three weeks of snatching what private moments they could to tear each other's clothes off and satisfy the need to be skin to skin.

And it was a need. He'd never been so preoccupied with sex, with getting a woman naked, in his life. Even when he'd been a spotty, horny teenager. Even when he'd been falling in love with Billie.

As usual, he shied away from any comparison between Billie and Angie. It wasn't a game he wanted to play. Billie was Billie, his beloved wife. And Angie was Angie, his good friend. And now his lover. Two very different women, even if they had been best friends when Billie was alive.

He shook his head. He didn't want to dwell on this stuff. He'd been working hard in recent days to simply take things as they came. To enjoy Angie and accept that they had a powerful physical attraction and that this was something that was happening, whether he was ready for it or not. God knew, he'd had enough unhappiness in his life over the past twelve months.

A motorbike roared around the corner, the harsh reverberation of its engine breaking the peace of the day. Michael took another swipe at the sweat on his forehead, then turned and started back down the mountain.

His thoughts shifted to the evening ahead as he ran. Angie was coming over and they were making dinner together and watching a movie. His body quickened as he thought about what would happen after dinner, after Charlie had been put to bed. He would undress Angie slowly, piece by piece, until he had her bare and panting for him. Or maybe he'd touch her through her clothes before sliding his hands underneath them, teasing her until she reached out and took what she wanted.

Without him consciously willing it, his stride lengthened. Even though Angie wasn't due at his place for another three hours.

Recognizing the foolishness of his own behavior, he slowed down to a more sustainable pace. Twenty minutes later his car appeared around a bend in the road, parked on the verge. He slowed to a walk and stretched his hamstrings before wiping himself down with a towel and getting behind the wheel. He collected Charlie from next door when he got home, gifting Mrs. Linton with a box of chocolates for her troubles. She assured him that Charlie was a pleasure to mind, even if he did insist on trying to swim in her koi pond every time they went out in her yard.

Sure enough, his son had dirty shoes and socks. Michael changed him and had a little chat with him about not swimming with the fishes, but it was hard to say how much he absorbed. Not much, if his bright smile and untroubled expression were anything to go by.

He was fixing Charlie a snack when Angie arrived at six. She was wearing a bright blue dress with a red belt and a pair of red espadrilles and she gave him her usual warm, slow smile when he answered the door. He smiled in response, aware of his mood lifting. Not that it had been grim, but everything always seemed better when Angie was around.

"Hey. You are so going to regret letting me choose the movie tonight," she said as she walked past him into the house.

Instinct told him to reach out and pull her close so he could greet her properly, the way he wanted to. But

Charlie was in the kitchen. He didn't want to confuse his son with what was happening between him and Angie.

Whatever that was.

"If it's *The Sound of Music*, all bets are off," he said as he followed her up the hall.

The soft fabric of her dress swished around her knees, drawing his gaze to her long, slim legs.

"My choice, remember?" She gave him a mischievous grin.

"All right. Put me out of my misery."

"I don't know. I'm kind of enjoying torturing you now."

She was, he could tell. Her blue eyes were sparkling, and she flicked her hair over her shoulder in a provocative, teasing gesture.

He shrugged as though he didn't give two hoots. "Fine. Keep your secret. You want a beer or wine?"

"Beer, thanks. Perfect for a nice hot day. Hey, Charlie Bear. What's happening?"

He waited until she was bending to kiss Charlie's cheek before he reached out and snagged the strap of her handbag, sliding it off her shoulder.

"Hey!"

Her response was lightning fast as she reached out to grab the body of the bag, foiling his plan to ransack her purse and find out for himself what celluloid punishment she'd devised for him.

"Not so fast, buster," she said, laughing and pulling the bag tight to her belly.

"Hand it over, Bartlett. I refuse to be held over a barrel." He tugged experimentally on the strap, but her grip remained firm.

"Haven't you ever heard that patience is a virtue?"

"Don't make me force you to hand it over." He was grinning, enjoying the foolish battle of wills.

"I'd like to see you try."

"Just remember, you asked for it."

He yanked on the strap, pulling her off balance and into his arms. He snaked an arm around her back and insinuated the other between her bag and the body, searching out the sensitive spot beneath her arm where he knew she was incredibly ticklish.

"Oh, you bastard!" she shrieked.

They swayed together, her helpless laughter echoing around the kitchen. The urge to kiss her, to taste her laughter and joy was almost too much to resist. He lowered his head, only remembering at the last minute that Charlie was watching.

He forced himself to let her go and step back, relinquishing his hold on both her and the bag. Sure enough, when he glanced over Charlie was watching them both with avid eyes, a questioning smile on his face.

"What's funny, Daddy?" he asked.

"Auntie Angie's being silly," Michael said.

Angie smoothed her dress and gave him a dry look. "I think Daddy's the one being silly. That move was worthy of the playground."

"Thank you. I believe I perfected it in grade two, actually."

Her smile started in her eyes before it curved her mouth. There was so much warm appreciation and affection in it that his chest got a little tight. He was suddenly deeply, fiercely glad that she was standing in his kitchen and that they were going to spend the night together. She made his world a better place. She loved his kids, and she understood him, and she never played games or pulled her punches. She'd held him together through the bad times and helped him find his way out the other side.

She was a gift, a godsend, and he knew with a sudden, sharp clarity that he was incredibly lucky to have her in his life. Despite the guilt. Despite the complications.

Even though Charlie was still watching, he reached out and caught her hand. He raised it to his lips and pressed a kiss to her knuckles.

Her smile faltered and she lifted her eyebrows in silent question. "Where's that move from? Grade four? High school?"

"Ten seconds ago. I'm glad you're here," he said simply.

She blinked, then she smiled again. "I'm glad I'm here, too."

For a moment the kitchen seemed very quiet as they smiled into each other's eyes.

"Up! Up!" Charlie said, jumping up and down, his arms raised beseechingly toward Angie.

"Your wish is my command, you little tyrant." She hoisted Charlie into her arms, rubbing her cheek against his. "Okay now?"

Charlie nodded, happy as a clam now he'd gotten his way. Michael shook his head.

"Lock up your daughters, Melbourne," he said as he started filling a pot with water for the pasta.

"It's true, he *is* too cute for his own good," she said.

"Worse thing is he knows it."

They worked together to make dinner. Angie cut Charlie's spaghetti into baby-proof pieces and they ate out on the deck, enjoying the last heat of the day. Michael bathed Charlie and got him into his pajamas while

Angie cleaned up the kitchen. When he returned with Charlie ready for bed, she revealed her DVD selection: *Bridesmaids,* which he'd somehow missed when it was on at the cinema.

"Phew. I can't believe you let me think it was *The Sound of Music*," he said, giving her a dark look.

"Careful, you're talking about one of my favorite movies. I might just bring it over and make you watch it next time."

"For you, I might just watch it. All three hours."

"It's not three hours. It's 174 minutes. Perfectly reasonable."

Her face was serious, but she was laughing at him with her eyes.

He resisted the urge to kiss her for the third time that night and occupied himself with settling Charlie on the couch. Not unexpectedly, his too-charming son was asleep after half an hour and Angie paused the DVD while he carried Charlie to bed. Angie had kicked off her shoes when he returned. He settled himself in the corner of the modular suite and patted the couch beside him. She came willingly, stretching out so that her head was in his lap, her body curled out at a right angle. He rested his hand on the nape of her neck and listened to her laugh, enjoying her enjoyment. He was too distracted by the weight of her head on his thigh and the length of her bare legs to pay close attention to the movie, and after a while he gave up the pretense and slid his hand beneath the neckline of her dress.

She stilled for a beat, then stirred, pressing her breast into his hand before lifting her gaze to give him a look as old as Eve. He smiled faintly and found her nipple with his thumb, teasing it to hardness. She moved restlessly, her gaze locked with his. He continued to stroke and tease her, gliding his hand from one breast to the other and back again until she pulled away from him and rolled onto her knees.

She crawled toward him, sinuous as a jungle cat, sliding one long leg across his body so that she was straddling his lap. They kissed, the movie playing in the background. He slid his hands beneath her skirt, smoothing them up her widespread thighs. She gave a giveaway shudder as he reached her panties. He found damp silk and heat and he stroked her with both thumbs, loving the little hitch in her breathing when he found a really good spot. He was painfully hard but he was enjoying himself too much to rush things. Stroking her tongue with his, he slipped a finger beneath the elastic of her underwear. He got even harder when he felt how wet and ready she was. He stroked her, finding the hard pearl of her clitoris and circling it lazily.

Her hand clenched into his shirt, her grip strong, demanding. She broke their kiss, her tongue tracing a path to his ear.

"Come on," she whispered. "Time to hit the study."

She slid from his grasp, standing and offering him her hand to help him to his feet. He stood and she started to lead him toward the study, the site of the bulk of their sexual encounters to date. Apart from that time in the kitchen and on the couch when the kids were in day care and at school, they had been careful to always make sure there was a locked door between them and his sleeping children. That door had never led to his bedroom, however, something he and Angie had never directly addressed. He knew without asking that she understood. He also knew that she would never push, because not once in their relationship had she asked for anything for herself.

He'd always been grateful for her generosity and understanding, but tonight for some reason it felt wrong to lay her down on the Turkish rug in his office and make love to her.

She deserved better. She deserved to not be some dirty little secret that he corralled off into his study, as though by doing so he could corral his feelings and lessen the importance of what they were doing. It was just sex when it was on the study floor.

Tonight, it didn't feel like just sex. It never really had, but he'd allowed himself to believe that because it had made it easier for him to reconcile himself to his own desires and needs.

He dug his heels in as Angie led him up the hallway toward the study. She glanced at him over her shoulder, a question in her eyes.

"Let's go to the bedroom," he said.

She went very still. "Are you sure?"

"Yes."

"Okay." The smile she gave him was a little tremulous. "Okay."

Without another word, he turned around. He led her now, through the kitchen and into the hall that led to the master suite. He entered the room, crossing to the bedside table to flick on the lamp. The curtains were open, and he crossed to the window and pulled them closed.

When he turned, Angie was standing beside the bed, an unreadable expression on her face. After a second she raised her gaze to his.

"It's stupid, but it suddenly feels more real, being in here."

It did. Very real. As though what was happening between him and Angie was important, and not just some itch they were both scratching or an extension of their friendship.

"It's just a bed," he said.

It was true, but it was also more than that. Angie nodded, then her hands went to the tie on her belt. They were shaking, and all of a sudden his own feelings weren't nearly as important as hers.

He crossed to her side, took her hands in his. She looked up into his face and he kissed her. After a few seconds her hands stopped trembling. Not breaking their kiss, he reached for her belt and started undressing her.

ANGIE LAY IN THE DARKNESS, her head pillowed on Michael's shoulder. She was almost certain he was asleep. Her mind was too busy to allow her to rest, however, going over and over what had happened tonight.

First there had been the way he looked at her in the kitchen, kissing her hand and telling her he was glad she was here. Then he'd encouraged her to put her head on his lap and rested his hand on the nape of her neck.

Then, instead of taking her to the study to make love, he'd led her in here. Into his bedroom. The room he'd shared with Billie.

He'd made love to her with passionate intensity, the need he stirred within her quickly pushing all other considerations aside. They were back now, though. With a vengeance.

How many times had she sat on this bed and watched Billie try on clothes or put on makeup? Too many to count. The walk-in wardrobe on the far wall had once held Billie's clothes. The vanity in the ensuite had once been cluttered with her perfumes and face creams and makeup. The chest of drawers had once played host to her jewelry box, a messy, crammed wooden chest overflowing with necklaces and bracelets and earrings.

Sometimes, it was very hard to remember that she wasn't stealing anything from Billie by being with Michael. That it wasn't a case of either/or. Billie was gone.

A single tear slid down Angie's cheek and onto the pillow. It would have all been so much easier if she and Michael had never connected, if he'd gone on being Billie's sad, widowed husband and she'd continued to be Billie's best friend. But that wasn't the way it had worked out.

Michael shifted beside her, his legs brushing hers. She turned her head to contemplate his profile in the dark. He was such a lovely man. A wonderful lover—passionate and patient and playful. A wonderful father, too. And a good friend. Having him fill so many of the empty corners of her life in the past few weeks had been…special.

She backed away from her own thoughts. This was all complicated enough without her getting carried away. No matter what happened when she and Michael were naked, no matter how many times they laughed and talked and shared their lives, it didn't change the fact that he was still in love with his dead wife. Only a very foolish woman would allow herself to turn great sex and companionship into a hope for more. And she'd always prided herself on a being a smart cookie. Most of the time.

Her gaze slid to the clock on the bedside table. It was late. She needed to get dressed and go home.

She eased her head off Michael's shoulder and shifted to the edge of the bed. She found her dress and

was searching for her panties when the bedside lamp
clicked on.

Michael propped himself up on one elbow, his eyes
squinted against the light. "You going?"

"Yeah."

She reached for her bra, aware that a very stupid part
of her brain was waiting for him to suggest she stay.

Wasn't it enough that he'd invited her into his bed tonight? Or was that what was making her greedy all of a
sudden? That and the way he'd kissed her hand earlier?

"You up to much tomorrow?" he asked as she slipped
her bra on and did up the back clasp.

"A friend has a show opening at a gallery in Flinders
Lane. I said I'd go along and hold his hand. What about
you?"

"The usual. Eva wants to practice riding her bike.
Charlie will no doubt attempt to defy death yet again."

She smiled before pulling her dress over her head.
Her shoes were out by the couch, along with her handbag and everything else.

"That's me, I think." Michael threw back the covers
but she held up a hand.

"You don't need to show me out. I know the way."

Michael gave her an admonishing look. "I'll see you
out."

He pulled his boxer-briefs on and she was aware of
him walking behind her as she collected her shoes and
bag and made her way to the front door.

"I had a nice night," she said.

"Yeah. So did I."

"You should watch the rest of the movie tomorrow.
It's really funny."

"It doesn't need to go back to the shop?"

"It's my copy."

"Wow. Up there with *The Sound of Music*. Impressive."

She punched him lightly on the biceps. "Funny guy."

He caught her hand and used it to pull her closer. They kissed, a deep, wet, languorous meeting of mouths that made her want to peel her clothes off all over again.

After a few minutes she pulled back. "I'll see you Monday, okay?"

"Okay."

He looked incredibly good standing there in the dim hallway, naked except for his boxer-briefs. She gave his body one last appreciative scan before stepping onto the front porch.

"See you."

She headed for her car, tossing her bag onto the passenger seat. She glanced across at the house before she pulled away from the curb. Sure enough, Michael was still standing in the doorway, making sure she got away okay. She raised her hand, not sure if he could see it in the dark, then pulled away from the house.

Twenty-five minutes later she was letting herself into her own apartment. For a moment she simply stood there, feeling oddly disoriented, as though she'd let herself into the wrong apartment or someone had come and moved her things around while she was out.

Or that she was simply in the wrong place, full stop.

She shook herself and the feeling passed as quickly as it came. Still, she read a few pages of a book to settle herself before turning off the light.

THE NEXT DAY SHE WALKED down to Brunswick Street and had breakfast at Babka Bakery, reading over the morning paper while stuffing herself with blintzes and coffee. Three times she caught herself reaching for her phone to call Michael to pass on some silly tidbit she'd read in the paper.

She'd left his bed barely ten hours ago. He didn't need to hear from her again. And she didn't need to get into the habit of telling him every little thing, either.

Her friend's opening was busy, thronging with arty types in severe black. Angie held her friend's hand until she was confident he could swim just fine on his own, then she slipped away and went home. She spent the night on the couch watching a documentary she'd recorded, pretending like crazy that she wasn't lonely for the sound of Eva's stomping feet and Charlie's beseeching demands and Michael's serious gray-green eyes.

She also told herself that she didn't deliberately wake up early the next morning so she could spend more time with him before he had to go to work. It was just a happy coincidence that she happened to be getting out of her car and walking up his driveway when he still had a full hour before he had to hit the road.

He answered the door before she could knock, wearing nothing but his suit trousers. His hair was damp from the shower and his aftershave was fresh on, surrounding her in a heady cloud of spicy masculinity.

"Hey," he said.

"Hey yourself."

He smiled and she knew he knew she'd come early to see him and that he was glad she had.

"Eva and Charlie are still asleep," he said. "I need to get them up soon or we'll be late."

"Good plan."

His smile broadened into a grin. Without saying a

word, he turned and headed up the hallway. She followed him without question, and when she entered his bedroom, she let out a small, grateful sigh when he pounced on her, pushing her up against the wall as he kissed her with almost savage abandon.

"Miss me?" he asked in a gravelly rasp as he pulled her T-shirt up and tugged her bra down.

"Yes."

She gave a small moan as he bit her nipple gently before soothing it with his tongue. Her hand found his belly, sliding down the front of his trousers until she felt his erection beneath her hand.

"Daddy...?"

Angie's head banged against the wall as she jerked away from Michael, her hands instinctively yanking her T-shirt down even as her gaze found Eva in the doorway, one hand knuckling the sleep from her eyes.

Oh, bloody hell.

Michael stepped back from her, his face very pale. "Hey, sweetheart," he said, his voice a dry croak. "I didn't realize you were awake."

"I just woke up. Why were you kissing Auntie Angie's boobies like that?"

Embarrassed heat rocketed up her chest and into her face. Michael was red, too, but he didn't take his gaze off his daughter.

"Auntie Angie and I were just having a cuddle," he said lamely.

Angie closed her eyes for a long beat. Why hadn't she closed the door? Better yet, why hadn't she just come at her usual time instead of giving in to impatience and racing to see Michael again?

"You mean you were sexing," Eva said knowingly.

Her eyes were big and questioning as she looked at Angie.

Angie had no idea how much Eva knew about the birds and the bees. Judging by the way she giggled whenever someone on TV kissed, she guessed not much. She had no idea what to say and she looked to Michael, not wanting to step on his toes.

"I guess that's one way of looking at it." Michael stepped forward and put his hand on Eva's shoulder. "Why don't we go out into the kitchen so we can talk about this?"

For a moment Angie thought Eva was going to protest, but she simply gave Angie one last, wide-eyed look before allowing Michael to lead her from the room.

CHAPTER FOURTEEN

ANGIE PRESSED HER HANDS to her face, utterly appalled.

Of all the ways for Eva to discover what was going between her and Michael…

She felt a little sick. More than a little, actually, when she thought of what Eva must have seen when she walked through the door. She stooped and collected her bag. She walked to the doorway, then realized that she couldn't exit that way without walking into the middle of what promised to be a complex father-daughter conversation.

She'd use the sliding door and cross the yard to the studio. Like a big old chicken.

She hovered, disliking the feeling that she was abandoning Michael to face the music. It wasn't like she was a stranger to his children, after all. Although there was no telling how Eva would handle the notion that her father might be interested in "sexing" with a woman other than her mother.

Voices echoed up the hallway from the kitchen as she hesitated. Eva's high tones, followed by Michael's deeper voice.

"You don't need to explain about sexing to me. Greta told me all about it. If you're sexing with Auntie Angie, does that mean she's going to be my new mummy?"

Angie closed her eyes. Poor Michael. Talk about a hairy question.

"No one is ever going to replace mummy, sweetheart." Michael's words echoed up the hallway, clear as a bell.

Angie swallowed. Then, before she could hear anything else, she crossed to the sliding door and let herself out onto the deck. She slid the door shut behind her and simply stood there, hands pressed against the cool glass.

She hadn't heard anything she didn't know already. Of course Michael still loved Billie. Of course he wasn't looking for someone to replace her.

None of it was new—except for the fact that she'd just realized that somehow, while she'd been looking the other way, she'd fallen in love with Michael.

Ironic that it had taken hearing him declare his continuing devotion for Billie to make her face the truth.

Feeling more than a little dazed and decidedly fragile, she made her way across the deck to the studio. She fumbled with her keys, then opened the door and stepped inside. She didn't bother turning on the lights, she simply went and sat on the chair at her workbench, her handbag pressed to her belly.

How had it happened? She'd gone in with both eyes open. She'd known from the get-go that he was never going to be emotionally available in that way. And yet she'd gone and fallen in love with him anyway.

All the breath left her body in rush. She felt so stupid. Really idiotic. She'd set herself up for hurt, big-time. And now it was heading her way like a Mack truck on a downhill run.

She didn't bother hoping. There was no point telling herself fairy tales. For the past year and more she'd watched Michael mourn Billie. He loved her with every fibre of his being. It was as incontrovertible and uncontestable as gravity. She'd always known it, she'd slept with him knowing it. She'd told herself that it didn't matter—and up until a few minutes ago she'd honestly believed it.

But somehow, in between the dinners and the days out at the beach and the bedtime stories and the laughter and the sex, she'd lost sight of the fact that Michael still belonged to Billie. She'd been lulled by his ready affection and the obvious pleasure he took in her company and her body. She'd always loved his children, but she'd allowed herself to sink into his family, to invest in them in a way she never had before.

That was why her apartment felt empty and foreign. That was why she'd rushed over here this morning, and why her heart gave a little kick whenever she saw him. Not because of the great sex, but because she loved him. Because he made her happy. Because she wanted his happiness more than anything in the world.

Footsteps sounded on the deck. Her gaze found the door as Michael appeared. He'd pulled on a shirt, but his feet were still bare. So typical of him.

"Is she okay?"

"A little confused. Which is hardly surprising."

"No."

"She asked me a few questions, but she seemed satisfied when I explained to her that sometimes adult friends like to cuddle and kiss when they really like each other."

She nodded, imagining how difficult that conversation must have been for him. "I'm really sorry."

He raised his eyebrows. "Why? It wasn't your fault."

"I should have shut the door."

"*I* should have shut the door." He shrugged. "It happened. I'm not wild about it, but it's not the end of the world. Eva's a smart kid. If she has any questions, she'll ask me. We'll work it out."

She stared at him. He was being so reasonable. So human and understanding and real. It was one of the many reasons she loved him.

For a moment, the knowledge that this special, lovely man would never, ever feel the same way about her was a physical pain in her chest. She blinked rapidly, swallowing the confession that was suddenly crowding her throat.

The last thing he needed was to know that she'd fallen in love with him. The very last. He had more than enough on his plate without having to take on responsibility for her pain. Which was exactly what he would do, because he was that kind of man.

The kind who worried about whether his friend was safe when she went to work in her crappy, run-down building. Who dropped everything to help the same friend clean up when she was overwhelmed by the bad luck that had come her way, and who never took her for granted or assumed anything where she was concerned.

She took a deep breath and tightened her grip on her bag. Then she took the plunge and did what needed to be done.

"Maybe it was a blessing in disguise. Things have been pretty crazy lately."

A faint wrinkle appeared between Michael's eyebrows. "Have they?"

"You know they have." She smiled, hoping she didn't look as anxious and close to tears as she felt. "And we always agreed that this would only last as long as it felt okay for both of us."

His head shifted, as though he wasn't sure if he'd heard her correctly. "Does that mean it's not feeling okay for you anymore?"

"I think it might be a good idea if we pulled back a bit. Took a bit of a break."

"Right."

He was confused. Why wouldn't he be? Not twenty minutes ago she'd been panting and hot for him, her hand down the front of his pants.

"Is this because of Eva?"

"No. We both know what this is, Michael. I don't want to lose sight of that. You're not looking for anything permanent. And I don't want to start believing in something that's never going to happen."

It was the truth, or part of it, anyway. It was enough to shock him. She could see it in his eyes—he'd never considered that she might fall in love with him. That was how wrapped up in Billie he still was.

Proof, if she'd needed it, that she was doing exactly the right thing.

"You know I care for you, Angie."

"I know. But you love Billie, which is exactly as it should be. She was incredibly lovable. Hell, if I'd been a man I would have given you a run for your money." Somehow, she forced a light little laugh out her mouth. "I'm just drawing a line before things get muddy, that's all."

If only that were true. If only she'd been smart enough to be that on top of her own feelings.

"I guess that's probably wise." He was frowning again and he shoved his hands into his trouser pockets.

"Yeah. I think it is," she said softly.

She stood and closed the distance between them. She set her hands on his shoulders, letting her fingers press into the warm, solid strength of him one last time. She closed her eyes and pressed a kiss to his lips, lingering longer than was wise, unable to stop herself from savoring one last moment of intimacy. He kissed her back, but when his hands came up to frame her hips she opened her eyes and stepped backward.

"I had a lot of fun," she said. "I'll never forget it."

The words almost choked her, but she said them. She even sounded convincing, miracle of miracles. Michael seemed convinced, anyway, because his face was suddenly shuttered.

"Yeah. Me, too."

She moved back to her chair, willing him to leave now that she'd set him free. As though he'd picked up on her silent signal, he glanced at his watch.

"I need to get the kids off."

"I know. I'll see you later."

She managed to stop her chin from wobbling until he'd disappeared through the door. Once he was gone, she set her jaw and took a deep breath, blinking rapidly.

*No tears. If he comes back and sees you crying...
No tears.*

Despite her stern self-talk, her eyes flooded. She made a disgusted noise and shot to her feet, crossing to her table and chairs. She snatched up her notepad and pen and sat and started composing a list of things she needed to do.

First up, she had to find a new studio, because she could not function if she had to come here every day and keep seeing Michael and the kids. She loved them all like crazy, but no way was she that big a masochist. Sitting on the outside looking in at something she wanted so badly would be pure torture.

So, a new studio. Which meant she needed to find a solution to Michael's child-care problem. She knew him well enough to know that if she moved workshops he wouldn't allow her to continue picking Eva up from school.

She would ask around her friends who had kids, see if they could recommend anyone. Even though it would kill her to reduce her contact with Charlie and Eva.

Although who knew how Eva was feeling toward her now that she'd caught Angie "sexing" with her father. She added a new note to her list: *talk to Eva*. Because she needed things to be okay with her goddaughter.

She was all out of things to do—except for the big one, of course.

Get over Michael. She laughed as her pen formed the words, the sound more of a hiccup than anything else.

She wasn't stupid, despite all signs to the contrary. It was going to take her a long time to stop loving Michael. There wasn't a corner of her world he hadn't touched. Stepping back from him was going to leave a big hole in her life.

She breathed through her nose. She needed to get through this as efficiently as possible. Just get it done.

She used the back of her hand to wipe away the few tears that had made it down her cheek. Then she pulled out her phone and started ringing real estate agents.

MICHAEL HAD TO WORK hard to keep his mind on the road and on his daughter's chatter as he drove her to school. He couldn't stop thinking about what had happened with Angie.

She'd ended things with him. What had she called it? *Drawing a line before things got muddy.*

"Daddy, stop. You drove past the school."

Michael braked and signaled to pull over. "Sorry, sweetheart."

"It's okay. I can walk from here."

She leaned across for his kiss and he bussed her cheek and gave her a one-armed hug.

"Have a good day, okay?"

"I will." Eva slid out of the car and shut the door. She turned to go, then just as quickly turned back and rapped on the window.

He hit the button to lower it. "What's up?"

"You know what we talked about this morning? About you and Auntie Angie?"

"Sure. What about it?" He braced himself for another difficult question.

"I wouldn't mind if it was her."

"Wouldn't mind what?"

"If she was my new mummy. Not that I would call her that, because Mummy is Mummy."

He looked into his daughter's earnest brown eyes and swallowed. "Yeah, I know."

"Auntie Angie is ace."

"Yeah. She's pretty cool."

"Okay. You think about it and get back to me," she said, stepping back from the car.

He couldn't help smiling at her take-charge attitude, but the smile quickly faded as he watched Eva disappear through the school gate and he pulled back out into traffic.

He'd done his best to explain what Eva had seen between him and Angie this morning, but he couldn't explain to her that Auntie Angie replacing Billie had never been on the agenda. He was nowhere near ready for that kind of commitment again. Not even close.

Which was why Angie had ended things between them this morning, because she didn't want to start believing in something that was never going to happen.

He remembered the way she'd said it, the way she'd laughed and told him that she knew he still loved Billie, that she understood. She'd always understood, right from the start. In the early days, she'd been the only one who knew how he felt, how empty life felt. She'd been the one to help him hold it together enough to look after the kids, and she'd been the one to kick him up the pants when he needed it. When he'd found himself viewing her as a woman and not a friend, she'd handled that, too, matching his honesty with her own.

She'd saved his ass. She'd kept him sane. She'd made love to him with abandon.

And now it was over.

She's still your friend. She's not going anywhere. You'll see her every day, she'll still stay for dinner and hang with you and the kids.

He knew it was true, but he also knew it was going to be next to impossible to stop viewing her as his lover and start seeing her as just a friend again. How was he supposed to look at her and not remember how she looked beneath him, her blue eyes cloudy with passion? How was he supposed to smell her perfume and not think of the soft, silky spot just beneath her ear? How was he supposed to hear her voice and not remember the things she said when he was inside her?

It wasn't possible. He couldn't just forget those things about her. They were etched in his mind, indelible. Better yet, he didn't want to.

And there's the crux of it, you selfish bastard. You want more, but you've got nothing to offer, and she knows it. And yet you still want it anyway.

It was a sobering realization, and it took all the heat out of his reaction. What right did he have to ask or expect or want anything from Angie when he had so little to give her in return? Hell, he'd only been generous enough to allow her access to his bed *this weekend,* for Pete's sake.

Yeah, he was a real catch. Positively irresistible.

He had a sour taste in his mouth by the time he arrived at work. He'd been so busy contemplating his own navel and wallowing in his own misery for the past twelve months that he'd turned being self-focused into an art form.

He made a promise to himself as he collected his briefcase and suit jacket from the rear seat. No matter what happened, he would honor Angie's decision. He would do everything he could to ensure that their relationship went smoothly back to the way it was before. It was the least he owed her. The absolute least.

ANGIE WAITED AT THE school gate for Eva at three that afternoon, one hand nervously jiggling her keys. She'd had a big day, talking to no less than six real estate agents and even dashing into the city to look at a couple of potential studios. Neither were suitable, but she was confident something would come up.

It had to, because she couldn't go on living in Michael's pocket.

She spotted Eva's blond head amongst the mob of children heading for the gate and lifted her hand to catch her attention. Eva smiled her usual sunny, open smile and quickened her pace.

The thought of the conversation that lay ahead of her made Angie feel sticky with nervous sweat, but it had to happen. After all, she was the grown-up in this situation, and she was also the closest thing Eva had to a female role model. She needed to get this right.

"Hey, Auntie Angie," Eva said. She slid her arm around Angie's waist and gave her a hug, business as usual.

Maybe this wasn't going to be as awkward as she imagined.

"Hey, sweetie. How was school?" she asked as they walked back to her car.

"Okay. Same old, same old."

Angie smiled, wondering where she'd picked up the new saying. "School can be like that sometimes."

They had reached her SUV and she opened the door for Eva before walking around to the driver's side. She slid into the seat and put the keys in the engine, but she didn't start the car. She'd planned to wait until they were home before they talked, but suddenly she just wanted it done.

Bracing herself, she turned to face her goddaughter.

"Eva, I wanted to talk about this morning. If that's okay with you."

Eva shrugged. "Sure. Why not?"

"Okay. First I wanted to check that you didn't have any questions. Anything you wanted to ask me or anything…?"

Eva's brow wrinkled as she thought for a minute.

Then she shook her head, ponytail swinging. "Nope. Don't think so."

"Okay." Angie paused, not sure where to go next. Eva seemed completely relaxed about what she'd seen. Which was good. She hoped.

"Actually, I do have a question. Do you like my daddy?"

"Of course I do."

"Do you like like him or *really* like him?"

Dear God. How to answer that?

"I think he's really, really nice. And I like him a lot."

"That's good. Because I told him this morning that I wouldn't mind if you were my new mummy. Not that I would call you *Mummy,* because you're my auntie. Sort of. And Mummy was Mummy. But you know what I mean."

Angie blinked, utterly blindsided. For long seconds she didn't know what to say. Then she realized Eva was watching her, waiting for her response.

"I do know what you mean. And I love being your auntie. It's one of my most favorite things in all the world."

She couldn't say any more. She was too busy trying not to cry.

"Don't be sad, Auntie Angie," Eva said, her face creased with concern.

"I'm not, sweetie. I'm really touched that you feel that way. I love you very much."

She leaned across and kissed Eva, pressing her cheek against the little girl's.

"So if Daddy asks, you wouldn't mind?"

Angie released her and sat back. As touched as she was by Eva's declaration and much as it made her heart ache, there was no way she could let this childish fantasy stand.

"Your daddy and I are just friends, sweetie. I don't think you should get too excited about him asking me anything like that."

"But he really likes you," Eva said stubbornly.

"And I really like him. But sometimes that's not enough."

Eva thought about it for a few seconds. "Sometimes I don't get adults."

Angie couldn't help but smile. "Yeah. Me, either."

She drove home, and when Eva ran off to change, she slipped out to the studio and pretended to be busy tidying her workbench to hide the fact that she was crying.

She'd never allowed herself to dream of being Eva's mother, just as she'd never allowed herself to dream of having a real relationship with Michael. Hearing those words from her goddaughter's mouth had been bittersweet and beautiful and incredibly painful.

After a few minutes, she mopped up her face and went inside to spend time with Eva. If things went to plan, these after-school hours would be a thing of the past, which only made what time she had all the more precious.

MICHAEL'S NEW RESOLVE to respect Angie's boundaries was tested after only two days. He came home from work on Wednesday to find dinner cooked and Angie helping Eva with her reading. Charlie wandered over to charm a hug out of Angie and Michael watched his son enjoy her embrace with envy in his heart.

Which went to show exactly how selfish he was.

"Let me guess—chicken casserole?" he said, trying to keep things light.

"Got it in one," Angie said with the same small, slightly distant smile she'd been offering him for the past two days.

"Have I got time to change?"

"Sure."

"Great."

He yanked his tie off as he walked to his bedroom. He threw his jacket on the bed, then followed it with his shirt and trousers.

How long would it be like this between them? Polite and cautious and wary? He didn't like it. He didn't like being jealous of his children because they were the recipients of her easy affection, and he really didn't like lying awake at night, his body on fire for hers.

He kicked off his shoes, pulled on his jeans and a T-shirt and returned to the kitchen. Eva was busy setting the table while Angie pulled the casserole from the oven.

"I had some good news today," she said, glancing up briefly as she eased the dish onto the counter. "A real estate agent called with a lead on a studio space in Collingwood. I went and checked it out this afternoon and I think it's going to work."

Everything in him went still. "I didn't realize you were looking for another studio space."

"I never really stopped. At least, I still had some feelers out. And this place came up and it seems perfect...." She was busy with the casserole, very careful to avoid eye contact now.

"I thought you were pretty settled here." He could hear the sulkiness in his own voice. The disappointment.

He didn't want her to move on. He liked coming home to her, even if it was an artificial construct.

"I know it's going to mess up things with Eva, but I was talking to my friend Tess and she recommended a retired teacher who her sister used for a while. Apparently she's really terrific, great with kids…. I don't know what her availability is but I got her number for you."

She looked at him then, and there was something in her eyes that made his gut clench. Something dark and painful and hurt. Then she blinked and it was gone and she was just Angie, endlessly kind and generous and helpful.

"Thanks," he said. "I'll give her a call."

"I won't do anything until you've got something sorted. I won't leave you in the lurch."

Won't you?

He almost said it out loud. Only the knowledge of how self-serving it would be stopped him. She'd put her whole life on hold for him and the kids. He had no right to expect more from her.

He shot a look toward Eva, checking to see if she was listening. She'd drifted over to watch the television, apparently oblivious to the conversation that was taking place in the kitchen.

"If this is because of us, I'm not going to put any pressure on you, Angie. I mean, if that's why you're leaving."

"I know that. I need to be closer to my suppliers, that's all. It's been great being here, but there are things I need that I can't get out here…."

It was the first he'd heard of it, but he wasn't going to argue with her. He'd just told her he wasn't going to pressure her, and he figured haranguing her about her decision came under that heading.

Eva provided the soundtrack to their dinner, chattering away about her day at school. Angie was silent, pushing her food around her plate. Michael chewed and swallowed, not tasting anything. He felt angry and baffled and shut out and he knew there was nothing he could do about it. They had agreed that their friendship was the important thing. Angie was doing what needed to be done to preserve it. He should be thanking her, not resenting her.

"I'll do that," he said when she started clearing the table.

She glanced at him and he slid the plates from her hands. "Thanks."

"I'm the one who should be thanking you," he said gruffly.

She shrugged off his thanks. "It's no big deal. I have to eat, too."

Except she'd hardly eaten a thing.

He dumped the dishes in the sink, watching as Angie collected her things.

"I've got some errands to run, so I probably won't see you tomorrow morning, okay?" she said.

"Sure."

She kissed the kids goodbye and waved to him from the doorway. Then she was gone.

Michael looked down at the mess in the sink. He wanted to go after her so badly it hurt.

Because he wasn't confident he could control the impulse, he went out onto the deck instead, breathing in the cool twilight air. Cicadas sang, their song sharp on his ears, and he stared at the studio and tried to get used to the idea that soon it would be empty again.

God, he didn't want her to go.

"Daddy, I think I did something bad today."

He turned to find Eva in the doorway, an uncertain look on her face.

"Did something happen at school?"

"No. It was after school, with Auntie Angie. I told her how I told you it was okay with me if she was my mummy but still my auntie. She said she was really touched but that you really liking her wasn't enough. And then when we got home, I went to change and Auntie Angie came out to her studio and cried." Eva paused for breath. "She doesn't know I saw her, and I didn't say anything because I could tell she didn't want anyone to know. But now I'm worried I made her cry."

Michael's chest was suddenly very tight. Angie had been crying. Over him. Over them.

He reached out and squeezed Eva's shoulder. "I'm sure you didn't make Angie upset. She's got a lot of stuff going on right now."

Eva looked doubtful. "I hope so."

"Trust me, you didn't make Auntie Angie cry."

No, he'd done that, because he'd been a blind idiot. He gave his daughter's shoulder a final squeeze, his mind racing furiously.

"Listen. I'm going to pop next door to see if Mrs. Linton would mind keeping an eye on you two for an hour or so, okay? Then I'm going to go see Auntie Angie and make sure she's all right. How does that sound?"

Eva brightened. "That sounds good."

They went back inside and he made sure Charlie was safely ensconced in front of the TV before leaving the house and starting down the driveway. He had no idea if his neighbors were home or if Mrs. Linton was available, but he hoped like hell she was because he needed to talk to Angie. Tonight. He needed to find out if what he was thinking was right. Because if it was—

He stopped in his tracks as he registered something that shouldn't be there: the dark green shape of Angie's SUV, still parked out the front of his house. He frowned, momentarily confused. Then he realized that Angie was sitting in the driver's seat, her head bowed.

The tight feeling in his chest got even tighter. He strode toward her car, a sort of hopeless fury building inside him. She'd huddled in her studio crying this afternoon, and now she'd left his house and was sitting in her car, looking lost and broken...

He couldn't stand it. Couldn't stand the fact that she'd hidden her pain from him. Most of all he couldn't stand the fact that he was the one who had hurt her.

He reached the car and curled his fingers around the door handle and pulled it open. Angie started, a four-letter word hissing between her teeth as she pressed a hand to her sternum.

"Michael..." Her face was shiny with tears, her eyes still swimming.

"What's going on, Angie?"

ANGIE STARED AT MICHAEL'S face. He looked pale in the moonlight, his features stony.

"Nothing's wrong," she said feebly.

He leaned forward, one arm braced on the roof of the car, the other on the open car door.

"Then why are you sitting out here crying?"

She didn't know what to say, so she simply stared at him.

"Eva told me what she said to you. She told me you were crying this afternoon, too."

Angie frowned. She'd been so careful to dry her tears. She'd even checked her reflection in the hand mirror in her purse.

"Tell me the truth, Angie. Is this because of me? Because of us?"

She couldn't hold his eyes and lie to him, so she looked away.

"No."

"Liar."

She pressed her lips together.

"Is that why you're moving your studio, too?"

He sounded so angry. Accusing, almost. As though she'd withheld some vital secret from him that he'd been entitled to know. She didn't like the fact that he was looming over her, either, so she got out of the car, forcing him to take a step back.

"What do you want to hear, Michael? What do you want me to say?"

"I want the truth. Not some sanitized half truth."

She was starting to get angry now, too. She didn't understand why he was out here acting all righteous and holier-than-thou. She'd tried to do him a favor, let him off the hook. He had no right to stand there looking *aggrieved,* for Pete's sake.

"Fine. You want the truth? You got it. I am in love with you. Probably have been for a while. Which just goes to show how bloody stupid I am. That honest enough for you?"

Despite the fact that he must have guessed how she felt, he rocked back on his heels a little. "You should have said something."

"Why? So you could let me down easily? I know the score, Michael. I loved Billie, too, remember."

"This isn't about Billie. This is about you and me."

That really got her goat. "Bullshit. It's not about Billie. She's been the third person in this relationship from day one. If you can even call it a relationship."

"You think I'd be out here if it was just a roll in the hay? If you weren't important to me?"

Suddenly all the fight went out of her. She pressed her palm against her forehead, searching for calm.

"I don't know what you want from me," she said quietly. "I was just trying to put things back the way they were."

"I don't think that's possible. Do you?"

His words made tears burn at the backs of her eyes again.

"That's why I didn't want to tell you."

It was all ruined now. Their friendship. Her time with the children. Nothing would ever be the same now that he knew. He'd feel sorry for her. Wouldn't know how to talk to her, whether she'd take things the wrong way...

"Angie. Don't cry."

She choked out a laugh. "It's a little too late for that."

"Come here."

He pulled her into his arms. She tried to push him off but he wouldn't let go and after a few seconds she gave in and let him comfort her.

He smelled so good, and she loved him so much. She pressed her face against his chest and sobbed, her fingers digging into the muscles of his shoulders.

"Angie. It's okay," he said, his arms tightening around her.

It wasn't, and she knew it, and so did he.

"I didn't do it on purpose," she said, her words muffled by his T-shirt. "I swear to you, I didn't. I loved Billie as much as you and the last thing I wanted was this. But it happened and I couldn't stop it."

"I know."

She felt him press a kiss to her temple—such a simple gesture, and such a perfect illustration of who he was as a man and why she loved him.

He was so loyal and kind and loving. It was why he still loved Billie, why he would never love her. She slid her hands from his shoulders and pulled away from him. He let her go, but she could feel his reluctance.

"You can't help me get over this, Michael. You know that, right?"

He took a moment to answer. "Yes."

The final nail in the coffin. She accepted the pain of it. Owned it.

"I need to go now. And you need to let me go."

He didn't move. She reached out and laid her palm against his chest. She could feel his heart beating, sure and strong. She looked him dead in the eye.

"I love you." It was the first and last time she would ever let herself say it. "Now let me go."

He still didn't move and she pushed him away, forcing him back a step.

"Come inside and talk," he said.

She shook her head. "No. There's nothing to say."

His gaze held hers and she could see how much he hurt for her, how much he regretted her pain and that he was the cause of it.

"It's okay, Michael. I'm a big girl. I can handle it."

She got into the car and started the engine, then reached for the door handle. He was blocking the door, and she looked at him, not saying a word. After a long beat he stepped out of the way and she pulled the door shut. She waited until he'd taken another step back before she pulled away from the curb.

She told herself not to, but she couldn't stop herself from looking in the rearview mirror. Michael was standing very still in the middle of the road, watching her drive away.

He faded into the distance, finally disappearing. She blinked away a fresh flood of tears.

It was all over. Now all that was left was the salvage operation. One day, they might be able to be friends again. She hoped so, because he'd been a wonderful friend.

But he was going to take some getting over first.

CHAPTER FIFTEEN

MICHAEL WENT INTO THE house. Charlie and Eva were watching TV, so he sat beside them and stared at the screen.

He had no idea what was on, but at a certain point he registered it was past eight and he hustled them both into the bath and into their pajamas and finally into bed.

He walked through the house, switching off lights, then made his way to his own bedroom. He lay on the bed staring at the ceiling, going over and over what had happened in the street, feeling the weight of Angie's head against his chest again, hearing her words.

I love you. Now let me go.

There had been a time not so long ago when he'd thought he was the luckiest man alive. He'd had a wife he adored, two great children, a career he loved. And then the heart had been cut out of his dream and for a while he'd been lost.

He'd found himself again, after a time in the wilderness. With Angie's help, he'd learned how to live again. But he hadn't been prepared to fully commit—to throw himself fully into the hurly burly and risk of life, with all its dangers and pleasures and perils—and his reticence had wounded Angie.

He fell asleep at some point. He woke with an ache in

his chest. A tightness that didn't go away even when he rubbed the heel of his hand against his sternum.

Under any other circumstances, he'd be dialing emergency services, but he knew the ache was not medical in origin. The ache was about Angie, a physiological expression of his regret for hurting her.

She was a wonderful woman. Creative and generous and smart and loving. She'd given him everything of herself. Her time. Her energy. Her empathy and sympathy. Her love. And he'd given her a broken heart.

He rolled onto his side and stared at the empty pillow beside him. He'd never had the chance to wake up with Angie in his bed. To share a morning talking and laughing and making love before slipping into a leisurely day. Everything they'd had had been hurried and furtive, shoehorned into whatever time or place had been available. He'd shortchanged her on every score—and she deserved the world.

"I'm sorry."

The words sounded woefully inadequate in the quiet of his bedroom. He hadn't said them to Angie last night. He'd said everything but, then he'd let her drive away.

He glanced toward the phone on the bedside table, wondering if she would be up yet, wanting to call to make sure she was okay.

A stupid idea if ever he'd heard one. What was he going to say to her, after all? *Hey. Still feeling crap because I'm a selfish, dead-inside bastard?*

Yeah. That would be really helpful.

Instead he showered and got the kids out of bed. He drove Eva to school and came home and settled Charlie with his building blocks. Angie's car hadn't been out front when he returned, but he walked to the French doors and glanced at the studio in case. It was locked tight, the windows dim. Pretty much what he'd expected, even though it made the ache in his chest intensify.

He rested his forehead against the cool glass of the French doors. He hated this. Hated knowing she was hurting, and that he was the cause, and that he could do nothing about it.

Except stay away from her, of course.

The day ground by. Every time the phone rang he hoped it was Angie, even though he knew it wouldn't be. Not today. Yet when the doorbell rang after lunch, his heart still gave a ridiculous, hopeful lurch. Maybe she'd had to come over. Maybe she needed something from her studio.

It was a courier, delivering some blueprints from the practice. He dropped them on the dining-room table and stood staring at the floor.

How long was it going to be like this? How long before he could see her and talk to her again?

It's never going to be the same, idiot. Even if you can go back to being friends, it will never be the same. You'll both know that the other thing happened. Every look or touch or phrase will be loaded. Time to face facts. You've lost her, and you'll never get her back. Not the way you want her.

The thought made him so angry he kicked one of the dining-room chairs, sending it skidding across the floor with a screech of wood on wood. He pinched the bridge of his nose in the thick silence afterward, aware that he was behaving like a spoiled child who'd had his favorite toy taken away.

More than a little lost, he retreated to his study, rubbing his sternum every step of the way. The phone num-

ber Angie had left him for the after-school carer lay to
one side of his desk. He picked the piece of paper up,
one thumb plucking at the corner. Then he reached for
the phone. Angie had said she wouldn't move until he'd
made alternative arrangements for Eva. Sorting something out ASAP was the bare minimum he could do.

IT HAD BEEN A LONG TIME since Angie had spent the day
in bed. She wasn't a moper, generally speaking, but after
last night's confession and resulting scene with Michael,
she didn't feel up to facing the day. So she didn't. She
ate toast in bed, then reread a favorite book, taking comfort from a story where she knew the outcome would be
good and just and right. She showered after lunch and
put on fresh pajamas and crawled back into bed to doze.
Michael haunted her thoughts throughout, slipping into
her mind despite her best efforts to block him out. His
body. The way he kissed her. The way he touched her.
The smell of his hair. The texture of his skin. The tim-
bre of his voice.

When she wasn't thinking about him she thought
about Eva and Charlie and how much she was going to
miss them. By midafternoon she'd worked up a good
head of misery and she gave in to the hot pressure behind
her eyes and pressed her face into her pillow and had
a good howl. She fell asleep with wet cheeks and woke
feeling thick-headed and sore-eyed. The bed felt like a
cop-out now more than a sanctuary, and she pulled on
workout gear and went for a brisk walk. When she got
back, she started making phone calls.

She spoke to the real estate agent, arranging to sign
papers for the new studio first thing the next day, then
she checked in with the removalist to see how quickly

he could accommodate her. If he wondered why she was moving again when she'd barely settled in to her new premises, he didn't say anything. Which was just as well, since she was pretty sure she wouldn't be able to provide even the most benign of excuses without getting emotional about it.

She took herself out for noodles at The Vegie Bar around the corner on Brunswick Street for dinner, then walked along the busy street, peering in at the displays in the many boutiques and jewelry stores. After she deemed she'd been out and about long enough, she went home and crawled into bed.

She dreamed of Michael, a sweet, beautiful dream where his arms were around her, his heart beating beneath her ear. She knew that he was hers and she was his, that everything was as it should be. Then she woke up to reality at three in the morning. Michael belonged to Billie. Always had, always would. Allowing herself to believe anything different was pure self-deception. She spent the rest of the night on the couch, curled beneath a rug while she stared at late-night television.

Her phone beeped with a text message the following morning as she was on the way to the real estate agent's offices. She saw Michael's name and her heart did a crazy, painful twist in her chest. She opened the message and read that he'd spoken to the woman her friend had recommended to look after Eva and Charlie. If their face-to-face meeting went well this afternoon, she was in a position to start the following week.

There was nothing more, but it was enough. This afternoon, in all likelihood, she would no longer be an integral part of Eva and Charlie and Michael's lives, and once she'd moved her studio to her new premises there would be no reason for them to see each other at all. Not that she intended to cut herself out of the children's lives. She wouldn't do that to them, even if she wanted to. But from now on she would simply be Auntie Angie again, a visitor.

Michael's confirmation came through later that afternoon, a brief text to let her know that he had Eva's child care sorted.

So. She was officially free to move. She took a deep breath and rang the removalist and booked in for the following Tuesday. Then she took herself window shopping again, just so she could be amongst the noise and energy of other people.

If Billie were alive, she wouldn't be so desperate for company that she was reduced to pretending to shop. If Billie were alive, she would be drunk on margaritas and Billie would be passing her tissues and coming up with painful punishments for the man who'd done her wrong.

But, of course, if Billie were alive, none of this would be happening. Angie would never have fallen in love with Michael. Her world would be whole instead of fractured and piecemeal.

Angie averted her gaze from her reflection in a shop window, not wanting to see the misery in her own eyes, and kept walking.

There wasn't much else to do, after all.

MRS. GRAFTON WAS FIFTY-FIVE, friendly and smart with a sense of humor. That she liked children was immediately obvious, and it took Michael all of five minutes to decide he would be comfortable leaving Eva with her. It took him a lot longer to text Angie to let her know she was off the hook for Eva's child care. He did it, though, and he got through the rest of the day, too, as well as the weekend.

He was late leaving for work on Monday and when he rushed out to the garage to warm up the car before loading up the kids he nearly plowed straight into Angie on the doorstep as she fished her keys from her handbag. She froze, her face a pale oval, her deep blue eyes darting to his face briefly before she looked away.

"Michael," she said.

She didn't sound or look happy to see him, but he was profoundly aware of the sudden rush of blood through his body as his heart began to pound away. He felt as though the sun was shining on his face for the first time in days, simply because she was standing in front him, because he could smell her perfume and hear her voice and breathe the same air as her. The urge to touch her, to reassure himself that she was real and warm and here, was almost overwhelming. He settled for tightening the grip on his briefcase and clearing his throat.

"Angie. How are you?"

He gave himself a mental kick for the question, but it was too late, he'd said it, and she was forcing a smile, pretending that everything was normal.

"I'm good, thanks. How about you and the kids?"

"We're all good."

They both fell silent. Angie didn't look at him again, her gaze instead fixed on the corner of the doormat. A small frown formed between her eyebrows, a faint, worried crease that told him more than words how hard this was for her.

The ever-present ache in his chest tightened its grip and he lifted a hand and rubbed the spot above his heart, a fast-growing habit that never seemed to have any effect.

"I guess you'll be packing today, with the removalists coming tomorrow," he said.

"Yes."

He nodded. For some reason he was having trouble swallowing and he cleared his throat again. "Well. I'd better get the car warmed up. Running a bit late."

"Yes."

She stepped aside so he could pass. He walked briskly to the garage, everything in him rejecting the stiff formality of their brief exchange. Was this what it was going to be like for the foreseeable future between them?

"Jesus," he muttered, rubbing his chest again.

Things only got worse. On Tuesday he came home to find Eva red-eyed from crying. He knew why—Angie had moved out today. He said all the right things to his daughter, assuring her that just because Auntie Angie was no longer in the studio didn't mean she wouldn't see her anymore. He knew without asking that Angie had delivered the same assurances, and that she would do her damnedest to honor her commitment to his children. None of it took the desolate, hurt look from Eva's eyes.

He waited until after dinner before he went out to inspect the studio. He went with a beer in hand and stood in the empty space, staring at the spot where Angie's workbench had once been.

He'd built this studio for Billie but in just a few short weeks Angie had made it her own. Now, whenever he glanced out the kitchen window and caught sight of the empty windows, he would think of her. Of how he'd hurt her and screwed everything up, and how he much he missed her.

Sick of himself, he returned to the house, locking the studio behind him. He put the kids to bed and went into the study and stared stupidly at plans for a house extension that he was supposed to be finessing. He couldn't stop thinking about Angie. About how empty his house felt without her, and how much he wanted to hear the sound of her voice and touch her soft skin and hold her close....

Everything felt wrong without her. Displaced. Over the last year and more, they had woven a life together, him and Angie and the kids. They had pulled together through their grief and they had come out the other side and found happiness again. Together. And he missed her. He needed her. He wanted her.

He loved her.

He sat back in his chair, stunned by the sudden moment of self-knowledge.

Of course he loved her. When she was around, the world was a better place. He loved her laugh, the way she smiled with her eyes, her slim, supple body, her generous heart, her boundless creativity...

He loved her. The only wonder was that it had taken him this long to recognize it.

A part of him wanted to deny it, to minimize the crime he'd committed against Billie's memory. But it didn't feel like a crime. It felt...real. And important. And precious.

No one knew better than he how valuable love was. How fleeting and priceless and vital. He hadn't set out to love Angie, just as she hadn't set out to love him, but it had happened and it was good and he wanted it. So badly.

He rubbed the heel of his hand against his chest,

knowing now what he needed to do. Understanding— finally—what the ache in his chest was about.

He went to bed, and the next morning he woke and went next door to beg a favor of Mrs Linton. She agreed readily, kind woman that she was, and he handed Charlie over into her care before dropping Eva at school.

He drove to the florist, the one that Billie had always favored, and bought a bright, colorful bouquet. Then he pointed the car east. The morning sun was harsh in his eyes by the time he parked and made his way along the driveway toward Billie's grave.

The lawn had been recently mowed and the smell of fresh-cut grass hung heavily in the air. He climbed the slope, his steps slowing as he approached the marble headstone.

The ever-present ache in his chest intensified as he knelt and set the colorful bouquet on the grass. He closed his eyes, remembering the first day he'd met her, the way she'd smiled cheekily when she'd mixed up his lunch order. He remembered how her hand had trembled in his when she'd said her vows on their wedding day, and the way she'd nearly crushed his fingers when she was giving birth to Charlie. He concentrated very hard, until he had a clear picture of her in his mind.

Then he said his goodbye, and he let her go.

Because he'd lost too much already. He wasn't going to lose again, not if he had any say in it.

After a long moment he opened his eyes and looked up at the sky. Not a cloud in sight. He took a deep breath. The ache was gone.

He'd lived with his grief for long enough now to know that it would always be with him. A scent on the wind, a phrase someone said, the sound of his daughter's laughter from a distant room—Billie would always be a part of his life. And he wouldn't want it any other way. He would always love her. But he would not live his life for her.

He couldn't. He had two children who needed him. And he had Angie. Amazing, miraculous, generous, gentle, incredibly lovable Angie.

His knees were sore by the time he pushed himself to his feet and walked away from Billie's grave. He headed for Collingwood and Angie's new studio, impatience and fear growing within him in equal measure as he wrestled with the traffic and his own doubts.

What if he'd made it too hard? What if Angie had changed her mind? What if he'd hurt her too much, taken too long to come to his senses...?

And why *the hell* was there so much damned traffic on the road?

Brow furrowed, he changed lanes and leaned on the accelerator.

ANGIE SAT BACK ON HER heels and surveyed the shelves inside her sideboard. All her reference books were out of order, but she didn't have the heart for making everything perfect today. Maybe in a few months' time she'd put a day aside to set her new studio up properly. Today, this week, she was all out of puff. Exhausted by loss and regret and grief.

She stood and looked around the compact, industrial space. She'd been spoiled at Michael's—the quiet, the view, the calmness. This new space was smaller and windowless apart from a thin aperture filled with wire-embedded glass high on one wall.

But it was *her* space, and she didn't have to run the

gauntlet of Michael and what could have been every time she came to work. For that reason alone, she would embrace this new studio with open arms.

The movers had set all the heavy pieces in their new places, but she still had lots to set up before she could do anything constructive. Dusting her hands on the seat of her jeans, she reached for the next box.

The scuff of a shoe on cement drew her gaze to the open door. Her heart stuttered in her chest when she saw Michael standing there, his eyes dark and serious as he filled the open doorway.

"Knock, knock."

Angie swallowed noisily. "Hi."

She'd had more than one fantasy over the past few days where Michael had simply turned up like this at her home or work or yoga class or the middle of the supermarket and told her all the things that she longed to hear. That he loved her. That he wanted to be with her. That he didn't want to imagine his life without her. That all the guilt and problems didn't matter when measured against how he felt about her.

Stupid, childish fantasies. Self-destructive and pointless, too. She'd known the score going in with Michael, and she knew the score now, too.

She wiped her hands on the seat of her jeans again, just to give herself something to do, and waited for Michael to explain why he was here.

"Can I come in?" he asked, gesturing awkwardly.

"Of course."

He entered the studio, his gaze taking in the white-painted brick walls, the stacked cartons, the yet-to-be-arranged table and chairs. His gaze returned to her, his eyes scanning her face with an unnerving intensity. Her belly tensed. If he was here to talk about the other night again… She didn't know what she would do, but she didn't want to go over it all again.

It was too painful, and she was still too raw.

"How are you?" he asked.

She made a vague gesture with her hand. "Okay. Good. The move went smoothly."

"So I see. But how are you?"

She took a deep breath. "Michael… I don't want to talk about us. If that's what you're here for. Not that there ever was an us. But you know what I mean."

He took a step forward. "There was an us, Angie. There still is."

Her heart stuttered again. Stupid heart, still hoping. She knew better.

"I need some time, Michael. A few weeks, a month… I don't know. I need to forget a little."

He moved closer, stopping next to the stump. He glanced down at it, resting his fingers on the scarred wood.

"I went to see Billie today."

He glanced at her and everything in her went very still. As though her body knew something that she didn't. There was something in his eyes….

"Did you?" She could barely get the words past the sudden tightness her throat.

"Ever since you drove off on Friday night, I've had this pain in my chest. Here." He touched the area near his heart. "I thought it was because I'd hurt you. Because I'd made you unhappy. It wasn't until you moved out last night that I got it. That's why I went to see Billie today. To say goodbye."

She forgot to breathe. Michael closed the final feet

between them, taking her hand in his. She shook her head, almost afraid of what he might say next.

"You don't have to do this, Michael. You don't have to make this right. I'm not your responsibility."

Because that was what this was. Michael trying to do the right thing. Trying to fix things.

He lifted her hand to his lips and kissed her knuckles. "Angie, I love you."

She closed her eyes. "Please don't do this."

"Open your eyes, Angie."

When she didn't, she felt him move closer. A sob rose in her throat. She'd dreamed of him saying those words and standing this close, even though she knew it would never happen. Yet he was standing here.

"Open your eyes, Angie."

She felt the brush of his lips on her cheek, on her eyelids, on the tip of her nose. She clenched her hands at her sides, refusing to reach out. Refusing to take what wasn't hers.

His mouth brushed her lips. "I love you, Angie."

"No, you don't. You feel responsible. You don't want me to be unhappy."

"You're right. I feel all those things. And I love you."

Finally she forced herself to open her eyes and meet his. "You love Billie."

It wasn't an accusation.

"I do. I won't lie to you, a part of me always will. But I learned something these past few months, Angie. I learned that no matter how much you hide from life, it comes looking for you anyway. I learned that even when I thought I was dead inside, I could still look forward to seeing you and hearing your voice. I learned that even though I thought I'd be happy being a monk, I could still look at you and want you more than seems sane or safe."

His hand slid into her hair, combing through the strands until he was cupping the back of her skull in his palm. He tilted her head back, his gaze holding hers, and she was utterly unable to look away from the light and fire and depth in his eyes.

"I learned that it's possible to love one woman while falling in love with another. And I learned that I don't want to give up on life, that I want a future, and I want it to be with you, Angie, because I've discovered that my life pretty much sucks without you in it."

A small, worried frown pleated his brow and his hand tightened on her skull.

"Don't cry, Angie," he said, his voice very low and ragged. "Please don't cry."

Only then did she register the tears streaming down her face. She wanted so much to believe what he was saying. So much.

"You love Billie," she said again, because it was a truth that was etched in her soul.

"I do. And so do you. And so do Eva and Charlie. And we always will. We will never, ever forget her. But she's gone, and we're not. Maybe there are people who will condemn us for snatching this chance at happiness, but I'm not giving it up, Angie. I'm not giving you up, because I need to hear your laughter and I need to make love to you and I need to be able to talk with you and to hold you close and to watch you play with and love my children and—"

Angie rose up on her tiptoes and pressed her mouth to his, the movement so abrupt and forceful she felt the hardness of his teeth against her lips, the smack of bone on bone as their noses and chins collided. She didn't back off, and neither did he, his hand clenching on the back of her head. She kissed him with all the hope and desperation and sadness and gladness in her soul. She gave him her all, because she wanted to believe, so badly.

And he gave her his all back, unreservedly, his body thrumming with the intensity of his emotion, every muscle taut with need and sincerity and urgency as he gathered her close, and suddenly the hope in her chest was expanding and filling her chest and belly and throat and pelvis and she believed.

She *believed*.

Michael loved her. As she loved him. He wasn't doing the right thing or trying to fix things. He wanted what she wanted. He wanted *her*.

Even though she wanted to kiss him for the rest of her life, she pulled back just enough to look into his eyes. He looked back at her, and she wondered if she looked as dazed and blown away and giddy as he did.

"Okay," she said a little breathlessly.

He smiled, the wonderful lines around his eyes and mouth creasing into familiar patterns. "It's going to be more than okay, Angie."

She knew he was right, even though there were going to be challenges and difficulties ahead. There would be raised eyebrows among some of their friends and family. There would be judgment. There would be teething problems with the children and between her and Michael.

None of it mattered. What mattered was that this man—this beautiful, loving, loyal, sexy man—and his two children were going to be hers to love and hold and protect and nurture.

Everything else was white noise. Dust. Insignificant.

Except for one last, very important thing.

"I want you to know that I will never begrudge you Billie." There was a quaver in her voice, because this meant so much to her. But it had to be said. She *needed* for it to be said. "I will never stop the children from talking about her. I will never not want to talk about her or how you feel about her. She's a part of me and a part of you and she will always, always be with us. She's not my rival, I don't want to replace her. I want to keep her alive as much as we can. For the children and for us. It's really important to me that you understand that."

Michael's eyes were suddenly swimming with tears. "Angie… God, I love you."

He pulled her into his arms, holding her tight. She wrapped her arms around him and held him in turn.

Michael was right—they were going to be more than okay. They had so much love on their side, and so much sadness behind them. They knew exactly how valuable this was. How precious.

Smiling slowly, she cupped his jaw gently in both hands and kissed him. It seemed her heart wasn't so stupid, after all.

* * * * *

Look for the next book from Sarah Mayberry,
SUDDENLY YOU coming in November 2012!
Available wherever Harlequin Superromance books
are sold.

COMING NEXT MONTH
from Harlequin® SuperRomance®
AVAILABLE SEPTEMBER 4, 2012

#1800 THE ROAD TO BAYOU BRIDGE
The Boys of Bayou Bridge
Liz Talley

Newly discharged from the navy, Darby Dufrene is ready to settle down. But not anywhere close to his family home in Louisiana. Then he discovers something that ties him here—and to his high school sweetheart Renny Latioles—much more than he imagined!

#1801 OUT OF BOUNDS
Going Back
Ellen Hartman

The budget from a fundraiser has been embezzled and Posy Jones tries to fix it before anyone finds out. Unfortunately, Wes Fallon has been appointed head of this charity. He's determined to prove himself and she's running out of excuses to avoid him!

#1802 PLAYING THE PART
Family in Paradise
Kimberly Van Meter

As an actress, Lindy Bell is used to drama. But she gets more than she bargains for when she butts heads with sexy single dad Gabe Weston.

#1803 THE TRUTH ABOUT TARA
Darlene Gardner

Tara Greer doesn't want to know if she was kidnapped as a child. To protect her mother—and herself—she must fight her attraction to Jack DiMarco, the man who could force her to face the truth.

#1804 THE WOMAN HE KNOWS
Margaret Watson

Darcy Gordon is on the run. If she gets complacent or tells anyone who she really is, her freedom—and even her life—will be at risk. So getting close to sexy FBI agent Patrick Devereux is a very bad idea....

#1805 SEEKING SHELTER
Angel Smits

Amy Grey lives one day at a time—no looking forward, and definitely no looking back. But when Jace Holmes rides into town on his motorcycle with surprising news, he turns the single mom's carefully constructed life on its head.

You can find more information on upcoming Harlequin®
titles, free excerpts and more at www.Harlequin.com.

HSRCNM0812

REQUEST YOUR FREE BOOKS!
2 FREE NOVELS PLUS 2 FREE GIFTS!

Harlequin *Super Romance*®

Exciting, emotional, unexpected!

YES! Please send me 2 FREE Harlequin® Superromance® novels and my 2 FREE gifts (gifts are worth about $10). After receiving them, if I don't wish to receive any more books, I can return the shipping statement marked "cancel." If I don't cancel, I will receive 6 brand-new novels every month and be billed just $4.69 per book in the U.S. or $5.24 per book in Canada. That's a saving of at least 15% off the cover price! It's quite a bargain! Shipping and handling is just 50¢ per book in the U.S. and 75¢ per book in Canada.* I understand that accepting the 2 free books and gifts places me under no obligation to buy anything. I can always return a shipment and cancel at any time. Even if I never buy another book, the two free books and gifts are mine to keep forever.

135/336 HDN FC6T

Name	(PLEASE PRINT)	
Address		Apt. #
City	State/Prov.	Zip/Postal Code

Signature (if under 18, a parent or guardian must sign)

Mail to the **Reader Service:**
IN U.S.A.: P.O. Box 1867, Buffalo, NY 14240-1867
IN CANADA: P.O. Box 609, Fort Erie, Ontario L2A 5X3

Not valid for current subscribers to Harlequin Superromance books.

**Are you a current subscriber to Harlequin Superromance books
and want to receive the larger-print edition?
Call 1-800-873-8635 or visit www.ReaderService.com.**

* Terms and prices subject to change without notice. Prices do not include applicable taxes. Sales tax applicable in N.Y. Canadian residents will be charged applicable taxes. Offer not valid in Quebec. This offer is limited to one order per household. All orders subject to credit approval. Credit or debit balances in a customer's account(s) may be offset by any other outstanding balance owed by or to the customer. Please allow 4 to 6 weeks for delivery. Offer available while quantities last.

Your Privacy—The Reader Service is committed to protecting your privacy. Our Privacy Policy is available online at www.ReaderService.com or upon request from the Reader Service.

We make a portion of our mailing list available to reputable third parties that offer products we believe may interest you. If you prefer that we not exchange your name with third parties, or if you wish to clarify or modify your communication preferences, please visit us at www.ReaderService.com/consumerschoice or write to us at Reader Service Preference Service, P.O. Box 9062, Buffalo, NY 14269. Include your complete name and address.

HSR11

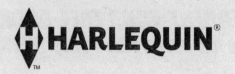

HARLEQUIN®

SYTYCW SO YOU THINK YOU CAN WRITE

Harlequin and Mills & Boon are joining forces in a global search for new authors.

In September 2012 we're launching our biggest contest yet—with the prize of being published by the world's leader in romance fiction!

Look for more information on our website, **www.soyouthinkyoucanwrite.com**

So you think you can write? Show us!